Remember When

A.D. RYAN

Copyright © 2015 A.D. Ryan

All rights reserved. No part of this book may be reproduced in any form or by any electronic or mechanical terms, including information storage and retrieval systems, without permission in writing from the author, except by a reviewer, who may quote brief passages in a review.

This book is a work of fiction. Names, characters, places, and incidents either are the product of the author's imagination or are used fictitiously. Any resemblance to actual persons, living or dead, events or locales is entirely coincidental.

Ryan, A.D.
Remember When / A.D. Ryan

ISBN 978-1508442011

Text and Cover design by Angela Schmuhl
Cover Image: Shutterstock, © Maksim Toome

I have loved to the point of madness, that which is called madness, that which to me is the only sensible way to love.
~Francoise Sagan

Contents

Acknowledgments	i
Prologue. Memory Lane	1
Chapter 1. I do it for Her	22
Chapter 2. So Many Memories	35
Chapter 3. Whispered Promises	44
Chapter 4. The Beach House	52
Chapter 5. Going Back	65
Chapter 6. Never Give Up	71
Chapter 7. Impasse	89
Chapter 8. Crossing the Line	105
Chapter 9. Breaking Free	120
Chapter 10. Three Leaps Back	127
Chapter 11. Reliving the Past	134
Chapter 12. Dreams Become Real	149
Chapter 13. Making Progress	155
Chapter 14. Back Sliding	164
Chapter 15. Breakthrough	169
Chapter 16. Wide Awake	178
Chapter 17. The Truth Comes Out	183
Chapter 18. The Pain of Healing	193
Chapter 19. Letting Go	201
Chapter 20. Within Reach	213
Chapter 21. Homecoming	221
Epilogue. Always With You	232

Acknowledgments

This book is for all the people who read it in its original form years ago. It is, by far, one of my favorite novels to have written, and I wouldn't have had the courage to formally publish it if not for the encouragement of all my online friends.

To my parents, thank you for constantly supporting me as I continue to chase after this dream. It means a lot to have you all in my corner.

My siblings, who drove me nuts when we were kids, but I now look up to for different reasons.

Lynda and Tiff, the two of you are, beyond a doubt, two of the best friends I've never met in person. Your attention to detail and constant support and cheerleading has been amazing. I don't feel like I can ever properly repay you for all you two have done for me. I'll find a way, though. Just you wait and see.

Two of my pre-readers, Sandy and Caroline, thank you for taking a chance on this emotional story. I'm so glad you enjoyed it, even if it stirred up emotions no one expected.

Marny, you were with me when I first wrote this story. You were the one to tell me to "just do it." And I did. I had second thoughts about certain parts of it, but it was you that encouraged me to stick with my original plans and do what I do best. I'm so glad you did, because this story is one of the best things I've ever written. It made me feel things I'd forgotten, and it touched the hearts of so many people. So, for that, I thank you for continuing to be my muse.

And finally, my husband and three amazing kidlets, to have each and every one of you respect the time I take to write means the world to me. You guys are my inspiration and my reason for doing everything that I do. Without you, I'd be lost. I love you.

Cheers,

Angela

A.D. Ryan

Prologue: Memory Lane

When I first saw her walking through the quad of Frederick High my senior year, I knew I had to have her. She was a sophomore and new to town. Apparently her father had been transferred here for work; I'd later find out he was the new principal at our school.

That first day was unforgettable. I was sitting at a table outside, on a particularly warm fall day, when I looked up and saw her wander through the crowd of students taking advantage of the warmth. I'd heard she'd transferred from somewhere in Oregon, so she was probably used to cooler temperatures. Her blonde hair shimmered in the sunlight as she cast her blue eyes nervously toward a group of guys tossing a football around, flinching slightly when Thomas Welch, the Warriors' starting quarterback, almost backed into her as he caught the ball. Truth be told, I jolted slightly in my seat in sync with her reaction.

She placed a delicate hand over her heart and laughed foolishly at herself as she continued on. Her smile was absolutely breathtaking, and I was in awe watching this beautiful woman walking toward me. Her eyes met mine, and as soon as I saw her blush, I knew I had to introduce myself.

I excused myself from my friends, Billy and Alex, who looked over their shoulders at whatever it was that had captured my attention. They both smiled while Billy started laughing and teasing me on finally being ready to give it up. He truly was — and still is — a crass pig, but he was also one of my closest friends.

I punched his shoulder — hard — as I walked past him and made my way to her. As I walked toward her, confusion flashed in her eyes before she looked back over her shoulder. I offered her a smile as I worked on closing the gap between us.

I was a few feet from her when the shouting began.

"Heads up!" My head snapped to the right as I watched the football closing in on her. Its height led me to believe it would easily sail over her head... Thomas' quickly advancing body, however, was on course for a major collision. His eyes were on the ball and not on where he was running.

In that moment, I made a snap decision and bolted toward her. She had no idea what was about to happen. Thankfully, my experience on the track team had paid off as I made it to her quicker than should have been possible. The look on her face was pure confusion and shock as I wrapped my hands around her slender waist and twisted our bodies. Thomas finally noticed a fraction of a second before he slammed into my back, and the three of us fell to the ground.

Her body was pinned beneath me, her blonde hair sprawled out on the grass. I stared down into her big blue eyes, drinking in her soft features. It wasn't until she groaned and reached for the back of her head that I grew concerned.

"Ooooh. What happened?" she had asked, trying to prop herself up on her elbows. I was too heavy on top of her, making it difficult, so I hopped to my feet.

Thomas jumped up and looked down at us as I helped her to hers. "Cassie, I'm so sorry. I didn't see you, and by the time I did, I couldn't stop."

Cassie.

She wobbled slightly on her feet. Acting quickly, I caught her around the waist and held her upright. She stood several inches shorter than my five-foot-ten frame, fitting perfectly against my side. She was slender and curvy, soft and womanly in all the right places.

"No, its fine. It could have been much worse if not for..." Her words trailed off awaiting my introduction.

"Jack. Jack Martin," I offered.

"Jack." My name fell from her lips in a breathy whisper, and she turned a deep shade of crimson. Her legs wobbled a little beneath her again.

"Maybe we should go to the infirmary. Just to be sure you're all right," I suggested gently.

"Um, yeah. Sure."

I kept my arm around her as we walked to the nurse's office, telling myself it was to ensure she stayed on her feet. Deep down, I knew it was because I never wanted to let her go.

That was day one. I asked her out two weeks later, and we never looked back.

∞ *forever*

For our first date, I took Cassie on a picnic in Vogel Canyon. As we sat on the thin blanket I'd brought, amidst the flowers of the early spring, we soaked up each other's stories as we ate the sandwiches I pretended I made. I couldn't have her know I was limited to peanut butter and jelly this early on in the relationship.

Then she laughed. I didn't think anything could

beat the melodious sound of her voice, or even how my name sounded when it breezed past her pouty lips, but I was proven wrong when she laughed at a memory of her mother.

"It was ridiculous," she had said. "I mean, my mom has done a lot of crazy things in her time, but skydiving? It took me a month to talk her out of it." She paused to take a breath and get her laughter under control.

That was when I kissed her. My lips brushed hers lightly, and I felt a spark as they connected. She pulled back immediately, her startled blue eyes searched mine for an explanation, and I struggled to find the words that could possibly justify my impulsive behavior. "I'm sorry," I whispered. "I just—"

She didn't let me finish. Instead, she leaned forward and pressed her plump lips to mine. As our mouths moved together, I felt Cassie weave her fingers into the hair at the nape of my neck before her delicate tongue peeked out and caressed my lower lip.

As we deepened our kiss, I wrapped my arm around her waist and we fell to the ground, our legs tangled up in one another's. Like the teenagers we were, we made out, sprawled upon the blanket, for what seemed like hours. It wasn't usual for me to be so impulsive upon meeting someone, but there was something about her that I just couldn't tear myself away from. I was drawn to her, like gravity.

We were so wrapped up in the moment as we groped and pulled at each other above our clothes that we hadn't noticed the sky darkening before the rain started to fall. Cassie's lips played up into a smile against mine, and she started to giggle when the rain pelted down on her back as she remained on top of me. We stood quickly, our bodies instantly soaked as the large drops assaulted us, and we rushed to pick up our blanket and basket before fleeing for the car, laughing all the while.

Once we were in the car, I turned the heater on to warm us up. I looked over at Cassie as she held her hands out over the dashboard vent awaiting the warm air to filter out. She tilted her head and looked over at me, a small smirk turning the corners of her mouth upward. Her hair was soaked from the rain and fell in damp waves over her shoulders, the water beading from the ends and falling onto her lap as she ran her hands together against the warm air.

I wondered if it was possible to love somebody with every fiber of your being after only a couple of weeks. Because I was fairly certain I was falling head over heels in love with Cassidy Taylor.

As soon as we pulled onto the highway, the sky opened up and a torrential downpour had begun, causing the road to disappear. The car ride back to town was mostly silent as I kept my eyes focused on what little I could see of the road ahead of me. I could feel her eyes on me the whole trip, though, and as much as I wanted to pull over and talk to her some more, I knew I should probably get her home, lest her parents worry.

I pulled up to her house and hopped out of the car. I ran to the passenger side and opened her door for her, draping my jacket over our heads to keep our still-damp bodies from being soaked through once more, and we jogged for the cover of her front porch. She unlocked the door before turning back to me and smiling. We stood for a moment in silence, just looking into each other's eyes nervously.

"I'm sorry," we both said at the same time.

I laughed. "What are you sorry for?"

Her cheeks turned a pale shade of pink, and she

pulled that delicious bottom lip between her teeth. "For what happened back in the field. I'm not usually so impetuous. I mean, we just met...and then you kissed me...I don't know. It's all so stupid, really." She dropped her eyes to her feet. "I just feel this deep connection to you. I can't explain it right, so this probably all sounds insane."

I cupped her face in my hands and lifted it gently so her eyes would meet mine. "Not even a little bit. I know exactly what you're talking about," I assured her.

"You do?" she whispered, placing her hands tentatively around my wrists.

I nodded as I leaned in to capture her lips with mine once more. We were inches apart when the front door opened, and her father, Principal Frank Taylor, stood in the doorway. His eyes were hard, and the same commanding presence he held at school radiated off him now, forcing me to quickly change course and place a gentle kiss to Cassie's forehead before saying goodnight to them both.

∞ *forever*

The more I got to know Cassie over the years, the deeper I fell. It seemed like we were with each other every waking moment, and we couldn't keep our hands off each other. When the time finally came for me to apply to colleges, Cassie grew sullen. It was the first true glimpse into her troubled past I'd been privy to, though I didn't realize it at first since I was just as upset about being apart from her. The only thing that kept me focused on my future was that I wanted to earn my degree in Psychiatry so I could make a life for us. I knew what all that entailed, and the sooner I started on it all, the better.

Being in a long distance relationship wasn't without its difficulties. Cassie really struggled—we both did. It was during our time apart that I learned more about Cassie and her struggles. She often broke down during our conversations, but by the time we said goodbye, she'd regained her composure. After a few months, her parents grew concerned enough with her erratic behavior to tell me that Cassie had a history of depression in her youth. It came as a shock, but not nearly as much as learning that she'd been backsliding since I left.

Naturally, when Cass announced that she wanted to move to Hanover with me when the time came for her to attend Dartmouth, her parents grew concerned. Rightfully so. Before they were okay with it, Cassie and I had to sit down with the two of them and discuss the positive changes in Cassie over the past year. She'd been seeing a therapist again who'd altered her med rotation slightly to level her out. Cassie and I both assured her parents that we would remain diligent with her treatment.

And we tried.

By the time Cassie joined me at Dartmouth that fall, I was two years away from earning my undergraduate degree before I started med school. Dartmouth was an amazing experience for both of us. We really blossomed there...eventually.

In the beginning, there was definitely an adjustment to be made. Cassie had more ups than downs, fortunately, but there were still days where I worried about her more than usual. Her emotions could change in the blink of an eye. I'd never seen her so out of sorts. It worried me, but I soon came to realize she'd been slacking on her routine with her busy course load.

Once I was able to pinpoint the reason behind her extreme mood swings, I was better equipped to help her through it. I used the information I'd learned in my classes and took it upon myself to help her through it to the best of my ability. I would gently remind her to take her meds before we both left for class; I checked in throughout the day if I knew we wouldn't see each other before the end of the day; and, most importantly, we made sure to have dinner together every night. No matter what.

Creating a routine helped.

I never once blamed or resented Cassie for the struggles we'd endured. I knew none of it was her fault, and, if anything, I loved her more because of it. What was important was that we didn't let it conquer her or dictate how we lived. We maintained control of it, and eventually, Cassie was able to enjoy her college experience to its fullest.

Two years into my three-year med school degree, Cassie graduated from Dartmouth. That was the night I proposed. There was never a doubt in my mind that we'd be together forever, and I was elated when she told me the same thing upon accepting my proposal.

I had waited until we were at dinner with our parents. I had spoken to Cassie's parents two weeks prior to that night and asked for their blessing, and they gave it wholeheartedly. The server brought dessert, and Cassie was just digging into her chocolate cake when I stood up.

"What are you doing?" she asked.

I smiled and looked down at her before looking at all the faces around the table. "I wanted to say a few words."

"About what?" she asked, casting a nervous glance at her parents.

"I'm so proud of you and everything you've accomplished these last four years, Cass."

She looked at me with slight confusion. "Um, thanks?"

"Since that day I saved you from that football in high school, I knew that we were fated to be together," I started with a light chuckle.

Cassie's eyes widened in realization. "What the hell do you think you're doing, Jack Martin?" Her chest began to heave with her heavy breaths. I pulled a small black box from my pocket and dropped to one knee beside her. "Put that away," she hissed.

I laughed and looked her in the eyes as I took her shaking left hand in mine. "Cassidy Lee Taylor, I can't imagine my life without you. Marry me?"

I opened the ring box, and her breath caught in her throat. "It's beautiful," she whispered as she looked down at the half-carat, princess cut solitaire ring nestled in the blue velvet pillow. She raised her tear-filled eyes and smiled. "Yes."

My heart soared with joy as I took the ring and placed it on her finger, where it would stay forever. I stood and pulled her into my arms, and our parents started to applaud, which only caused the rest of the restaurant to join in on the celebratory cheers.

I pressed my lips to Cassie's and could feel her smile against my mouth. "Forever, Cassie. Without a doubt, you are my forever."

"And you're mine."

∞

We set the date for that December, during our winter break.

After her graduation, Cassie stayed in Hanover,

New Hampshire while I finished up my final year at Dartmouth. She was able to land a job at a small graphics design company with hopes of starting her own some day.

Getting started on our life together was important, but not as important as starting our careers and putting money away for a down payment on a house.

My older sister, Jennifer, helped plan the perfect wedding in a church back home in Frederick. Always one for overdoing it, she was the perfect choice. The morning of the wedding, my closest friends, Billy and Alex, as well as my father, Robert, and I all got ready together.

"So, you're actually doing this, huh?" Billy asked jokingly, blue eyes alight with jest. His dark hair was combed neatly, and his tie was immaculately straight.

I chuckled as I fastened my tie around my neck. "I really am."

Dad approached me and held out a key ring. The lines around his brown eyes were made more prominent by the proud smile he wore. "Here are the keys to the beach house in California. Your mother and I want you to take Cassie there for your honeymoon. We know you two said you didn't have anything planned, so we took it upon ourselves to plan it for you."

"Dad, I...thank you." I took the keys from him as he wrapped his arms around me.

"Congratulations, son. We couldn't be more proud," he told me.

The time finally came for me to head downstairs and wait for my fiancée—I never tired of saying that—to arrive. My parents sat in the front row, holding hands. Dressed in a lovely purple dress, her light blonde hair pulled away from her face, my mother dabbed at the corners of her green eyes with a tissue in an attempt to keep her tears of joy at bay.

Once Cassie's bridesmaids—two of her close friends from her hometown—were in place, the music shifted into the traditional wedding march. My eyes travelled to the top of the aisle, and my breath caught in my throat when the doors opened for one final time and Cassie started her ascent toward our new life together. She was stunning in a handmade gown by my sister, and I had to ask Billy to pinch me, because I was afraid it was a dream and I would wake at any moment.

The priest started the ceremony as soon as Cassie was by my side, her fingers laced through mine. "Family and friends. We are gathered here today to witness the joining of two people." He continued to talk about the meaning of matrimony and love, but I failed to hear most of it as I took in the exquisite beauty of my soon-to-be wife.

"Cassidy, do you take Jack, whom you now hold by the hand, to be your lawfully wedded husband?" he had asked.

With a sniffle and tears brimming her eyes, she whispered, "I do."

He then turned his attention to me. "Jack, do you take Cassidy, whom you now hold by the hand, to be your lawfully wedded wife?"

The first tear fell onto her rosy cheek, and I brushed it away with the pad of my thumb. "I most definitely do," I breathed.

With a smile, he looked to my best man. "Now is the time for the exchange of rings."

I turned to Billy, who reached into his tux jacket pocket and pulled out two simple white gold bands. I plucked the slender silver circle from him and turned back to Cassie. I slid the ring over her knuckle and held it in place as I spoke. "With this ring, I pledge my love and commitment." I leaned forward and placed my lips against the ring, making Cassie sigh.

Cassie reached forward and took my ring from Billy's hand and slid it onto my ring finger. "With this ring, I pledge my love and commitment."

Finally, the priest closed his book and smiled proudly. "It is my pleasure to announce you both Husband and Wife. Jack, you may kiss your bride."

Our first kiss as husband and wife was…incomparable to any other kiss we shared. Tears of happiness had begun to spill onto Cassie's cheeks as I leaned forward to capture her lips with my own. Cassie stretched up onto her toes, throwing her arms around my neck, and kissed me passionately.

Feeling nothing but love in that moment, the rest of the world slipped away and we kissed like nobody else was in the room. In fact, it wasn't until Cassie's father started clearing his throat that I pulled away.

We turned our bodies to face our guests and made our way down the aisle…toward our future.

The rest of the night was a blur of happiness and love as we greeted out-of-state friends and relatives, while still finding those few select moments to steal away for ourselves.

With Cassie securely in my arms, we moved in the centre of the dance floor. "Enjoying the party, Mrs. Martin?"

With a soft giggle and blushing cheeks, she said, "That'll take a while to get used to."

"I'm certain we have a while," I assured her as I leaned down and kissed her once more. From all around us cameras flashed, capturing our love forever.

We left before the reception and dance were over

since we had a plane to catch. Cassie slept the entire way, utterly exhausted from the long and arduous weeks of planning our wedding.

She awoke, only briefly, as we got off the plane and into the town car that would take us to our home for the next few weeks. When we arrived outside the oversized—and incredibly private—beachfront property, Cassie's jaw dropped.

"Wow," she whispered as I unlocked the front door.

I looked slyly down at my wife and scooped her up into my arms. I carried her through the house, turning on each and every light as we made our way around. The floors were a dark wood throughout as I walked through the open-concept living and dining rooms and toward the hall that would lead to the bedrooms. At the end of the long hall was the master bedroom. It was large and white with a floor-to-ceiling window that looked out toward the ocean.

I set her down on her feet. "I'll go get the bags," I said quietly, suddenly nervous.

It seemed silly that we were both as nervous as we were. It wasn't as though we'd never made love; we'd been together almost six years, living together for more than half of that. But this—making love as husband and wife?—it felt like an enormous amount of pressure.

When I returned, I found Cassie at the large picture window, staring at the gentle waves as they lapped up against the shore. She saw my reflection in the window and melted into my embrace as I wrapped my arms around her waist and held her close.

She laid the back of her head against my chest and sighed. "It's beautiful."

I lowered my lips to her neck and kissed her tenderly. "I couldn't agree more," I whispered as my lips ghosted a trail down to the pale flesh of her shoulder.

"I was talking about the ocean." Smiling, Cassie slowly turned her body to me, her eyes full of love and apprehension. "I love you, Jack." She must have seen the same emotions in my eyes, because she laid her hands on my jaw and smiled. "We don't have to... If you're tired, I mean."

Eyes wide with surprise, I smirked. "I'll never be too tired, Cass," I replied thickly, lowering my face to hers and kissing her softly.

Cassie's fingers found their way into my hair as she pressed her body closer to mine. I lifted her off the ground and spun us around so I could walk us to the oversized bed. I lowered Cassie back to her feet and stared into her lust-filled eyes as I lowered my hands to the hem of her shirt.

We worked quickly to undress each other, our nerves from earlier quickly taken over by our hunger for one another. With our clothes discarded, I pulled her body to mine and kissed her with everything I had.

Our hands explored each other's bodies, memorizing each curve of every muscle before we fell onto the bed where we made love...

...and our daughter.

The day Cassie told me she was pregnant was one of the best days of my life.

Right before the wedding, Cassie and I had found a nice little apartment to rent in Hanover until the spring when I finished school. I had arrived home one Friday evening at five and was surprised to find

Cassie's Toyota already in its parking spot. She always worked until six. Always.

"Cassie?" I called as I took my shoes off at the front door.

"In the kitchen," she replied.

I walked through the hallway and found Cassie sitting at the kitchen table, sipping a cup of tea. I walked to her and placed a kiss upon her temple. She felt warm. "How have you been feeling today?"

She smiled weakly and shrugged. "No better, no worse. Listen, we should talk," she said, her face suddenly taking on a very serious, and honestly quite frightening, expression.

My stomach rolled as I pulled the seat out next to her and sat down. "What is it?"

She closed her eyes and took a deep breath in through her nose and exhaled through her mouth. "I love you, obviously, but something's happened."

I couldn't help the multitude of thoughts that crashed through my mind regarding what she could be talking about. I swallowed thickly and finally found my voice. "I know that. I love you, too. But, Cass, you're scaring the hell out of me. What's wrong?"

Her brow softened, and a small smile started to spread. "Oh, no! It's nothing like that," she said, intuitively knowing what I must have been thinking. She placed her hands on my knees. "I'm pregnant. I know it's much sooner than either of us even expected, but…"

"What?"

The expression on my face must have scared her, because she instantly pulled her hands back and averted her gaze. "I…um, it wasn't on purpose…"

"You're certain?"

She nodded meekly. "I met with the doctor this

morning. He confirmed it. I'm about six weeks along," she said quietly, her voice shaking and her chin quivering. "I'm sorry." She dropped her gaze from mine, and I saw a tear fall onto her lap.

I shook my head. "Sorry? Why on Earth are you sorry?"

Her head snapped up, and she wiped her cheeks. "Y...you mean you're not mad?"

"Not at all. This is... Cassie, this is fantastic!" I exclaimed, jumping from my seat and sending it clattering to the ceramic tile. I pulled her into my arms and kissed her.

"Really?" she asked, her tone full of the relief she felt at my reaction.

"Definitely."

With a smile and a tender kiss, she looked up at me. "You're going to be a daddy."

We called our families immediately to tell them the news.

Cassie's morning sickness lasted the first three months, and nothing we did seemed to help. There wasn't much she was able to keep down, and it was starting to concern us, even though the doctor said it was quite normal. Once she hit that second trimester, though, her appetite was back in full force. I honestly don't think I had ever cooked that many waffles in my life. It was all she ever craved for weeks.

If I never saw another waffle in my life, that would be fine by me.

Watching her body change with each passing week was the most amazing thing I had ever experienced. The way her stomach grew with the life that was inside of her, the way I would catch her rubbing her protruding abdomen and singing soothing lullabies...

Such beautiful memories.

We tried to find out the sex of the baby at our twenty-week ultrasound, but the baby was uncooperative. Cassie was convinced we were having a boy, while I had no preference one way or the other, as long as the child was healthy.

With Cassie and I now expecting, it was very important for us to be close to family. So, I had my upcoming residency transferred to Denver, Colorado and, after I finished up with school, we moved back to Frederick and started house-hunting. It took two days and five houses before we found "the one."

It was love at first sight. It was a newer two-story home with four bedrooms on the upper floor and a large backyard. There was a den off the main entry where Cassie had set up her home office for the graphic design company she had started.

Then came the day Cassie went into labor. It was probably one of my more terrifying life experiences. It was September first, two days before Cassie's twenty-fourth birthday. I had just walked through the door to find Cassie hard at work in her office on her latest project. Not wanting to interrupt her, I headed for the kitchen to start dinner.

I had just pulled out the vegetables from the fridge to start chopping when I heard Cassie groan. I stopped what I was doing and waited. I heard the clicking of her keyboard start up again, so I turned back to dinner.

"Ooooh," she groaned again, a little louder this time.

I put the knife down and moved to poke my head into the hall. "Cass?"

"It's nothing. It must have been the Mexican food Jen brought by for lunch. I'm fine," she assured me.

"You know, I have half a mind to talk to her about bringing that stuff over for you when it doesn't agree with you right now," I muttered.

I heard Cassie laugh as she continued to work. "You know as well as I do your sister wouldn't listen to you anyway. What the baby wants, the baby gets," she reminded me.

Ten minutes had passed, and I had just cut into the peppers for the salad I was preparing when Cassie came hobbling into the kitchen. I looked at her, and my smile quickly vanished as she looked back at me, her eyes full of distress. "Sweetheart?"

"Um, either I just peed myself, or my water just broke." Suddenly her body hunched over, and her knuckles turned white as she death-gripped the fridge handle. "Ooooh my God!" she cried.

I dropped the knife immediately and turned the burners off before rushing to her side. I grabbed her bag that sat by the front door for the occasion and helped my very pregnant wife out to the car. We rushed through the busy streets, breaking multiple traffic laws in the process. I called our families to let them know what was going on while Cassie groaned and practiced her breathing in the background.

When we reached the hospital, I helped Cassie out and took her inside to be admitted. Once we were in our private room, the labor really kicked itself into high gear, and I had never seen Cassie so uncomfortable. Dr. Morris arrived an hour later and did a quick examination of Cassie's stomach.

He was a portly, middle-aged man with salt-and-pepper hair. His bedside manner was impeccable, and Cassie was instantly comfortable with him when we first met with him. After finishing his examination, he looked at us both solemnly. "It would appear that some time in the last week, your baby has flipped into a breech position. We'll have to perform a cesarean."

Cassie's worried eyes met mine, and I forced a smile in hopes of reassuring her. Dr. Morris looked at us and went over everything that the procedure would entail before he left the room to get ready. Nurses came in with a pair of scrubs for me and a blue cap for my hair. They prepped Cassie for surgery and then wheeled her off to the OR.

I waited in the hall until the doctor came for me. When I stepped foot in the brightly lit room, I saw my wife lying on an operating table, her arms spread wide and strapped down. There was a blue privacy sheet draped above her chest, and her stomach was bare and exposed.

Nervous, I took my place beside her head and placed a kiss on her forehead to reassure her that everything was going to be fine. The steady sound of the monitors kept me sane while my wife's body moved gently under the doctor's ministrations. I stroked Cassie's head soothingly as she smiled up at me.

We sat in silence for ten minutes before Dr. Morris told Cassie there would be a little pressure, and then she gasped. It didn't take long before tears of happiness spilled from the outer corners of her eyes.

"Here she is," he announced.

"She?" I asked, looking down at Cassie.

Dr. Morris moved away from Cassie momentarily, and in his arms was a tiny, pink bundle. "Congratulations—it's a girl."

After whisking her away to be cleaned up, the doctors proceeded to finish stitching up Cassie before wheeling her to recovery. I went with our daughter to the nursery where I got to help with her first bath and hold her. She opened her eyes almost immediately, and I realized I was staring into Cassie's eyes.

I got to introduce Cassie to our daughter an hour after her birth. When I walked into the room, holding our baby in my arms, Cassie began to cry. I placed our daughter in her arms and sat next to them as Cassie got acquainted with her. Cassie seemed extremely tired as she held the tiny bundle in her arms.

"So, what are we going to name her?" I asked, hoping to rouse her slightly. "You were so convincing that we only had a boy's name set."

Cassie looked up at me with a slight smile. "I was thinking maybe, Charlotte."

I looked at her with an arched brow. "Charlotte?"

"Yeah. I really liked Charlie for our baby boy's name, and I think she looks like a Charlotte." She looked at me and pursed her lips. "You don't like it."

I chuckled and looked down at our sleeping baby girl. "I think it suits her perfectly." I kissed Cassie's forehead softly before I noticed her eyes flutter closed in contentment and exhaustion. I took Charlotte from her and held her while Cassie rested her head on my shoulder and slept.

∞ *forever*

Four years later, I stood in Charlie's doorway watching her sleep soundly. Her soft blonde curls framed her cherubic face as she snuggled her little stuffed kitten close to her heart and smiled.

"Hey," a soft voice said from behind me.

I closed Charlie's door before turning to Cassie. The moonlight that shone through the window in the hallway cast a silver glow across her perfect features and she offered me an apologetic smile. "You're late." There was no hiding the edge of anger in my voice.

She tilted her head to the side and placed a hand on my cheek. "I'm sorry. I'm here now, though."

I brushed past her and headed to our bedroom.

Her soft footfalls were heard behind me as she followed. "For tonight," I said, closing the door once she had crossed the threshold.

And like every other night for the last two years, we argued until we were both too tired to say anything else.

Chapter One
I do it for Her

I slapped the "off" button on my alarm clock and opened my eyes to see the sun streaming in through the bedroom window. I turned away from it, reaching across the bed only to find it empty...and freshly made. I was instantly wide awake and flopped back over onto my side of the bed, running my fingers through my messy hair as I stared up at the ceiling.

Our fight the night before was no different than any other in the last few years...

With the door closed, I turned to Cassie and waited for her to say something, but she only looked at me, smiling. That infuriated me even more than her missing out on an evening with her family.

"You said you'd be home for dinner," I reminded her angrily, keeping my voice down so as not to wake Charlie.

Cassie sat on the edge of the bed looking up at me calmly. "Jack, you know it can't be helped. I get home when I can."

"Then leave earlier!" I fumed. "This shit is unacceptable, Cassidy. You're not here for her anymore. She needs a mother."

Tears welled in Cassie's eyes, and she swallowed thickly. "Don't..."

I ran my hands through my hair in frustration. "Don't what? Don't tell you that your daughter needs you? Don't tell you that she doesn't even ask about you anymore?"

Cassie stood from the bed and approached until she stood inches from me. "You think I don't want *to be here with the two of you? Do you think I love the fact that I've been away for as long as I have? I'll tell you something, Jack Martin, you don't know a damn thing about what I'm going through," she seethed.*

"Because you don't talk to me! This is all we do anymore!" I shouted, waving my hand between the two of us. "Well, I refuse to keep doing it. You need to make a choice."

Her head snapped back as though I had struck her. "You…you know it's not that simple."

*"*Make it *that simple," I instructed as I walked toward the bathroom, slamming the door. I placed my hands on the countertop and dropped my head. I took several deep, cleansing breaths in an effort to gain control over my raging emotions, then I opened the medicine cabinet, noticing the empty bottle of anti-anxiety meds. I closed the cabinet and closed my eyes as I continued my breathing.*

When I finally reached a state of calm, I lifted my face to look in the mirror and didn't fail to notice how worn out I looked. My light brown hair was messy from my earlier game of hide-and-seek with Charlie, my brown eyes were shadowed with the dark circles of exhaustion, and my forehead was etched with lines of worry for the future of this family. Not wanting to dwell on it anymore for fear I might go crazy, I grabbed my toothbrush and brushed my teeth.

By the time I had emerged, Cassie was already beneath the covers on her side of the bed. I pulled the blanket on my side back and sat down to set my alarm. I turned out my light, and with a deep breath, I lay down next to her — facing the opposite direction. It felt like miles between us on the queen-size bed, when really it was only a couple of feet.

Mere minutes had gone by before I felt her delicate hand on my bicep and her chin rest on my shoulder. "I'm sorry," she whispered.

"You always are," I stated monotonously.

I felt her lips brush lightly over my shoulder. "I am trying. It's just hard for me."

I turned over and took her hand in mine, placing it over my heart. "I know."

She looked deep into my eyes. "Do you, though? I want to be here all the time...but I just...can't be."

"Why not?" I asked, begging her with my eyes to finally open up and tell me what was really going on with her.

She dropped her gaze from mine. "You know why," she breathed.

"I need you to say it. Out loud," I told her softly.

She tilted her head and offered me a smile. "Isn't it enough that I'm here now, and that I love you both more than my own life?"

I brought her hand up from my chest and kissed it. "It is...for now." I pulled her down to me, and she rested her head on my chest while her finger ghosted lazy designs over my upper body. I ran my fingers through her thick blonde hair, and soon we both fell fast asleep.

And yet, like every other day, I woke up alone, only to find her side of the bed fixed up. She always left before dawn in order to make it to her office in Denver before eight. Just over two years ago, Cassie merged her company with another in an effort to expand it globally—the long workdays were proof of their success.

I suggested we move to Denver in those first few months, even though the commute was only forty minutes on a good day, but she assured me that wasn't going to happen. She loved our home and the life we had built here and would hate to start over in a new city. She was confident that it was only temporary and that once the new company took off, she'd be home a lot more.

She was wrong.

It was so frustrating dealing with everything alone on a daily basis. There was only one reason I did it — and she was peeking her head in through the half-opened bedroom door at that very moment.

"I see you, bug," I whispered to the little head of blonde ringlets.

She giggled before flinging the door open and running across the carpeted floor toward my side of the bed, her hair bouncing wildly about her cherubic face. "Daddy!" she squealed as I hoisted her onto the bed and snuggled her up next to me.

I inhaled the sweet smell of her hair as she started tracing her teensy fingers along my forehead. "How was your sleep, Charlie? Did you have nice dreams?"

"I don't renember," she said quietly, her big blue eyes looking into mine inquisitively. "Why you look so sad, Daddy?"

I smiled and pressed a delicate kiss to her forehead. "Not sad, baby girl, just sleepy."

"Sleepy?" she asked in disbelief. "But it's mornin' time! When the sun wakes up we're s'posed to wake up with it so we can go to Gramma and Grampa's house!" she exclaimed excitedly as she stood and began bouncing on the bed.

She hopped up and down the length of the bed until she reached the footboard and began climbing one of the posts toward the ceiling. "All right, you little squirrel, let's get down from there before you hurt yourself," I said, sitting up quickly. I unhooked her arms and legs from around the solid wood beam before slinging her onto my back.

Her arms wrapped around my neck as I exited the bedroom. "Gid me up, horsey!" She was too cute to correct as I walked briskly down the stairs and to the kitchen. I knelt down next to one of the stools at the island and let her climb down onto it.

"Okay, so what would Miss Charlotte like for breakfast today?" I asked, clapping my hands together and rubbing them furiously.

She put her elbows up on the counter and placed her chin in her hands, furrowing her brow in contemplation. She pursed her lips, looking very much like her mother, and it hurt my heart just a little bit more to think of how many mornings Cassie had missed.

"Hmmmm..." Charlie pondered for a moment before her face softened and her eyes lit up. "Can I have French toast, please?"

I turned to the fridge and grabbed the eggs and milk, placing them on the counter in front of her. "What milady wants, milady gets." Charlie watched with rapt attention as I grabbed everything I would need. "So, what do you and Grandma have planned for today?" I asked as I placed the egg-soaked bread on the griddle.

She slapped her hands down on the marble countertop. "Ugh, she said I have a playdate with *Seth*." She wrinkled up her tiny nose as she sneered his name.

"And what, pray tell, young lady, is so upsetting about a playdate with Seth Marshall?" I asked, barely able to keep my laughter under control.

"Daddy, you wouldn't even understand. He's so 'noying. He says he's this many," she said, cocking her eyebrows and tilting her head while holding up five chubby digits. "But he acts like a big baby. I just want to punch him."

I looked at her disapprovingly. "Now, Charlie, you know that's not how we raised you."

"I know, Daaaad," she said with an exaggerated

eye-roll. "I won't *actually* punch him. You're imposs'ble." I snickered. "Anyway, Gramma says after we see the Marshalls we're going to go to the zoo." She was practically vibrating off her seat as she told me what her afternoon included.

"The zoo, huh? And what on Earth is at the zoo that could have you so excited?"

Charlie's mouth dropped open into a large "O" shape. "You have got to be joking with me, Daddy. Oh my gosh, they have *everything* at the zoo. There's lions, and tigers...and bears!"

"Oh my," I teased as I flipped the French toast over. "Sounds like you girls are going to have a lot of fun today."

"Oh, we are." Suddenly, she gasped and it startled me. "You should come!"

"I would love to go to the zoo, but unfortunately I have to go to boring old work today," I reminded her as her bottom lip jutted out into a pout. "But..." Her eyes lit up for a moment. "What if you take Daddy's camera? That way you can take a ton of pictures of all your favorite things and we can look at them together."

She drew in an excited breath. "Oh, yes! Daddy, please?"

"Okay, let's eat and then we'll go get ready and grab the camera," I said as I placed our breakfast on our plates and pre-cut Charlie's for her before sliding the plate in front of her.

"Thank you, Daddy," she said licking her lips and placing her napkin in her lap.

"You're welcome, baby girl." I took my seat beside her and we ate our breakfast.

When we finished, I took our plates and put them in the dishwasher before turning back to her as she wiped her mouth with her napkin. "All right, let's head back upstairs so we can get dressed and brush our teeth, shall we?"

I helped Charlie jump down from her stool, and we headed back upstairs together. I went into her room with her and watched as she ran over to her dresser and stopped before opening the top drawer. "Daddy, can I wear a dress today?"

I smiled as she looked up at me with those pleading blue eyes. "Of course you can. Would you like me to help you pick it out?"

"Um, no thank you." She darted over to her closet and flung the white door open and reached for the frilly yellow sundress that Cassie's mother and father bought for her this past summer.

"Okay, I'm going to go and change. I'll set the timer and meet you for tooth-brushing in ten minutes. Got it? Ten," I told her as I backed slowly down the hall.

Once back in my room, I made the other half of the bed and picked out my clothes for the day. I grabbed my camera from the top of my tall dresser and put it in my pocket before heading to the bathroom, where I found a three-foot-tall blonde staring at me with her arms crossed.

"You're late," she told me, to which I laughed.

"I apologize." I walked into the room and grabbed our toothbrushes, and we proceeded to go about the rest of our morning routine. With everything in order, I looked down at her. "Okay, you ready for a fun day at Grandma's?"

Charlie looked up at me skeptically. "I think you forgot one thing, Daddy." I scrunched my forehead and thought about what I could have forgotten. "The morning time isn't going to be fun because *Seth* is going to be there, too."

I knelt down so I was at eye-level with her. "Oh

sweetheart, I think if you'd just give him a chance, the two of you might become friends. Best friends, even."

She shook her head, cupping my jaw in her small hands. "You're crazy, Daddy." I chuckled softly as she walked around me and headed for the stairs, with me in close pursuit.

I helped Charlie into her long coat and tied her shoes for her before grabbing my own jacket and briefcase. I slipped my shoes on quickly and ushered us out the door and toward the Audi. Charlie hopped into her booster seat and strapped herself in before I double-checked to make sure she was secure, and then I slid behind the wheel.

We drove through Frederick, playing a game of "Eye Spy," and singing along with the radio until we pulled into the oversized driveway of my parents' house.

My mother, Helen, had been watching Charlie every day since Cassie started working in Denver. She ran her own bakery and had an amazing staff that allowed her to liaise from home most days, so she was able to juggle both that and her only grandchild effectively.

As we made our way up the walk, the front door opened and my father, Robert, stepped out. His dark hair was neatly combed, face freshly shaven, and he was wearing a suit and tie and had his briefcase in hand as he descended the front steps and walked toward us.

"GRAMPA!" Charlie shrieked as she took off running for him.

His smile spread from ear to ear, and his eyes lit up as he knelt down and braced himself for her impact. "Well, here she is!" he exclaimed as he wrapped his arms around her. "I was just beginning to wonder if I would see you before I had to leave for the hospital." He looked at his watch and tsk'ed. "You cut it pretty close, young lady," he teased.

Her little brow furrowed, and she turned her head to me briefly before looking back at my father. "It's not my fault, Grampa, I swear. Daddy told me I had ten minutes to meet him for us to brush our teeth, and *he* took...I don't know, like, twelve," she tattled.

Shooting me a quick smirk, he looked at her and winked. "Well, it sounds like Daddy needs a turn in the naughty corner, doesn't he? And do you know who can make that happen?" he asked.

They looked into each other's eyes and then back to me. "Gramma," they said in unison.

"Dad, don't encourage her," I begged jokingly as Charlie pecked him on the cheek and skipped up the front stairs yelling for my mother.

My father laughed as he stood up straight, watching Charlie's retreat. "Jack, she's your daughter. She doesn't need encouragement," he reminded me before turning and meeting my tired eyes. Concern flashed across his face. "You feeling all right, son?"

Not wanting to burden him with the issues Cassie and I were going through, I simply smiled and nodded. "Yeah, I just didn't sleep very well last night. I'm fine, though. Thanks."

He eyed me skeptically for a moment. "All right. Well, if you need anything, just call me."

I smiled at him appreciatively. "Will do, Dad." I looked up and saw my mother and Charlie standing in the doorway. Mom was struggling to keep a straight face while Charlie looked rather proud of herself. With a heavy sigh, I looked at my father again. "I have to go and face my fate now...thanks to you."

Laughing, he placed a hand on my shoulder in passing. "Better you than me."

I walked the rest of the way, and my mom smiled wider. She was dressed casually in jeans and a long-sleeved shirt, her hair pulled up into a ponytail. Her appearance was likely in preparation of a day full of chasing a four-year-old around the zoo. "Good morning, Mom. What's up?"

"Well, my granddaughter has just informed me that you were late after you specifically told her to meet you in ten minutes this morning. And that two minutes almost made her miss her hugs from her grandfather." She snorted quietly as she tried to stifle her laughter. "Now, what do you think your punishment should be?"

With a soft chuckle, I responded, "I'm not sure. Why don't we ask the one I seem to have wronged so horribly." I knelt down. "Charlie, sweetheart. I am terribly sorry for almost making you miss Grandpa. I am ready to accept my punishment."

She looked deep in thought for a moment. "Well, when I'm naughty, I have to sit in the naughty corner for four minutes, 'cause I'm four years old. How old are you, Daddy?"

"Twenty-nine," I told her.

Her eyes grew wide, and she started shaking her head from side to side. "That's a lot," she whispered. "Okay, I'll make you a deal."

I cocked an eyebrow and leaned in close to her. "I'm listening."

"I get *double* scoops of ice cream tonight after dinner, and you don't hafta sit in the naughty corner for all those minutes," she said, holding out her hand for me to shake.

I eyed her carefully, pretending to think about her bargain, before I took her hand in mine and shook it. "You drive a hard bargain, Miss Martin. But, I accept your terms. Tonight, after dinner, you will get double the ice cream."

Charlie squealed in delight before running into the house. "Auntie Jen! Auntie Jen! It worked!"

I stood up, shaking my head. "I was just played by a four-year-old, wasn't I?" I asked my mother with a laugh.

She shrugged, pulling me through the front door. "To be fair, your sister had something to do with it."

"I should have known," I said with a quick nod.

My older sister entered the foyer, laughing. She looked like a younger version of my mother, her green eyes bright and cheerful, but she had our father's dark hair. It was cut short, falling just beneath her chin. "Yes, you really should have." She stopped in front of me. "I figured ice cream would be better than a half hour in the naughty corner, though. You can thank me later," she said playfully.

"I'll let you know how thankful I am tonight when she's running around the house like a hamster on speed," I told her, chuckling. I glanced up at the old grandfather clock that stood in the entry and groaned. "Well, I suppose I should be heading to work now. Charlie?" I called out.

I heard the pitter patter of her little feet running through the house. "Yeah, Daddy?"

I knelt before her and took her hands in mine. "I have to go to work now. You have fun with Grandma today, okay? And do me a favor?"

"Uh huh."

I smiled. "Play nice with Seth, all right?"

Charlie rolled her eyes. "Fine."

"And before I forget," I said, reaching into my pocket. "Don't forget to take lots and lots of pictures at the zoo this afternoon." I handed her the slim black camera.

She took a deep breath and held it as her eyes

shone with excitement. She cupped her hands together and held the camera as if it were a precious glass figurine. "Oh, thank you, Daddy! Thank you! I will! I'll take lots of the best pictures on the whole planet!" she squealed.

"Good to hear." I pulled her into a hug and gave her a kiss before I stood to leave. "Mom, call if you have any problems." I turned to Jennifer and shook my head. "Jen...I'll be seeing you around Charlie's bedtime tonight?"

Jen laughed. "You think that's going to be bad? Just wait till you come pick her up...I'm going to the zoo with them. Do you know how many different kinds of sugary treats they have there?" she asked teasingly.

"Mom, you keep her in line," I instructed, pointing at my sister.

My mom picked Charlie up and snuggled her. "Jack, you forget that I am the one that has to deal with this precious angel all day long... Your sister won't get a drop of sugar near these pouty little lips," she cooed, brushing her nose against Charlie's. Charlie started laughing at her grandmother's affection.

I opened the door to leave. "Okay, I'll see you guys at six. Charlie, be good." I walked to my car and headed to work.

Once I was alone, though, I couldn't stop myself from dwelling on the fact that my marriage was on the fast-track to self-destruct. When I pulled my car into its spot at the office, I picked up my phone and dialed Cassie's number. It went straight to voicemail, which was no surprise since she rarely had her phone on when she was at work.

When the beep sounded, I took a breath and left her a brief message. "Hey, it's just me. I just wanted to tell you to have a good day today since we missed you this morning, and to say we should maybe organize a family outing for this weekend. Call me later. I love you."

I ended the call and grabbed my briefcase before heading into the building, ready to start my day. Sadly, I couldn't stop myself from feeling that this one would be no different from the rest.

Chapter Two
So Many Memories

The end of the day couldn't have come soon enough. Most days I truly enjoyed my job, but I was so worn out from the night before that I just couldn't find that same drive. That's not to say I didn't listen to my patients and give them the best care they deserved. I was still a professional. However, today was a particularly low traffic day, and when I had fewer patients, I had more down time to think of the shit-storm my life had become these last few years.

I packed up my briefcase and exited my corner office as quickly as possible, anxious to pick Charlie up and hear all about her exciting day. I passed the receptionist on my way out and waved. "Goodnight, Jill. See you tomorrow."

"Goodnight, Dr. Martin," she replied with a flirtatious smile.

I shook my head as I pushed my way through the doors. It didn't seem to matter to other women that I was married—happily, or not—they all seemed to think I would succumb to their advances. It grew quite tiresome after a while.

I climbed into my car and checked my phone to see if Cassie had returned my call from earlier. She hadn't, not that I was surprised. After taking a moment to try to remind myself she was probably really tied up with work all day, I finally started the car and headed through town to my parents' house.

When I arrived, I found Charlie outside with Jen

and one of my best friends — who also happened to be my sister's husband — Alex, playing a game of "Tag." I laughed as Alex ducked and rolled to evade my sister's touch. When he got up, he had bits of grass and leaves scattered in his brown hair. I put the car into park and stepped out.

"Daddy!" Charlie cried, rushing across the lawn to come see me. "We need a time-out! My daddy's here!"

Alex stood up and furrowed his brow. "Hey! No fair! When I asked for a time-out, you said they weren't allowed," he teased, acting petulant.

Charlie laughed at him as she hopped into my awaiting arms and squeezed me. I returned her embrace as I spoke. "Hey, sweetie. How was your day?"

She wriggled free and looked me square in the eyes. "It was so good!"

"Fantastic," I said happily. "Are Grandma and Grandpa inside?"

She nodded excitedly. "Mmm hmm. Gramma's cookin' dinner."

"Thanks. You go and play with your aunt and uncle. I'm going to go and say hi and then we'll head for home, all right?" I suggested.

Her smile lit up her face as she turned and ran back to the lawn. "Time-on!" she squealed as she ran for Alex. He picked her up and carried her quickly away from Jennifer as she continued to try and tag them both.

"That's not even close to being fair, Alex!" Jennifer cried out as I walked through the front door. Sometimes it was hard to believe she was a year older than me.

Once inside, I removed my shoes and padded through the massive entryway. As I walked through the hall on my way to the kitchen, I couldn't help but look at each and every picture of happier times. Pictures of mine and Cassie's wedding adorned the wall, along with pictures of Jennifer and Alex's. Then, there were oodles of pictures of Charlie, some with only her and Cassie, others of her and me, and then a few of the three of us together. It didn't escape my notice that the last family picture we had of the three of us was when Charlie was two.

Shaking my head, I made my way to the kitchen, promising myself that we would go and have some more taken soon. When I walked through the doorway, I found my father hard at work over the stove, and my mother was peeling carrots.

"Hey," I greeted, leaning on the counter across from my mom as she meticulously peeled the bright vegetables. "How did everything go today?"

Mom laughed. "Well, your daughter has about three hundred pictures to show you from today. Though, I think only seventy are from the zoo. She and Seth were taking pictures of absolutely everything today while he and his mother were over." She laughed softly. "You should really just arrange their marriage now. I'm pretty sure they're meant to be together."

"She's only four and you're already trying to marry her off to the neighbor boy. Nice, Mom," I teased just as the front door opened and Charlie ran into the room, closely flanked by Jen and Alex, who took a seat at the table.

I scooped Charlie up in my arms and held her close. "Besides, Charlie is quite sure she doesn't even like Seth."

"Oh no, Daddy. Seth is my very best friend now," she informed me seriously, her eyes as wide as saucers.

"Is that so? And what made you finally come to

this conclusion?" I questioned.

Charlie smiled brightly. "He shared his cookies before lunch," she whispered, chancing a glance over at her grandmother to be sure she hadn't heard.

My mother didn't look up to acknowledge Charlie's pre-lunch snack, but she smiled knowingly as she continued to prepare dinner. "Jack, will you and Charlie be joining us for dinner tonight?" she asked, looking up to meet my gaze.

"No thanks. I think we're going to try for a quiet family dinner tonight," I declined politely.

Mom arched her brow and glanced at me disapprovingly. She shook her head quickly and returned her attention to the vegetables in front of her. "You know, Jack, I'm worried about you two," she told me.

I took a deep breath and forced a smile as I looked into Charlie's bright eyes. "Don't, Mom. Not now," I pleaded, hoping for Charlie's sake that she wouldn't bring up my marital discord with Cassie.

"I'm sorry, but I am," she continued.

I sighed exasperatedly. "Look, everything is fine. I should get Charlie home, though. I'll see you guys tomorrow." I turned and started for the door.

I was just putting Charlie's shoes and jacket on when my dad joined us in the doorway. "Son, don't be upset with your mother. We're both concerned. Ever since—"

"Enough!" I shouted, causing Charlie to jump at the volume of my voice, and her eyes instantly filled with tears. I swept her up into my arms and stood quickly. I narrowed my eyes at my father and clenched my teeth together. "It's really none of your concern."

Wrapping her arms tightly around my neck, Charlie buried her face into my shoulder, and I could feel her warm tears seep through the fabric of my shirt. Her quiet sobs soon caused her breathing to shorten as she gasped for air.

"Shhh, Charlie. Daddy's sorry for yelling." I turned back to my father. "Look, I have to get her home. I'm sorry."

With an unspoken understanding, he nodded as I turned and opened the door. I walked to the Audi and placed Charlie in her seat, strapping her in tight as she swiped at her blotchy red eyes and sucked in an unsteady breath of air.

I kissed her forehead softly before looking into her eyes. "Baby, I'm sorry for shouting. I didn't mean to frighten you."

"I...I know," she said between sobs.

I offered her a wide smile and rested my forehead to hers. "What do you say we go home and make dinner? Then after dinner you can have your ice cream?" I suggested, hoping to take her mind off the argument I had just had with her grandparents.

She raised her eyebrows at me and sniffled once more. "Double ice cream, renember?"

"Right, double."

With Charlie feeling a little better, I closed her door and slid behind the wheel. Charlie was quiet the entire trip, which was incredibly out of character for her. She was usually exuberant while she spoke about her day with her grandmother. Not today, however. I looked back at her through my rearview mirror and saw her looking sadly out her window. She took a deep breath and sighed, and my heart broke a little inside.

I pulled the car to a stop in our driveway and turned to look at her. "Charlie, baby? Are you all right?"

She turned her head to face me slowly and nodded. "Mmm hmm."

"Okay, as long as you're sure," I said, a hint of worry in my voice.

It upset me that she was affected so deeply by my disagreement with her grandparents, and I had no one to be angry with but myself. I had always tried to shield her from this sort of thing, only I failed miserably this time around.

Sighing, I grabbed my briefcase and exited the car before going around to help her out. We walked side by side up the front steps, and she waited patiently as I unlocked and opened the door for her. Once inside, she slipped out of her jacket and shoes and put them away before padding slowly toward the kitchen.

Always one step behind her, I watched as she pulled her chair at the table out and sat down. She placed her palms flat on the table and rested her chin on the tops of her hands. I was silent for a moment as I waited for...something. *Anything.*

"So, what would you like for dinner tonight?" I asked, hoping that involving her would rouse her a little.

She turned her head to me, keeping her chin firmly on the tops of her hands, and shrugged. "I don't know. Sgabetti?"

I chuckled at the cute way she always mispronounced the word. "Sounds delicious," I told her as I headed for the fridge to start preparing it. "Would you like to watch some television before dinner?"

"No, thank you. Can I color pictures instead?" Her voice was so quiet, withdrawn.

I offered her a big smile. "Of course you can. I'll go get your stuff," I offered before exiting the kitchen for Cassie's home office. Charlie's pad of art paper and her crayons were on the corner of the desk, so I scooped them up and took them back out to the kitchen table.

"Thank you, Daddy," she said as she opened up her box of crayons and leafed to a fresh piece of paper.

I kissed the top of her head and smiled. "You're welcome, bug." I headed back to the kitchen and continued to prepare dinner, every once in a while looking up at Charlie as she colored. I couldn't help but smile every time I witnessed her tongue occasionally peek out from her lips and her forehead furrow with deep concentration. She was truly something else, and I couldn't imagine my life without her. She brightened up every day.

I just wished that Cassie saw it that way.

As dinner cooked, I kept glancing up at the clock, always wondering if Cassie would actually make it on time tonight. Seven o'clock arrived and dinner was ready; sadly, Cassie was still absent. With an aggravated sigh, I plated the pasta and sauce and carried it over to the table. Charlie pushed her artwork away from her place to make room for her plate, and she dug right in.

"So, you had a good day today?" I asked, hoping for details.

With her little mouth full from the bite she had just taken, she simply nodded in response. "Mmm hmm."

"And you got a lot of pictures?" I inquired before I took a bite.

She swallowed her spaghetti quickly. "Oh, yes. I took a billion pictures today. Can we look right now?" she asked excitedly. Her eyes seemed to brighten as her mood shifted significantly back to my Charlie.

"How about after bath time we come to the living room and snuggle. Then you can show me and tell me all about your day," I suggested.

"Okay!"

We continued to eat our meal, occasionally talking about her day and what she and Grandma had planned for the next day. When we finished, I took our plates to the kitchen to begin the cleanup and grabbed Charlie her ice cream. As she ate, I filled the dishwasher and washed the pot and pan.

"Please may I be excused?" she asked from the table.

I looked up and smiled. "Of course. Can you please bring me your bowl?"

Charlie hopped down from the table and cradled her bowl between her hands as she crossed the floor to me. I put the dish in the dishwasher, turned it on and gave the counter one final wipe-down before turning to her. "All right, who's ready for bath time?"

Charlie jumped up and down, raising her arm in the air. "I am! I am!" she squealed. We walked upstairs together and I ran her bath, being sure to add plenty of bubble bath as she got ready and climbed in.

Charlie snatched up her toys and played until it was time to wash her hair. Once she was clean, she played some more until the water was chilled and her fingertips pruned. She pulled the plug as I grabbed her towel, and I bundled her up tightly before pulling her from the tub.

She held her towel tightly as I combed the tangles from her hair and helped her brush her teeth. Once we finished in the bathroom, I walked with her to her room and stood in her doorway.

I bent down until I was face-to-face with her. "All right, now. How about you get into your jammies and I will go and do the same? Then, we'll meet downstairs and look at the pictures you took today. Sound good?"

"Yup!" she exclaimed, darting over to her dresser for her pajamas.

I went off to my room and got ready for bed before heading back down to meet Charlie for our date. When I entered the living room I saw Charlie sitting on the couch dressed in her two-piece blue flannel pajamas. With her back right against the couch, her little legs stuck straight out in front of her, and as I got closer, I saw she had the camera resting on her lap.

I snuggled up next to her as I picked the camera up and turned it on. "Okay, so what are we looking at here?" I asked as I started flipping through the multiple images.

Charlie narrated the entire time we looked at the pictures; my mother wasn't kidding when she said Charlie and Seth had taken hundreds around the house. The pictures were ranging from the fresh flowers on the dining room table, to pictures of Jen reading on the couch in the family room.

We finally got to the zoo pictures and Charlie squirmed excitedly next to me. "Oh! These are the lions, Daddy! They were neat! There was a daddy lion and a bunch of mommy lions and some babies, too!" she exclaimed.

We flipped through the rest of the animals, each one more exciting than the last for her, and I hadn't realized we were at the end of her zoo adventure until I flipped to a picture of Cassie and me sitting at our piano.

In an instant, my mind drifted back to that day; it was one of the last days we were truly happy.

Chapter Three
whispered promises

Cassie had just hoisted a two-year-old Charlie into her arms and carried her upstairs for bed while I stayed downstairs and finished tidying up the toys scattered about the living room. When everything was put away, I sat down at the piano and started playing.

I looked up when I heard Cassie's soft sigh, and I melted inside when she smiled. "I love hearing you play," she said softly as she crossed the room to me, stopping momentarily to grab the camera from the shelf.

She sat down next to me as I continued to play for her. She pressed a series of buttons and placed the camera on the sleek black wood. She leaned her head on my shoulder and, with a smile, I pressed my lips to her forehead as the camera flashed, capturing that moment forever.

She picked the camera up and flipped it over. "That's a keeper," she announced.

"Why don't you play anymore, Daddy?" Charlie asked, her tiny voice pulling me out of the beautiful memory.

I sighed, looking over at the piano that sat untouched for the last two and a half years. "I don't know, baby. I guess I've just been too busy."

She looked up at me with wide, innocent eyes. "Will you play for me tonight?" she pleaded.

I looked over at the clock on the mantle, my gut

churning with upset, and then back down at her apologetically. "It's already past your bedtime tonight, sweetie. But, how about we make a date for tomorrow after dinner?"

"Yes! Okay!" she agreed animatedly as she bounded off the couch and rushed toward the stairs.

I followed her to her room and watched as she climbed under her purple comforter and pulled it up under her chin. I moved to her bedside and knelt down, placing a kiss on the top of her head.

"Are you tucked in tight enough?" I asked only to have her nod her reply. "All right, sleep tight, Charlie. I love you."

"Love you, too, Daddy," she responded as I moved to the door. She snatched up her stuffed kitten from behind her and snuggled down further into the blankets. I flicked off her lights and pulled the door closed most of the way before heading back downstairs. Being just past eight-thirty, I wasn't ready to turn in, plus I still had to wait for Cassie to get home.

I walked into the kitchen and poured myself a glass of wine. As I stood at the island, I eyed the sleek, black baby grand that stood in the far corner and took a drink before heading toward the regal, abandoned instrument. I placed my wine glass on the top of the piano and lifted the fallboard. Eyeing the keys nervously, I took a deep breath and reached out. My fingers gently ghosted over them, familiarizing myself with the smooth surface. Then, without thinking, my fingers pressed down and began to dance fluidly over the ivory, causing melodies to fill the house completely.

As the music took control, I closed my eyes and got lost in the same memory from earlier.

Cassie set the camera back down and tilted her head

upward and pressed her lips to mine firmly. The music stopped instantly as I lifted my hands and twisted my fingers into the hair at the nape of her neck, deepening our kiss. With a soft moan against my mouth, Cassie twisted her body closer to mine.

I broke our embrace and scooped her up in my arms, quickly carrying her upstairs to our room where I set her on the bed and pulled her shirt over her head. She began to unbutton my jeans as I pulled my shirt off. With my pants pooled around my ankles, I stepped out of them and leaned forward, capturing her lips once more. As I moved forward, Cassie reclined down onto the bed, and, with one hand, I unfastened her pants and helped her remove them before I hovered over her near naked body.

I pressed my body into hers and she hitched her legs up around my waist as we molded together. Twisting her body, she successfully rolled us over until she was straddling me, and her lips created a delicious trail down my neck and chest while her hair fell in a curtain around her face, tickling my skin on her descent. She continued kissing her way down my body until she was standing at my feet.

I propped myself up on my elbows and looked at her with confusion. "Where do you think you're going?"

With a seductive smile, she tucked her hair behind her ears and leaned back over me, kissing me sweetly. "To take my pill before I forget."

I sat up as she stood again and I grabbed her hand, pulling her across my lap and kissing at the hollow below her ear. "Well, what if we didn't worry about it," I whispered huskily, nipping her earlobe gently and moving my hand up her inner thigh.

She pressed her hands to my chest, pushing me back slightly, and laughed. "Funny."

With an arched eyebrow, I attempted to read her expression. "Why is that funny? We've talked about this for a while now."

The look in Cassie's eyes was no longer one of lust as she sighed and rolled her eyes. I could sense her frustration as she stood from my lap and snatched her shirt off the floor. The mood had shifted drastically. Sex was no longer on the table. "No, you talked about this. I kept telling you it wasn't going to happen."

"Cass—"

She shook her head and pulled her shirt over her head, reaching behind her neck to remove her long hair from the collar. "No. I'm not going to chance another pregnancy. I'm not ready, and you, of all people, should know not to press this issue."

I stood from the bed and gripped her waist firmly as I placed a kiss to her nose. "We always said we wanted more than one," *I reminded her.* "You loved being pregnant."

She placed her hands on my jaw and smiled. "I did. It was wonderful, and one of the best experiences of my life. But the year after?"

The memory of that dark time stung to the very center of my being. Cassie had fallen into a deep depression. Her anti-depressants did little to nothing to help bring her out of it, and she was in such a state of denial about the whole thing, that there was nothing I could do to help. She refused it all, pulling away from everyone around her until she hit rock bottom.

We were finally able to get it under control with a new anti-anxiety prescription in combination with her regular meds. The combination made her a little foggy, but it was better than the alternative. Without them, her moods were the worst I'd ever seen. It was one extreme to the other, and I feared what she might do to herself during one of her low points.

"There's a chance that you wouldn't experience that again," *I breathed, trying to forget.*

She shook her head. "And also a chance I could. Jack, you were there, you saw just how bad it was. I missed most *of the first six months of her life."*

I smiled reassuringly and spoke softly, "I remember, but now that we know what to look for, we'd be better prepared to handle it."

Her face fell. "I'd be medicated again," she whispered sadly.

"Again?" Placing my fingers beneath her chin, I forced her eyes to mine. "Cassidy, have you gone off your meds completely?" She didn't have to answer; her eyes spoke volumes. "Love, was Sienna okay with that? You know the risks."

Cassie pulled her bottom lip between her teeth. "It's been a year since I started them. You know what they did to me...how they made me feel. So, I stopped taking them slowly. And I've been doing really well these last two months." She paused for a moment before looking at me with conviction. "Even you couldn't tell the difference," she tried to explain.

I pinched the bridge of my nose in frustration. "So, you're telling me you came off your meds, and your doctor has no idea?"

"I am," she replied confidently. "I'm also telling you, I'm not interested in having any more children. At least...not for a while." She turned from me then and closed herself in the bathroom, ending the discussion.

When I opened my eyes, I was surprised to see Cassie leaning on the piano in front of me with the biggest smile on her face.

"You're playing," she said happily. "Geez, it's been what? Two years?"

Instantly, I lifted my fingers from the keys and brought the fallboard back down. "Two and a half. Not since the night—"

Her smile faded, eyes filling with sadness as they dropped to where her fingers danced along the smooth black finish. "Yeah," she interrupted with a soft nod. "I remember."

A wry laugh escaped my lips as I picked up my glass and stood from the piano. "Wine?" I asked, holding the glass out to her.

"Jack, you know I can't drink." It shocked me that I had forgotten that.

I shook my head. "Oh, right. I'm sorry." I finished the rest of my drink and rinsed my glass before placing it in the sink. When I turned around, I found Cassie sitting on the counter behind me.

"How was your day?" I asked her.

"The same as always," she said with a shrug. "Charlie's asleep?"

"Where else would she be?" I really tried not to sound annoyed.

"Sorry," she quickly apologized upon hearing the inflection in my voice. "How was she today?"

"She was fine. Mom took her to the zoo," I explained, my irritation growing since she could have known all of this had she been home for dinner.

Cassie smiled. "How fun." I couldn't help but scoff and shake my head, which only caused Cassie to cock her head to the side. "What?" she inquired.

I clenched my teeth together tightly to keep myself from saying something I knew I would regret. "Nothing."

Hopping down from the counter, she approached me. "No, that's not a 'nothing' face. What is it?"

The words spewed forth before I could stop them. "You could have known all of this had you shown up. This shit's been going on almost three years, Cassie. You'd think a person would want to spend time with their family. Especially when that person's marriage is ready to fall apart any day."

"Is that really how you view all of this?" she asked incredulously.

Frustrated, I pinched the bridge of my nose. "You're something else, you know that?" I raised my eyes to hers. "How else should I view this?"

"I think you should start to see things for what they really are," she said cryptically, an edge of anger lacing her tone.

"What the hell is that supposed to mean? What exactly am I not seeing?" My eyes widened as a new thought entered my mind. "Is there someone else?" It was something I never once considered before, and I was terrified for her response.

Raising her eyebrows and releasing a sigh, she looked at me. "Look, I don't want to fight tonight. I'm going to go and lay with Charlie for a bit. I'll come to bed soon, okay?" She took a small step forward, placing her hands on my chest and standing up onto her tiptoes to kiss me. Her lips brushed mine so softly I almost didn't feel them.

I watched as Cassie left the room, and I heard her light footfalls overhead as she entered Charlie's room. Feeling the deep desire to calm my nerves, I snatched my glass from the sink and poured another glass of wine. The house was silent as I stood against the counter, drinking the smooth liquid, and I couldn't help the myriad of thoughts that ran through my mind. Was she having an affair? It certainly made sense, what with the late nights and all. But, could she really do that to her family? To Charlie? To me? It didn't take long before my glass was empty and my head was foggy, so I put it back into the sink, ready to retire for the night.

Once I was sure I was calm enough to face her again, I took a breath and headed for the stairs. As I walked past Charlie's bedroom, I peeked in and saw

Cassie lying on the outer edge of the bed, running her fingers through a sleeping Charlie's golden hair.

Could she? I looked at the image before me—the smile on her face as she whispered something to our sleeping daughter—and shook my head in disbelief at my mistrust.

"Cass?" I whispered into the dimly lit room, and she looked up at me sadly. "Are you coming to bed?"

With a brief nod, she leaned forward and kissed Charlie's cheek before rising from the bed. "Mommy loves you, bug."

As Cassie led the way to our room, I felt the deep desire to believe that everything was going to get better from this point on. Of course, there was still something that hung thick in the air as it tried to suffocate us, and it refused to change. With both of us ready for bed, we climbed beneath our comforter, and I couldn't help but notice that Cassie still seemed as distant as ever when I pulled her into my arms.

"I love you," Cassie whispered, pressing her body impossibly closer to mine. "Forever."

I pressed my lips to the top of her hair. "I love you, too. I always will," I assured her, and my words were one hundred percent true. I loved her so much that I would fight for her—for us—until I drew my last breath.

That was a promise.

Chapter Four
the beach house

It was the end of the work day. As the remaining sunlight of the day streamed in through the window, I sat in my leather office chair staring at the computer monitor. The images that flashed before me served to remind me of the wonderful times we used to have together. Christmases, vacations, family dinners... So many beautiful memories.

One particular picture caught my attention, and I sat forward in my chair to stare at it intently. It was a picture of Cassie and an almost three-year-old Charlie looking at shells on the beach.

After our honeymoon in California, our families always took two weeks at the end of every summer to spend at my parents' beach house. As I stared at the picture, it didn't take long for the memories of that last summer vacation to come flooding back.

"Tell Daddy what we found, Charlie," Cassie said quietly as she padded across the sand with our daughter at her side. Her blonde locks and white sundress flowed behind her in the gentle ocean breeze, and as her eyes met mine, she offered me a smile. However, there was something behind her expression that had me worried. She looked tired — exhausted, even — and there seemed to be a hint of sadness behind her blue eyes.

With an empathetic smile in Cassie's direction, I set

the camera down on the beach towel next to me and shifted onto my knees to see what Charlie held so delicately in her tiny hands. "What did you and Mama find, bug?" I asked excitedly.

"Sea shells!" she told me with a level of enthusiasm only a toddler could have.

I pulled Charlie onto my lap as I sat back down on the ground. My concern for my wife returned when I looked over at her as she knelt down next to us, running her fingers through her hair and exhaling a heavy sigh.

I reached over and rubbed her back soothingly. "You feeling all right, sweetheart?"

With a small smile, she nodded. "Yeah. I'm just tired."

"You sure?" I asked, only to have her smile and place her hand on my cheek. I turned my head and placed my lips to the inside of her wrist before turning my eyes back to Charlie's treasures.

The sun was beginning to set as we sat there together with Charlie showing me all the beautiful shells she and Cassie had collected. I glanced over at Cassie again and noticed that she seemed terribly withdrawn from the moment we were sharing as a family. As Charlie continued to leaf through the shells she had dropped into the skirt of her dress, I wrapped my arm around Cassie's waist and pulled her against me. She scooted over until she was sidled right against me, leaning her head on my shoulder with a sigh, and I kissed the top of her head.

"All right, you three, dinner is on the table. Let's not keep everybody waiting," my mother announced from behind us.

Knowing the wrath we would face for keeping our fathers waiting, we hurried and collected our things before heading inside. I stayed a step behind Cassie and Charlie and couldn't help but notice how sluggish Cassie seemed, even just walking to the house. Once we were on the porch,

I pulled her aside and placed my hand to her warm forehead.

"Cassie, you don't look well. Are you sure you're okay?" I knew the concern was audible in my voice, but I couldn't help the worry that came over me whenever she acted out of sorts. Especially since she had admitted to coming off of her medication five months ago.

"Yeah, I think I just got too much sun. I'll be fine." She stepped up onto her tiptoes, softly pressing her lips to mine before taking me by the hand and leading me to the dining room.

I took my seat next to my father's place at the head of the table while Cassie sat between me and her mother. Through my periphery, I watched as she draped her linen napkin across her lap before running her fingers through her hair again. I could see her jaw clench as she inhaled deeply, and I placed my hand upon her lap in silent reassurance.

Her mother, Gayle, reached over and placed a hand to Cassie's now-glistening brow. "Sweetheart, you feel clammy, and you're as white as a ghost."

Cassie laughed it off as she removed her mother's hand from her head. "Mom, I've always been pale." Her comment got a laugh out of everyone at the table as my mom made the rounds with the wine.

Mom had just touched the neck of the bottle to the rim of Cassie's glass when Cassie threw her hand over it. "Oh, um...none for me, thank you." Casting a nervous eye around the room before finally resting on me, she dropped her gaze and stammered, "I've had so much sun today that I don't want it to go straight to my head."

My eyes snapped wide open, and I stared at Cassie as she meekly raised her eyes to mine. Her bottom lip instantly found its way between her teeth as she watched me put the pieces together. She gave me a pleading look and head-shake that begged me not to say anything, so I didn't.

Her cheeks flushed as our mothers eyed her skeptically. "I'll just go and grab a glass of water. The rest of you can start without me. I'll be right back," Cassie said, sliding her chair back from the table and exiting the room.

I sat in stunned silence for a while as our families conversed back and forth. The only thing that was going through my mind was what was going on with Cassie and what she could possibly be feeling. This wasn't something she wanted, and I had promised to stop pushing the idea after that night two months ago. Sure, I wanted more children, but marriage was about compromise, and sometimes one had to make sacrifices. Not having a large family was mine.

Unable to focus on anything other than Cassie, I was on my feet in a flash, excusing myself to go off in search of her. I walked into the kitchen to see her leaning against the counter next to the sink, a glass of cold water clutched tightly in her right hand while her left death-gripped the edge of the tile countertop so hard her knuckles were white. Her eyes were focused on the floor, and I could hear her sobbing softly.

"Cass?" I whispered.

Upon hearing my voice, she jumped and quickly placed her glass on the counter. She used both hands to wipe the tears from her eyes as she met my gaze. "Oh, hey," she said, forcing a smile.

I crossed the room swiftly and pulled her into my embrace. She wrapped her arms around my waist and held me tightly. "So, you're sure? You're pregnant?" I asked her quietly.

"I took the test this morning," she mumbled into my shirt, fingers curling, gripping tighter.

Even though I knew this wasn't what she wanted, I couldn't help the smile of pure joy that spread across my face. We were going to have another baby. Charlie was going to be a big sister. Every part of me was over the moon with happiness, but as I held Cassie, I could feel her fear and despair as it rolled off her body in waves.

I pulled her away from me and held her at arm's length as I stared into her eyes. "You're not happy about this, are you?"

Her shrug was one of defeat and her smile was weak and forced. "I'm happy that you're happy." She sensed my unease with her answer and quickly added, "I just...I don't know... I need time to adjust, I think. It's not like this was exactly planned, you know?"

I moved my hands up to cradle her face. "Cassie, everything is going to be fine," I assured her.

"I know you think that, Jack, but it doesn't absolve my fear. I don't want to be that person again. The woman who resented her child, who found fault in everything, who could barely pull herself out of bed most mornings." A loud sob escaped her, and fresh tears spilled over her cheeks. "It wasn't fair to you or Charlie." She looked down between us, placing her hands on her flat stomach. "It wouldn't be fair to this baby."

I enveloped her in my arms again. "I promise you, everything is going to be fine this time."

Her slender arms snaked up my back until her hands firmly gripped my shoulders, and she pressed her cheek to my upper body. "You shouldn't make promises you can't keep," she whispered into my chest.

That was the last summer we had spent there. Just before we left for California that year, Cassie had merged her company with the one in Denver; she was actually fortunate to get those two weeks off. Her business had picked up shortly after we had returned, and we didn't see much of her after that.

There wasn't a single part of me that didn't want to recapture the magic of our summers away. I took one look at my calendar, and my impulses took control as I reached for my phone and rang Jill.

She picked up instantly, almost as though she were sitting on the phone. "What can I do for you today, Dr. Martin?" she purred into the receiver.

Rolling my eyes, I replied. "Jill, I need you to reschedule all of my appointments for the last two weeks of August. I'm going away."

Papers started rustling frantically. "Oh, um, that's the week after next?" she said, her voice rising at the end as though she were confused.

"Yes, I know," I told her monotonously.

"Right, okay. Well, you don't have too much lined up, so I'll see what I can do," she stumbled through her words.

"Thank you." I hung up the phone and began to gather my things so I could go and pick up Charlie. Suddenly, there was a gentle knock on my door. "Come in," I called out, putting the last of my papers into my briefcase.

I looked up when the door opened and my colleague, Dr. Sienna McKay, popped her head in. "Hey," she said quietly as she crossed the room to my desk, walking around until she was next to me, and perched herself upon the edge.

I offered her a smile. "What's up?"

She arched an eyebrow. "I didn't mean to eavesdrop or anything, but did I hear correctly that you're going away for a couple of weeks?"

I sat back down in my chair. "Um, yeah. I need to get away for a bit. You know, clear my head." I paused for a moment and saw the look in her eyes. "That's all right, isn't it? I mean, I know it's short notice, but I think I just need some family time away from home."

Sienna's face warmed as the smile stretched across her face. "Don't be silly. You deserve a little break. In fact, I was wondering if you wanted to maybe go and get a drink tonight? Would your parents mind keeping Charlie for an extra hour?"

Having been so long since the last time anyone hit on me, I wasn't quite sure if that was what was going on. There was a certain glint in Sienna's eyes, but it could have been nothing more than collegial concern. Regardless of her intentions, I was—no, *am*—one hundred percent dedicated to my marriage, even if Cassie wasn't always around.

Still, there was no doubting Sienna's beauty and her ability to charm most men. She was smart, funny, confident...

Shaking the thoughts from my head, I leaned forward onto my desk. I clasped my hands together in front of me and addressed her. "Sienna—"

She placed her gentle hand over mine. "One drink, Jack. You look like you could use it." Her hand was so warm as it laid above mine, and her thumb moved soothingly over my hands.

My breathing faltered slightly as I looked up into her hazel eyes and swallowed thickly. "I really don't think that's a good idea. Charlie's waiting for me," I told her hoarsely.

The shine in her eyes seemed to dim upon my declining her offer, but her warm smile remained. "I understand. Another time, then?"

I watched her stand and my eyes followed her, betraying me and the vows I made as they stared intently at her sashaying across the room. "Sienna, I don't know that any time is going to be good for me. Things at home are...complicated. I think it's best if we keep things between us professional."

She pulled the door open and turned back around, her eyes meeting mine. "It's just drinks, Jack. Nothing more."

The door closed with a soft click behind her, and I slumped back into my oversized chair. I let out a large breath and ran my hands through my hair, gripping it tightly for a moment as I tried to figure out exactly what I was thinking. Yes, my marriage wasn't ideal, but I couldn't cheat. Not ever. Cassie was my life.

Feeling the need for some fresh air, I picked up my briefcase and headed for the door. As I exited my office, I saw Sienna discussing something with Jill, and she shot me that dazzling smile she often did, raising her hand to wave. I simply nodded in response and kept walking toward the main doors.

Once I was in my car, I started it quickly and peeled out of the parking lot, suddenly in a hurry to get home to my family. I reached my parents' house in record time, and when I walked in, I found them in the kitchen with Charlie perched on the counter near my mom, licking a popsicle.

"Daddy!" she cried excitedly when I entered the room.

I kissed her temple and smiled. "Hey, bug. How was your day?"

With a big smile, she told me everything. "Gramma and me went to Denver today! She had to shop for work stuff and then she took me for lunch! We even drove by Mama's building!"

"You did?" I asked, looking up at my mom briefly.

Charlie nodded quickly. "Uh huh. I renembered that she worked in the city and I asked if we could see where."

"I see," I said. "Well, I'm glad you had a fun day. That's wonderful."

Mom let out a short breath and smiled. "How was your day, Jack?"

I pulled out a stool and took a seat. "It was busy, which was good. Keeps me out of my own head. I'd hate to have to psychoanalyze exactly what goes on in there," I chided. When my mother didn't laugh with me, I quickly changed the subject. "I actually had a pretty great idea before I left for the night."

She lifted her gaze to meet mine, and my father turned from the stove to look at me as well. "You did?" he inquired.

"I thought maybe we could all go back out to the beach house for the last two weeks of summer," I suggested. "I thought it would be fun to start doing the family summer trips again."

My dad moved to my mother's side, and they locked eyes for a moment before looking back to me. "Really?" he asked before a smile spread across his face. "Son, I think that's a wonderful idea."

"I figured it was time to try and get back to old traditions." Upon hearing this, my mom's eyes glistened, and she came around the island to hug me tightly. "Relax, Mom. It's really not a big deal."

She let go of me before cradling my face in her hands. "You may not think so, but I always enjoyed our family summers in California. So to hear that you're ready to start going again after everything that's happened...it makes me beyond happy." She wiped the few tears of happiness that had fallen from her eyes. "Oh! I'll have to call Frank and Gayle and see if they would like to join us. You're staying for dinner tonight, right? I won't take no for an answer."

The look of resolve on her face was hard to say no to, and I knew the chances of Cassie being home in time for dinner were slim since she never was. So, I smiled and nodded happily. "Of course we'll stay."

"Wonderful," she cheered as she took her place behind the counter again. "I think your father and I have everything under control out here. Why don't you take Charlie and go find something to do?" she suggested.

Charlie looked at me excitedly before her grandmother lifted her off the counter, whispering something in her ear. Whatever my mother had said caused Charlie to bob her head up and down exuberantly. "Daddy, can we go to the park? Gramma says we have an hour before dinner!"

"We sure can. Come on, let's go get your coat and shoes on." I took Charlie by her free hand and led her to the entry, where we put our shoes on and headed out the door.

We made our way down the sidewalk toward the park; Charlie was mostly silent as we walked. As soon as we reached the playground, though, she took off for the jungle gym. I stayed close as she climbed the ladder and went down the slide, repeating this cycle a few times before heading for the swings.

"Daddy, will you push me?" she asked as she jumped onto one of the available swings. I complied and began pushing her gently. She giggled and squealed in delight as she swung higher and higher. It was always a joy to hear her having fun and to watch her be so free...something that reminded me so much of how her mother used to be.

We laughed and ran around the park for a while, just playing and losing track of the time. It wasn't until I noticed the light in the sky change that I looked down at my watch and then to Charlie, who seemed to read my face. "We have to go now, huh?" she pouted.

I knelt down to her level and looked her in the eyes. "We do. But, I guarantee you Grandma has something yummy waiting for us back at the house." I smiled and gave her a wink. "Come on, I'll give you a piggy-back ride."

Charlie's face brightened, and she rushed around to hop on my back. I stood and adjusted her slightly as she wrapped her arms around my neck and rested her chin on my shoulder.

We walked in silence for a bit before Charlie spoke softly. "I miss Mama."

"Aw, baby. Mama misses you, too," I told her. "And she tells you so whenever she kisses you goodnight."

Charlie lifted her head from my shoulder quickly. "She does?"

We had reached the end of the driveway by that point, so I got down on one knee and Charlie slid off my back. I took her by the hand and pulled her around in front of me. "Every night," I said. "Now come on, I can smell Grandma's roast and my stomach is rumbling."

Holding my hand tightly, Charlie tugged on my arm in an effort to help me to my feet before pulling me toward the front door. As soon as we passed through the threshold, the aroma of the roast propelled us in the direction of the dining room, where my mother was just placing the last few table settings down.

"Oh good, you're just in time!" she exclaimed.

Charlie and I took our places at the table, and I dished up her dinner. Once Charlie had her plate in front of her, I started filling my own as I tried to make conversation. "So, what do you guys have planned for the weekend?"

"Oh! Actually I wanted to see if Charlie wanted to sleep over this weekend," my mom suggested. "You're father's busy at the hospital, and I was going to see if Charlie wanted to keep me company in this big lonely house."

Charlie's eyes went wide, and she turned her big, blue-eyed stare to me. "Oh, yes I do! Daddy, please may I stay with Gramma and Grampa?"

It had been awhile since she had stayed with them overnight, and it was difficult to look into her puppy-dog eyes and tell her "no." Plus, maybe it would give Cassie and me some much-needed time alone to talk through everything.

I smiled down at Charlie. "Of course you can sleep over. I'll pick you up Monday after I'm done work, if that's all right with Grandma."

My mother beamed from her spot across from me. "That would be perfect." Taking a bite of her dinner, she looked at me as though she had remembered something. As soon as she swallowed the bite, she spoke. "And before I forget, I called the Taylors and they would love to join us at the beach house this summer."

"Oh my goodness!" Charlie shrieked, bouncing wildly in her seat. "Gramma and Grampa Taylor are gonna come, too?"

My dad laughed and leaned forward. "And that's not all. Because it's so close to a certain little girl's fifth birthday, we're going to have a special family birthday party there," he announced, to which she replied with more exuberant shrieking and bouncing.

As we continued eating our dinner, we talked about the upcoming trip. My parents were extremely happy that we'd be participating in another family vacation. However, I knew convincing Cassie to take time off would likely be difficult, but I was hopeful—especially since it was likely our only shot at saving our fast-imploding marriage.

It was eight o'clock by the time I was ready to head for home. Once my shoes were on, I knelt down and pulled Charlie forward. "You be good for

Grandma and Grandpa this weekend. I'll call you tomorrow to say goodnight." I gave her a quick kiss before standing back up. "Call if there are any problems," I instructed my parents.

Mom laughed, placing her hands on Charlie's shoulders, causing her to squirm at the ticklish gesture. "I'm sure Miss Charlie will be on her best behavior. I foresee no problems."

After saying our goodnights, I hopped in my car and drove home. When I walked through the door, I removed my shoes and propped my briefcase up against the bench in the entry before making my way toward the kitchen. I poured myself a glass of wine and turned for the living room to watch some television. The sight before me caused me to stop dead in my tracks; Cassie was on the couch with a smile on her face.

"Well, well, well," she said, cocking an eyebrow. "Look who's late tonight."

Chapter Five
going back

Cassie laughed softly and winked at me as I stood there in complete shock. I couldn't believe that she was home before me. "Y...you're home," I blurted out, gaping at her in surprise.

She nodded happily, but her smiling face quickly transformed into a look of perplexity as she sat forward on the couch and looked behind me. "Where's Charlie?" she asked.

"Oh," I started. "My mom wanted to keep her this weekend. I figured that would be okay...I guess I should have checked with you first. I'm sorry." I shook my head in disbelief. How could I have completely overlooked Cassie's opinion on where our child stayed this weekend? That wasn't like me or conducive to my partnership with my wife.

"No, it's fine. She always has fun over there. Plus, this way we can spend some one-on-one time with each other." She sank back into the plush sofa and tilted her head to the side, silently inviting me to join her. Her posture was more relaxed than I'd seen her in a long time. Would this be the weekend we took the first steps to reconciling all that was wrong with our marriage?

Smiling at the possibility, I crossed the room and sat down next to her. She bent her legs, tucking her feet underneath her, and turned toward me. "So, how was your day?"

With a low sigh, I dropped my head to the back of the couch. "It was good," I replied. "Busy, for the most part." I paused and looked at her apologetically. "I'm so sorry. Had I known you'd be home early, I wouldn't have stayed out so late."

Cassie shook her head and placed her hand on my cheek. "You have no need to apologize...least of all to me. I'm just glad you're here now," she whispered softly, placing a tender kiss upon my lips before prodding me for more information. "So, tell me more about your day."

"You don't want to hear about my day," I assured her as she ran her fingers through my hair and then down the length of my neck, causing a slight shiver to pass through me.

"Try me," she said, her soft voice permeating every fiber of my being.

My body tingled as her fingers traced lazy designs over my neck. "Well, after delving into the minds of about seven people, I sat around at my desk for an hour looking at old pictures," I began, lifting my head and turning to face her.

"Sounds productive," she teased, her finger tracing the collar of my dress shirt.

I chuckled. "Oh, it was." I took a sip of my wine before continuing. "As I was looking at the pictures, I came across one from the summer before Charlie turned three. You remember...when we were at the beach house?"

Cassie's entire body stiffened and she pulled her hand back quickly, almost as though she'd been bitten. Instantly, I knew what she was remembering. "Seems like a lifetime ago," she breathed as her eyes drifted to her hands, which were now fidgeting in her lap. I could sense her anxiety creeping up based on her behavior.

I set my wine on the coffee table and placed my hands over hers to still them. "Remember how much fun we had? Charlie loved the water so much," I said with a smile, hoping to keep her from thinking of the tragic weeks that followed the trip.

A smile graced her face, and her eyes sparkled as she answered. "She really did, didn't she?"

"And I know you enjoyed our time there." I could tell by the softening of her rigid posture that I was breaking her down slowly. "Please, just try to remember all the good times we had there and not about the tragedy after we returned before you make up your mind…"

"Daddy, peas we go back to the wadder?" Charlie asked in the broken English that was common in toddlers.

I smiled as I scooped her up into my arms. "Charlie, it's too dark out now. The sun has gone to sleep, so that means it's time for you to go to bed, too," I explained in a way I hoped she would understand.

As if on cue, Charlie yawned. Chuckling, I let her down to go say goodnight to her grandparents and her aunt and uncle.

"Goodnight, pumpkin," Frank cooed when Charlie went to him last. He hugged her to him tightly, and she giggled. "You have a good sleep, okay? We'll see you in the morning."

I picked her back up and carried her down the hall toward her room. On our way, I stopped in the doorway of the room Cassie and I shared and found her lying on the bed with her back to me as she stared out the over-sized window at the gentle waves.

She never returned to the dinner table after we spoke in the kitchen. Instead, she asked me to tell our families she was feeling a little under the weather and needed to go lie down. I offered to go with her, but she told me she just needed some time to herself. When I returned to the table, both Gayle and my mother gave me knowing glances; I really should have known they would figure it out.

Unsure what state of mind I would find her in, I took a moment before I addressed her. "Sweetheart?" She twisted herself to face me. "I'm taking Charlie to bed now. Would you like to come and read a story with us?"

A small smile played at the corners of her mouth, and my concern for her lessened slightly. She stood from the bed and walked over to us. When Charlie reached out for her, Cassie took her from me and carried her the rest of the way to her room.

After tucking Charlie into bed, we lay down on either side of her, and I listened raptly as Cassie read "Goodnight Moon." The words flowed melodically from her mouth, and by the time she had finished the book, Charlie was already asleep. I looked up at Cassie as she watched Charlie's sleeping face wistfully. I knew she was upset by our situation, but I couldn't help the overwhelming feeling of happiness that coursed through me. My cheeks actually hurt from the smile that was constantly plastered on my face.

She raised her hand and began to stroke Charlie's golden curls away from her little face, smiling poignantly before looking up at me. I could feel the right corner of my mouth turn up in a half-smirk before I stood from the bed. "Come on. We should let her sleep," I whispered.

When she moved to my side, she twisted her fingers through mine and led me from the room. I pulled Charlie's door closed behind us and then turned to Cassie. "So, we're doing this?" I asked her quietly, barely able to contain my elation.

Cassie's brows knit together and she shrugged. "Well, what else can we do?"

"Cass—"

She held up a hand to silence me. "I just...I need time, Jack. I'm absolutely petrified of what's to come. But, I know this is what you want. And, in time, I'm sure I'll be fine."

The look on her face was one of immense fear, and I felt the undeniable need to comfort her. I pulled Cassie into my arms and pressed my lips to hers tenderly. Her resistance was unwavering as I embraced her, but I was confident she needed time, like she said. She had a lot to work through emotionally, and I was going to help her as best I could. I pulled Cassie's rigid body closer to mine and wrapped my arms around her waist as she ended our kiss. I rested my forehead to hers as she looked up at me through her thick lashes nervously and bit her bottom lip.

"So, I guess we should go and tell everyone?" she suggested quietly.

"Remember how happy they were?" I asked with a reserved smile.

She nodded sadly, her face slowly contorting as the trauma of past events came back to haunt her, even after all this time. "I do. I also remember how devastated they were three weeks later."

I hated to see her in such despair as she remembered that part of our life. Her pain was my pain, and it tore at me to watch her face twist like that. "Sweetheart, their reaction wasn't solely from the miscarriage. You were verging on catatonic. It was starting to scare us."

With a slow nod, Cassie sniffled and swiped the few stray tears that had fallen from her eyes. I wanted nothing more than to make things better for us, and I felt that there was only one way to truly do that. Knowing what reaction I was likely in for, I bit the bullet and spoke. "I want us to go back this summer. I'm desperate to fuse this family back together." I paused for a moment to gauge her reaction. "My mother even called your parents already. They're going."

Her head snapped up, and her eyes were still rimmed with tears. "No," she said breathlessly. "You *know* I can't."

"Cass, honey," I whispered soothingly as I brushed more tears from her cheeks with the pads of my thumbs. "We can't keep living in fear of the past."

Her head continued to shake from side to side in outright defiance to my request. I squeezed her hands gently and smiled at her, hoping to soften her resolve. I knew I had to do this to save us, so I pleaded. "Please?"

Cassie's eyes were filled with regret as she answered. "I'm sorry. You know I can't. I won't."

Chapter Six
never give up

I stared at her a moment, dumbfounded. How could she so readily dismiss this? Whatever the reason, I wasn't ready to give up quite so easily.

"Are you afraid we're going to repeat history?" I asked her.

Cassie's brow furrowed. "No, it has nothing to do with that."

I gripped her hands firmly in mine and looked deep into her eyes. "Listen, sweetheart, I know our life these last two years has been difficult, and our loss..." I took a moment to choke back my tears before continuing "...completely unbearable at times. But the Cassie I knew was so alive and carefree, and would fight the pain with everything she had. That's the Cassie that I remember...the Cassie that I fell in love with."

Cassie's eyes overflowed with tears as she stood, running her hands through her hair. "I lost a baby, Jack," she rasped, folding her arms around herself.

"*We*," I corrected her quietly, leaning forward and resting my arms on my knees as I watched her pace the room. "*We* lost a baby..."

"What do you think of 'Hannah' for a girl?" I asked excitedly, looking up from the baby naming book I had picked up on my way home from work. Charlie was in bed,

and Cassie and I were sitting on the couch watching "The Office" on television as I flipped through the pages. I was seated in the middle, while Cassie sat in the far corner, her legs pulled across my lap as she held the remote in her hand, waiting to swap the channel on the next commercial.

"Uh huh," she agreed less than half-heartedly.

Slightly discouraged, I furrowed my brow in discontent and continued to flip through the book. Excitement reclaimed me a few pages later, though, and I had a feeling this was the one. "Oh! Or there's Max? For a boy, I mean."

Cassie shrugged and flipped the channel with an annoyed sigh. "Whatever you want."

I closed the book and placed it down on her thighs as she tried to shift away from me. It was frustrating, but I knew I had to keep trying to get her involved. "I was also thinking we could maybe paint the room beside Charlie's in soft neutral tones. You know, keep the gender a secret on purpose this time. Remember how incredible it was when Dr. Morris told us Charlie was a girl?"

Cassie turned onto her side and propped her elbow on the arm of the sofa, allowing her head to rest in the palm of her hand. "Not really," she mumbled with a shrug, changing the channel again. There were no words to describe my shock as I absorbed her words. I stared at her with wide eyes, and she must have sensed my shock because she quickly added, "I was exhausted."

My spirit was crushed as I took in her despondent tone of voice. I had been trying since California to help her move toward acceptance and happiness for the new addition coming into our lives, but my efforts were being thwarted time and time again.

I didn't stop trying, though. Every day we would still talk and laugh, and when I figured she was in a good mood, I would bring up the baby in some way. In an instant, her mood would shift and she would become withdrawn from the subject. There were times that she seemed a little bit happier, however, the simple fact remained; Cassie never once started the conversations regarding the child that was growing within her. Instead, she preferred to talk about work.

We had been back from our family vacation for almost two weeks, and both Cassie and I had returned to work a few days after we arrived home. Considering Cassie's company merger was still pretty fresh, things were going smoothly. The late nights had begun shortly after they signed their largest client yet, and I offered to take care of things at home until work slowed down for her. I hoped that this would alleviate a lot of her stress, and that maybe that was her reason for being so withdrawn from the pregnancy.

Then came the day that would ultimately change our lives forever. It was Friday — Cassie's birthday — and we had Charlie's party planned for the following day. It was fortunate that Cassie had been able to get the weekend off, and my parents had even offered to take Charlie for the night so I could take Cassie out.

My breath hitched when Cassie descended the stairs wearing a form-fitted royal blue dress that cut off just above her knees. She looked sensational, and I told her as much when I held out my hand for her as she took her final step into the entry. Thoughts of staying home and skipping our dinner reservations altogether flew through my head upon seeing her. The only thing keeping me from scooping her up in my arms and taking her back upstairs was the rarity of being without Charlie. With my resolve steeled for the moment, we got into the car and drove to Cassie's favorite Italian restaurant.

We were about halfway through dinner when Cassie winced slightly. The look of pain on her face alarmed me. "Sweetheart? Are you okay?"

She looked up at me with a smile I was sure was sup-

posed to put me at ease, but it did no such thing. "Yeah. I've been having cramps all day," she said as she waved her hand dismissively. "I'm sure it's nothing, and I see Dr. Morris on Monday for blood work. Plus, I cramped off and on with Charlie, too," she reminded me.

I wasn't entirely reassured as I watched her carefully. She stabbed a spear of asparagus onto her fork and brought it to her mouth, narrowing her eyes at me as she chewed. "Your food is getting cold, Jack. I'm fine.*"*

I was skeptical, but I resumed eating my meal, my eyes never straying from her. Barely five minutes had passed when her entire body tensed and she clutched her stomach. "That's it," I said as I stood and reached for my wallet. "We're going to the hospital." I took out more than enough money to cover the meal and tossed it on the table before helping Cassie to her feet.

"Jack, you're overreacting," Cassie told me, picking up her pace so she wasn't being dragged in my haste to leave the restaurant.

Pushing through the immense fear I felt in that moment, I smirked at her. "Are you really surprised?" I asked with a wink.

"No, I suppose not," Cassie replied with a laugh as I opened her door and ushered her in. Her dress crept up her legs as she lowered herself into the passenger seat, and I was just about to close the door when my laugh died and my blood ran cold.

Cassie looked at me with mild concern before her eyes followed my intensely focused gaze. "Jack what's wr...?" Her words trailed off when she saw the thin crimson trail on her inner left thigh.

A sharp gasp echoed around me, jarring me from my paralyzed state, and I slammed her door before I rushed to get behind the wheel. Panic consumed every part of me. So much so, that I wasn't aware of time or speed limits as I sped through the streets of Frederick. I could only hope I was actually stopping for red lights. By the time we reached the hospital, Cassie's breathing was surprisingly in control, and she was calmly wiping at her leg with some wet-wipes she had found in the console. She must have been in shock, because the look on her face was far from the pure terror that mine likely portrayed.

My heart was hammering painfully against my ribs, and my hands were shaking as I threw the car into park. "Cassie, it could be nothing. We just have to try not to panic," I told her in the calmest voice I could muster given the circumstances.

Very slowly, she pushed her hair off her face. "'Kay," she said in an emotionless tone. She didn't sound panicked at all, and this only served to increase my fear.

We walked as quickly as we could through the doors of the Urgent Care facility at the hospital before stopping at the front desk. A woman, whose name tag read "Grace," looked up at us.

"Hi, what can I do for you this evening?" she asked cheerfully.

"We need to see a doctor as soon as possible," I said frantically.

Grace looked at her computer monitor and cocked an eyebrow as she looked for an opening. "All right. And what is it in regards to?" she inquired as she clicked the mouse.

"My wife is about seven or eight weeks pregnant and she started bleeding." My voice started to rise as my calm exterior began to crumble, and I could feel my anxiety spiking.

Grace's head snapped up, and her eyes shifted from mine to Cassie's. "Oh! Okay, well, I need all your information, and I'll enter you into the system ASAP."

As I rambled off our insurance information and the reason for our visit, I looked over at Cassie, who was standing stoically by my side. It was strange, but the look in her eyes was empty...almost completely void of any particular *emotion as the shock seemingly pulled her under. Once I had given all the information I could, we were told to take a seat and we'd be seen as soon a doctor became available.*

Sitting there didn't help put me at ease, though. My leg bounced rapidly, and I continually looked up at the time. Fear seeped in, invading every part of me, as I ran my trembling hands through my hair. With each passing millisecond, my anxiety level increased exponentially and my breathing became more and more shallow. It was too much; I was starting to lose my shit.

After looking at the clock for the hundredth time in two minutes, I glanced over at Cassie. She sat on the edge of her seat with her hands on her thighs, and her eyes appeared to be glazed over as she stared through the wall ahead of us. Seeing her slip into a near-catatonic state only served to remind me of the last time she was like this, and my chest tightened.

"Jack? Cassie?" The voice that called out to us seemed far away — as though it were cutting through the fog in my mind.

I raised my eyes toward the familiar sound. "Dad!" I cried, jumping to my feet as he approached.

"What are you guys doing here?" he asked, looking down at Cassie, whose expression was still emotionless and unfocused. "Cassie, sweetheart," he began, looking worriedly at me as he knelt before her. He took her face in his hands and gently coaxed her gaze to his. They were completely glossed over — staring through him. "What's wrong?"

Her voice cracked as she answered monotonously. "I think I'm losing the baby." She sounded cold — detached — and she blinked rapidly to focus her eyes on my father.

Just hearing the words caused my stomach to roll and my head to spin. I sat back down next to Cassie, resting my elbows on my knees and burying my face in my hands. Everything went black for a minute, and I was startled when I felt a hand on my shoulder.

"Son, come on. I'll take the both of you to an exam room and see if we can figure a few things out," Dad offered.

I looked over at Cassie, whose eyes were now wide with fear as she noticed me falling apart. I took her by the hand and we stood, following my father down the corridor. I could feel the bile churning in my stomach

"Cassie, I'm going to try and acquire an ultrasound machine," he said, shifting his eyes back and forth between the two of us. For the first time ever, he sounded nervous. "However, with you being so early in the pregnancy, it would have to be an internal procedure. I would understand if you'd prefer to wait for another doctor to become available."

Cassie bit her lower lip as she looked at me to gauge my reaction. I squeezed her hand in reassurance before she met my dad's eyes. "It's fine. I need to know now."

With a nod, he patted her shoulder as he moved past her toward the door. "Well," he began as he stopped and looked at her awkwardly, "Why don't you hop up on the table then? Just drape the paper sheet over your lower half, and I'll see if I can locate an ultrasound machine."

My father was gone in a flash. I began pacing the room, pushing my hands roughly through my hair while Cassie walked toward the exam table. Her face went deathly pale and she cringed as she shed her blood-soaked underwear and climbed up onto the paper-covered table.

The door opened just then and Dad entered, wheeling in an ultrasound machine. Cassie lay back, mechanically putting her feet up in the stirrups as my father started the examination. To say the situation was uncomfortable would be the understatement of the millennium, but we all tried to ignore the awkwardness for the sake of this crisis. He was silent as he looked at the monitor, and I tried to see what he was staring at so intently while he clicked a series of keys to zoom in.

I lowered my gaze to Cassie in hopes of reassuring her, but she was staring up at the roof, her eyes glazed over once more. Any emotion she was feeling earlier dissipated. I leaned forward to place a tender kiss on her head, but she was completely unresponsive.

The silence in the room was maddening, and finally I couldn't take it anymore. I exhaled loudly before speaking. "Dad, what the hell is going on?"

Then the air in the room changed, suddenly poisoned by the news my father gave me with just one look. When I squeezed Cassie's hand she turned her head slowly, and I looked down at her regretfully.

"I'm sorry, you two," *he said quietly as he removed his latex gloves.*

It felt as though the rug had been ripped out from under me in a matter of minutes, and I sank to the chair behind me, never releasing my grip on Cassie's hand. I could feel the hot tears spill forth onto my cheeks, but I couldn't find the energy to lift my free hand to wipe them away.

Cassie sat up slowly, clutching the thin paper sheet around her as she drew in deep breaths. "Y...you're sure?" *she asked in a wavering voice, her eyes fixed on me as I broke down emotionally.*

"I am," *he said before explaining his findings.*

I didn't hear much of what he was saying because I was in complete shock. Familiar words and phrases like "no fetal pole" *and* "unable to detect the heartbeat" *seemed to stick out most prominently.*

"We should do a D and C as soon as possible, Cassie." *I heard my dad say, his voice finally coming through loud and clear.*

I snapped my head up in his direction. "What?" *I asked, the tone in my voice only proving that I was still in denial.*

"Son — " *he started, looking at me with sympathy.*

Cassie interjected before he could continue. "Do it." It unnerved me just how steady and sure her voice was as she asked my father to end this pregnancy.

"Cassie!" I gasped, looking over at her with wide eyes.

When her eyes met mine, they were impossibly more vacant than they were when we first arrived. "It's already too late, Jack," she said, her voice entirely steady in pitch.

"Son, we could just let nature take its course, but in some cases it poses too much of a risk to the woman and possibly her fertility," Dad tried explaining.

I knew what I was being told to be true, but I just couldn't accept it. How could she accept it so readily? Why did she seem...fine? The confusion was starting to cloud my mind, making me dizzy. I buried my face in my hands as I tried to cross that fine line to acceptance, and I could feel the wetness from my tears on the palms of my hands. With a shuddering breath I whispered, "I know."

I felt a strong hand on my shoulder, and when I looked up, I was staring into the sympathy-filled eyes of my father. "I'll go and get everything in order, and when I return..." he paused and turned his focus back to a zombie-like Cassie before continuing "...we'll go through the details of the procedure, all right?" He left us in the room alone as we grieved. My eyes never left the floor as I tried to come to terms with everything that had happened in a matter of just a couple of hours...if that.

"Jack?" Cassie said softly. I looked up at her slowly, afraid to let her see how weak I was. I needed to be strong...for her. "Are..." she took a breath "...are you okay?"

"Yeah," I said in a low voice that even I didn't recognize. I stood and ran my fingers through my hair. "Everything is going to be fine. We'll figure things out from here. Together." Taking her hands in mine, I offered her what was meant to be a warm smile, but it likely came across as forced as it felt. "How are you?" I asked.

Cassie's eyes became lackluster as she swallowed thickly and nodded. "I'm fine."

There was a soft knock at the door, and when it opened, my father and a small, dark-haired nurse slipped in. The next hour and a half was pure torture. I didn't think I would survive the agony that tore its way through my body as I sat next to Cassie. I was shocked to hear Cassie tell my father she'd prefer to be awake for the procedure — I didn't even want to be awake for it.

They gave her a local anesthetic after she had changed into a hospital gown and positioned herself back onto the exam table. I watched her face the entire time, just waiting for this to hit her. It was bound to...I just wasn't sure when.

Toward the end of the procedure, one lone tear fell from the corner of her right eye — no sound, just the visual proof of her pain — and I leaned over and kissed it away. "It's going to be okay, Cass," I whispered into her ear.

After the nurse left the room, Dad gave us a laundry list of things that were normal after this "procedure," and things to watch for. He assisted Cassie into an upright position and kissed the top of her head before telling her she did an exceptional job. His words didn't seem to reach her as she inhaled deeply and stared through him.

Whispering his condolences once more, he turned to leave the room. Just as he opened the door and slipped out, the nurse popped back in, and nestled in her arms was a pair of light blue hospital scrubs. "Mrs. Martin? Dr. Martin asked me to drop these off for you," she said, setting the scrubs down on the table.

Cassie shook her head clear momentarily and looked at the small woman. "Thank you," she told her kindly as the nurse slipped back out into the hall. Cassie looked down beside her, and lying atop the pile was a pair of disposable hospital underwear. "Well," she said as she held them up. "Just when I thought this couldn't get any worse." Her tone was meant to come off as a joke, but neither of us really found the humor in her words.

When Cassie was changed, she slipped her dress over her arm and we left the exam room to find my father right outside. He pulled Cassie into his arms and told us to head home.

"But Charlie?" Cassie spoke up.

Placing his hands on Cassie's shoulders, he stared into her eyes. "Sweetheart, you've just been put through something no one should ever have to experience. Go home and rest. Charlie is probably sleeping right now, anyway. Helen and I will bring her by for the party tomorrow."

Cassie nodded solemnly in silent agreement, and I wrapped my arms around her. "Thanks, Dad," I said as I led Cassie toward the exit.

When we arrived home, Cassie walked to the kitchen, dumped the dress she wore that night straight into the trash, and grabbed a bottle of wine and a glass before retiring to the couch. I stood in the open space between the two rooms, watching her for a moment as she drank her first glass quickly.

"Cass, we can have the dress cleaned," I suggested.

"I don't want it," she snapped. "I don't want to ever remember tonight. I want it to be as though none of this even happened." Her expression hardened, and I watched her pour another glass of wine.

I couldn't disagree. It was a pretty shitty day, and one I would love to forget about. But the simple fact remained that it did happen, and it was what forced our lives into a downward spiral.

When we awoke the next day, the sun was out, which was a shame, because both of our moods were sullen. It was as though the world was trying to rub our noses in our recent loss. We remained in bed for what seemed like an eternity, neither one of us speaking or touching, just staring up at the ceiling in complete silence.

I heard the front door open when my parents showed up with Charlie at noon. She was as exuberant as ever. I climbed out of bed and tried to get Cassie up also, but she told me that she needed a minute.

I went downstairs to find Charlie at the table coloring, so I joined her and just watched her. I made the effort to be happy for her birthday, but it was hard. Charlie lost someone, too. She just didn't know it, and likely never would.

My mom came up behind me and kissed the top of my head before wrapping her arms around my shoulders. That one gesture caused fresh tears to prickle at my eyes, so I took a breath and blinked rapidly to hold them back.

Cassie's parents showed up shortly after, and the looks on their faces told me that they knew already. Gayle came into the room and hugged me. "I'm so sorry," she said quietly.

"Thank you. But, today is about Charlie. We'd prefer not to take away from that," I said, hoping she would understand.

She nodded, placing her hand on my cheek. "Of course, dear. Where's Cassie?"

"In bed, last I saw. She's...not taking it very well." I knew that was an understatement.

Gayle and my mom went upstairs to try and convince Cassie to come down for the party, and while they were gone, Jennifer, Alex, Billy, and his girlfriend, Sarah, showed up. News travelled fast in this family, so I wasn't surprised — nor was I angry — that they all knew. It was easier this way.

Cassie came downstairs by one o'clock, closely flanked by our mothers. Her hair was brushed, but fell limp around her face, and the look in her eyes hadn't changed. She had exchanged the hospital scrubs that she had slept in for a pair of jeans and white T-shirt. One piece of clothing that concerned me was the knitted brown button-up sweater that she was pulling closed across her chest as she held her right hand over her heart.

It was the same sweater she wore almost every day during her depression two years ago.

Charlie ran for Cassie when she saw her, and Cassie smiled and hugged her, her eyes still unable to register anything around her. "Hey, baby," she whispered as she buried her face in Charlie's blonde curls and inhaled deeply.

When Charlie wriggled free and ran over to her grandmothers, Cassie stood up and walked over to the far corner of the couch, sitting and bringing her knees up to her chest. Jennifer made a move to go to her, but I shook my head in a silent plea to not say anything that could make this worse – for any of us. She nodded her understanding and sat next to Cassie, who looked at her with sad eyes before she laid her head on her shoulder.

The following week didn't get any better for either of us. Being in my final year of my residency, I called my colleague, Sienna, Sunday night to ask if she'd mind me taking a few days to stay with Cassie, and she was more than willing to fill in for me. She expressed concern for Cassie and me, and even offered to stop by in a few days time to speak with us if we were ready.

Also, even though Cassie and I both had some time off, my mom still offered to come and pick Charlie up to keep her in her routine. I was certain she was only trying to keep Charlie sheltered from the depressing atmosphere of our home.

Cassie would stay in bed for hours most mornings and even refused to eat when I brought her food. Her behavior was familiar territory, and quite frankly, it was beginning to scare the shit out of me. If she wasn't in bed, she was huddled in the far corner of the couch with her legs bent up against her body, or at the table as we attempted to eat a meal together.

Cassie wouldn't eat much, instead pushing the food around on her plate.

"Cassie, you should eat. I can make you something else if you'd prefer?" I suggested carefully.

She shook her head weakly. "I'm not hungry."

"Well," I said, still trying to tread carefully. She hadn't snapped yet, but she was wound so tight, I knew it was coming. "Do you want to talk about it? It might help you move past — "

Her head snapped up, and her eyes were the most alive I'd seen them all week. They weren't the sparkling eyes I was used to, though...they were blazing with her anger as it bubbled to the surface. She slammed her fork down on the table and stood quickly. "Don't you dare try to psychoanalyze me, Jack Martin. You're not my fucking therapist!" she screamed as she rushed from the room, pulling her sweater closed around her, and locked herself in our bedroom.

She was right; I wasn't her therapist. But Sienna was. I called her immediately and asked for her to stop by when she could.

Cassie wasn't too thrilled when Sienna showed up the next night after work, but she complied — for the most part. We sat in the living room, Cassie all folded in on herself in her usual spot on the couch, and I sat beside her while Sienna took a seat on the loveseat across from us.

"Cassie?" Sienna started. "How are you feeling?"

"I'm fine," she spat, keeping her gaze averted from Sienna's. I knew that if she looked into Sienna's eyes that she would crack...and so did she.

"Cassie, don't forget that I know you. I'm only here to help." Sienna was good at her job. It was almost as though she held the power of compulsion in her hands and was able to make people do what she wished just by speaking in a certain tone of voice. "So, Cassie. How are you feeling about all of this?"

I watched Cassie carefully as she turned her head to meet Sienna's gaze. Her eyes weren't focused and seemed to stare right through Sienna, dead to the world and emotionless as she spoke. "Undeserving. Responsible. Guilty." There was a heavy silence in the room before Cassie continued. "Failure." Her eyes darted to mine very briefly before finding sanctuary in Sienna's. "Like, if I had wanted this baby from the beginning, this wouldn't have happened."

Shock hit me from every angle as I learned her true feelings, and I turned to her, aghast by this revelation. I opened my mouth to speak, only to have Sienna interject. "Jack, Cassie is allowed to express how she feels."

"I know that, but she shouldn't feel that way. This wasn't her fault," I said quietly, my eyes never leaving Cassie as her gaze fell to the cuff of her sweater so she could tug at an imaginary thread.

Sienna offered me a sympathetic smile before returning her focus to Cassie. "How have you been sleeping, Cassie?"

"I don't. Sleep, I mean. Every time I close my eyes..." She took a deep breath. "I just can't."

"Are you eating anything?" Sienna knew she wasn't; I had discussed all of this with her earlier.

"I'm not hungry," Cassie responded with no emotion.

Sienna sat back in her seat for a moment, waiting for one of us to say something. Minutes ticked by on the mantle clock before she spoke again. "Well, I'm going to prescribe some sleeping pills. And also an anti-depress – "

"No!" Cassie shouted, jumping to her feet. She crossed her arms around herself protectively as she looked at Sienna with an anger I had never before seen. "I lost a baby less than a week ago! I'm allowed to grieve!"

Sienna held her hands out in front of her in surrender. "I know that, Cassie. I'm not saying you have to take them now. But, in my experience, someone with your medical history and who has gone through the level of post-partum depression you did a couple of years ago has a chance for relapse in the wake of another trauma," she said calmly.

"I won't be medicated again," Cassie stated firmly.

"I understand. You have every right to feel what you feel," Sienna said. "I'll leave the prescription with you. Keep it...just in case, okay?"

Cassie shook her head in frustration. "Whatever. I'm going to bed."

Once Cassie left the room, I leaned forward and rested my arms on my knees, looking up at Sienna. "It's not good, is it?"

With a slight head shake and smile, she answered, "Jack, her pain...and your pain...is still so fresh. It's hard to say what's going to happen. Her reaction is expected. You're a psychiatrist, you know this...hell, you've dealt with it." She leaned forward and locked eyes with me. "Now, how are you feeling?"

I cocked an eyebrow at her. "Are you seriously trying to evaluate me?"

"Jack." Her tone was serious with an air of threat behind it.

I exhaled loudly as I flopped back into the couch. "I feel..." I took a minute so I could try and put into words what I was feeling. "Sad. Angry. Frustrated. Maybe if I hadn't been so damn happy about this pregnancy and forced Cassie to accept it, then she wouldn't be hurting right now."

"Do you really feel as though you forced her acceptance?"

With an exasperated groan, I looked at Sienna. "You're far too good at this, you know that?" She smirked, and I rolled my eyes. "I guess I didn't really force her acceptance, but that's how it feels. It feels like once she's done grieving her loss – "

"Your loss, too, Jack," she corrected.

"Obviously that goes without saying," I said snarkily. "Anyway, it feels like once she's done grieving, she'll resent me and begin to pull away," I admitted.

"Cassie loves you, Jack. You both just need some time." Sienna's eyes drifted to her watch. "I have to get going, but if either of you need anything, you just let me know. I'll leave the prescriptions with you, all right?"

We stood, and Sienna handed me the papers before I walked her to the door. Before walking through the threshold, Sienna turned to me and pulled me into a friendly hug. "I care about you, Jack. About both of you. She'll come around, just give her some time."

"Thank you," I said as she pulled away, and I watched her walk to her car and drive down the street from the doorway. After locking the door, I headed upstairs to find Cassie lying in bed, wide awake.

"I'm sorry," I said. "I just thought it would be easier for you to talk to her than to me."

Cassie sighed. "I'm so tired."

I knelt before her and stroked her hair. "Then sleep."

Tears fell rapidly from her eyes. "I can't, because every time I close my eyes...all I see is..." she sobbed loudly before finishing "...the look on your face when your dad told you I had lost the baby." She buried her face behind her hands and wept hysterically for the first time in a week. "I didn't want the baby, and you were so excited. And now...I've failed you so many times."

Knowing it was my anguish that kept her from sleeping destroyed me. "Oh God, Cassie," I whispered, moving to embrace her as she remained on the bed. I tried to make her feel better, but I knew the exhaustion was taking its toll on her. I pressed my lips to her forehead as she sobbed into my shoulder.

I didn't want to leave her right then, but she needed to sleep, and clearly that wasn't happening on its own. "I'm going to go and get the sleeping pills that Sienna prescribed. I'll be back in fifteen minutes, okay? I'll see if my mom can keep Charlie tonight, too." I stood and walked to the door, stopping before leaving the room entirely. "I love *you."*

Cassie raised her head and wiped her eyes as she sniffled. "I love you, too."

Reliving such a painful part of our past was the hardest thing I had ever had to do. I knew it was what we needed in order to move on from it, but it didn't make it any less difficult.

I looked down at Cassie and could feel my eyes burn with tears. "Cassie, I'm afraid that if we don't try harder that our marriage won't survive."

The faint sparkle that was left in her eyes burned out, and she sighed sadly. "I think it's too late to worry about that."

Chapter Seven
impasse

"What?" I asked in a hoarse voice after a beat of silence. Too late? What did she mean it was too late? I stood there, staring at her in shock as she looked me dead in the eye and told me that our marriage was over. My mouth opened and closed as I tried to find the words—any words.

I pinched the bridge of my nose in frustration. "So, what? You're telling me you don't love me?"

Cassie's eyes widened, and her head snapped back at my assumption. "No! That's not what I said at all. You know I love you. Both of you. God, Jack, I'd sacrifice my soul for you if I had to." Cassie took a deep, trembling breath as her eyes hardened with resolve, and she broke the silence. "Look, we've both rehashed a bunch of shit that should have stayed buried for obvious reasons. So, before either one of us says anything else we don't mean, I'm going to go upstairs." She turned from me in that moment and started to walk from the room.

It only took me two long strides to catch up to her. I took her by the hand and turned her to me. "No, you don't get to walk away from this that easily. Not this time."

She raised an eyebrow and stared me down. "You think that any of this has been *easy* for me, Jack?

For two years I've been struggling to come to terms with my choices. Each and every time I'm ready to move on from it all, you won't allow it. It kills me to know that I've hurt you this deeply." Cassie placed her right hand on my cheek and smiled up at me. "I know you don't want to keep hurting. You don't *deserve* to keep hurting."

"And you telling me that our marriage is over is supposed to help me how, exactly?" I demanded angrily. "I don't get how can you say that there's no hope to save our marriage? Our *family*?" I moved my arm back and forth between the two of us. Cassie only stood there, silent, as I continued on my tirade. "Shit, Cassie! Why now?"

Her eyes finally registered a sliver of remorse as they locked with mine. "It's not that I don't *want* to work on our marriage. I would love to be able to go back in time and fix it before it got to its breaking point. But we can't."

"So, what? You want out?" I was furious that everything seemed so far out of my control.

Cassie's soft hand brushed my cheek. "Is that what you want?" she asked in a voice so small I almost didn't hear it.

"Of course not," I responded. "I want things to go back to the way they were."

Cassie inhaled deeply. "So do I, but we can't ignore the things that brought us to where we are now. We need to come to terms with them in hopes of being able to move forward. We need to keep Charlie's best interest at heart."

"That's all I *have* been doing!" I shouted, moving away from her touch. To hear her disregard how much I actually did for *our* child on a daily basis seriously pissed me off. *I* was the one that was there day-in and day-out taking care of her. *I* was the one who ran to her bedside when she had a bad dream. I was a single father, regardless of the fact that I was married to our daughter's absent mother. How completely fucked up was that?

When I was certain I could keep my temper in check, I spoke. "She needs parents, Cassie. Parents...plural. Not one, but *two*."

"I couldn't agree more," Cassie responded with a small shrug. "I *want* to be there for her." Her voice cracked as the tears streamed down her cheeks and she wiped them away furiously. "God! What I wouldn't give to sit with her on the couch and read to her...or even just *hold* her and ask her about her day!"

I rushed toward her, wrapping my hands gently around her biceps. "Then *do* those things. It's not too late."

She struggled to free herself, her eyes wild as she moved to the other side of the room. "But it is! I fucked up, Jack!"

With the shake of my head, I furrowed my brow. "Regardless of whether or not you fucked up, you can change your relationship with her. Be there *now*."

That was when Cassie shut down. The expression on her face went blank and her shoulders slumped ever-so-slightly. The room was filled with an uncomfortable silence as we stood staring at each other. Cassie's breathing was still shaking with the sobs that were slowly dying. Seconds turned to minutes before her eyes finally locked with mine. Without a word, she quietly moved forward, reaching out to place a hand on my chest.

I pulled away and turned from her, running my hands through my hair as I tried to absorb all that had been said between us. I walked to the mantle and placed my hands on it before slumping forward in defeat.

"I'm so lost, Jack," Cassie whispered. I could feel her presence right behind me, and it took everything in me not to turn around and embrace her...not to kiss away this whole messed up night. "I don't know where to go from here." The pain in her voice broke my heart, and my chest tightened as I turned to face her. Her big brown eyes were red and swollen from crying, and she was sniffling against the residual sobs that refused to relent.

"Go?" I asked incredulously. "Cassie, you're not *going* anywhere." I cupped her face in my hands and looked into her fear-filled eyes.

She brought her hands up to encircle my wrists. "Jack—" I quickly pressed my lips to hers to silence her. "You really want me to stay?" she mumbled against my mouth before pulling back slightly, her chilled hands circling my wrists.

I shook my head, but not in disagreement. "No, I *need* you to stay. I can't ever be without you." I rested my forehead against hers and inhaled deeply, my eyes closing as everything *Cassie* consumed me. "How can you be so ready to give up on this?"

"Because everything that's happened is all my fault. I don't deserve your forgiveness." When I opened my eyes, I saw the despair that was trying desperately to claw its way to the surface of her soul.

I kissed the tip of her nose softly and offered her a comforting smile. "What happened two years ago...the miscarriage? That wasn't your fault. I never once blamed you. Everything happens for a reason. Everything."

Cassie sighed despondently. "It may not have been my fault in the literal sense, but afterward? The way I treated you? The way I—?"

I quickly kissed her again. "Don't..." I pleaded against her lips, not wanting to hear the rest of her sentence. The truth would only make things worse. Deep down, I knew I wouldn't be able to handle hearing the truth. "Just don't, please. You need to stop shouldering the blame." I stilled my lips against hers and ended the kiss, moving my hands from her face and down her arms until I gripped her hands firmly in mine.

"I just need you to understand," she said, her eyes falling to our hands.

Leaning my forehead against hers, I squeezed my hands gently. "Come on," I said, tilting my head a fraction of an inch toward the stairs. "It's late. Let's go to bed."

Cassie sniffled lightly and nodded her head, her eyes still focused on the floor. We trudged up the stairs together, our bodies both physically drained from everything that we had unleashed tonight. As I headed for the bathroom, Cassie sat on the edge of the bed, fidgeting nervously until I emerged from the bathroom and knelt before her.

"We can fix this," I assured her quietly, tenderly coaxing her gaze to mine.

A single tear trailed down her cheek, and I reached to brush it away, but she beat me to it. "I love you for your undying commitment, Jack. I just wish it wasn't so misplaced. I don't deserve it. If only you could see that."

I stood up, pulling Cassie to her feet with me, and pulled the blankets back. I ushered her beneath the thick comforter before climbing in behind her. I folded her into my embrace and inhaled the sweet scent of her hair as I intertwined our fingers. "Yes, you do. *We* do." She turned to protest again, but I quickly interceded. "Shhh. Sleep," I whispered against her lips.

As I listened to Cassie's breathing deepen and

even out, I thought back to everything we had talked about in the last few hours. It had been a long time since we had discussed any of the past in such detail, but it needed to be done. We needed to reopen old wounds to get to the source of the problem so that we could force our minds into acceptance. It still hurt to remember the emotional pain and suffering that we had been forced to endure at the hands of fate, but I just kept telling myself over and over again that it was needed. That from here on out, things would be different.

My focus on the glowing red numbers of the alarm clock started to blur as the exhaustion took hold, and I couldn't fight it anymore.

"Cassie! We're home!" I called as I walked through the door. I set Charlie down and helped her out of her shoes and jacket. "All right, bug. Let's go put on the cartoons for you while I go see what Mommy's been up to today."

Charlie and I made our way into the living room, and while she hopped up onto the couch, I turned on her favorite evening programs and headed off in search of Cassie.

"Love? We're home!" I called again. There was no answer, and it unnerved me. The feeling of dread was all too present in the air around me as I slowly climbed the stairs. "Cassie?" When I heard the sound of glass shattering, I jumped into action, taking the steps two at a time. "Cassie!" I shouted as I ran toward our bedroom, only to find the bed wasn't made and the bathroom door was slightly ajar. That's when the feeling of abandonment seeped in...

My eyes snapped open, and I knew instantly that I was alone. I felt the walls of blind panic start to close in all around me as I looked frantically toward the bathroom door. My breathing faltered and my heart skipped a beat when I saw that it was only open a sliver...*just like in the dream.* Feeling the bile churning in my stomach, I bolted from the bed and ran to the door. The force I used to open it caused it to crack the drywall upon impact.

The room was empty as I rushed for the toilet and threw up. My esophagus burned as I continued to heave into the porcelain bowl. I could feel the sweat beading on my forehead as my body shook and shuddered with the final remnants of the dream I just had.

"Jack?" I snapped my head in the direction of the wide-open door to find Cassie standing there, concern marking her angelic face. "Are you all right?" she asked timidly as she stepped closer to me.

I reached out and took her by the hand, pulling her to me as I crawled on my knees to meet her halfway. She looked down at me and pushed the hair from my forehead as she tried to search my eyes for an explanation. The only thing I wanted to do in that moment was hold her, so I wrapped my arms around her waist and pressed my cheek against her stomach as I gripped her almost too tightly.

"Jack, what's going on?" she asked, her voice full of bewilderment.

I clenched my eyes shut, only to relive the final moments of the dream before I shook my head violently against her. "I just had a horrible dream where you were gone. And when I woke up, you were nowhere to be found. I panicked."

My body instantly relaxed as Cassie's hands tenderly caressed my cheeks until she found my chin. With very little force, she was able to gently persuade me to look at her. "I'm here, Jack. I'll always be here."

I had just opened my mouth to speak when my phone vibrated on the nightstand. I looked over at it for a moment but quickly decided against it as I stood up and walked to the bathroom sink. Cassie walked over to the bedside table and picked it up.

"Just answer it," she instructed, holding it out to me. "It's Billy."

I had just pushed the toothbrush into my mouth as I spoke. "You answer it," I mumbled around the plastic.

She continued to hold it out. "He's not calling for me."

With a playful glare, I took the phone from her and spit in the sink before putting the receiver up to my ear. "Hey, Billy."

"What the hell, man?" he bellowed into the phone.

I rinsed off my toothbrush thoroughly before placing it back into the holder. "What?"

"Um...what time is it, asshole?" he asked in a very stern tone.

I exited the bright bathroom and looked at the clock by the bed. "It's eleven-thirty," I responded flippantly.

"Uh huh..." he said, dragging out the last syllable longer than should have been acceptable for a man his size. "We were supposed to meet at eleven for lunch."

Throwing my head back, I smacked my forehead with the heel of my palm and groaned. "Oh right. I am so sorry. I must have forgotten. Can we take a rain check?"

Cassie rushed over to me and shook her head vehemently. "No, don't stay for me. Go...have fun with Billy. I'll be here when you get back."

"You're sure?" I inquired quietly. Cassie nodded her head happily and stood on her toes to kiss me softly before retreating downstairs.

I shook my head and tried to time how long it

would take me to get ready. "Um, okay, I'll be there in...a half hour?"

Billy huffed exaggeratedly into the phone. "Fine. But I'm starting without you. I'm fucking starving, man."

With a chuckle, I said, "Yeah, yeah, yeah. What else is new? I'll be there as soon as I can." I hung up the phone and scrambled about the room getting ready so I wouldn't be any later than I already was. Once I was dressed, I ran my fingers through my messy hair in an effort to tame the unruly locks and headed downstairs to find Cassie curled up on the couch reading.

"You look nice," she said, setting her book in her lap. "Where are you guys eating?"

"Um, the diner downtown. Did you want me to bring you anything?" I asked as I frantically searched for my keys, finally locating them on the island in the kitchen.

Cassie arched an eyebrow at me and smirked. "No thanks. I'm sure I'll be okay."

Keys in hand, I walked to her side and leaned forward, placing a tender kiss on her awaiting lips. "I won't be long," I promised.

She shook her head and laughed at me. "Don't be silly. Take your time. I'm not going anywhere." With a final goodbye kiss to her forehead, I turned from her and headed for the door.

Since I was already extremely late, and I didn't want to have to force Billy to watch me eat — okay, so realistically I didn't want him to pick off my plate even though he'd probably have already eaten a few appetizers and a full meal by the time I arrived — I drove faster than was entirely necessary. I pulled into the parking lot at twelve-oh-four and quickly made my way into the restaurant to see Billy sitting at the far table, several French fries in his fist as he chewed the previous mouthful.

His eyes widened as I approached the table. "Well, it's about fucking time!" he exclaimed, his speech muffled by the copious amounts of food. He looked past me, confused. "Where's Charlie?"

I arched an eyebrow as I eyed him questioningly and shook my head. "Nice. So you didn't even know if Charlie would be here, and you chose to greet me in that way? Miles to go, buddy. Miles." I sat at the table with him and picked up my menu before addressing his question. "She's with my parents for the weekend."

Billy's eyes widened in excitement, and I couldn't help but compare the look on his face to that of a four-year-old on Christmas morning. "Sweet! So you got an all-adult weekend? Nice!" he exclaimed, throwing his hand in the air, waiting for me to slap it.

"What are we, twelve?" He raised his eyebrows, and when he didn't put his hand down, instead tilting his head toward his upraised hand in an effort to encourage me, I shook my head and complied. "You are such a child. No wonder Charlie likes you so much; you fit right in with her age group," I teased.

"Hi, there," a female voice cooed beside me, and I turned in her direction. "Can I get you something to drink?" The tone in her voice was soft, and her eyes seemed to be focused intently on me as she licked her lips invitingly.

"Yeah, can I get a coffee, please?" I asked before turning back to my menu.

She giggled lightly. "For sure. I'll be right back."

I rolled my eyes as she walked away, and Billy began panting like a dog. "Damn, she was fine."

"Dude," I chastised, my eyes darting up to meet his. I was completely shocked that he was checking out another woman.

Billy scoffed. "Please, like you didn't notice."

"I most certainly did not. And you shouldn't be, either. You're engaged...to Sarah." He looked at me with raised eyebrows. "How do you think she'd react to hearing what you just said?"

Billy rolled his eyes at my reaction. "You're kind of a prude, huh? In fact, I don't know that I want to have lunch with you anymore," he joked, shoving another handful of fries into his mouth.

The server returned with my coffee. "Are you ready to order, sir?" she purred.

I sighed exasperatedly before closing my menu and answering. "Yeah, I'll get the club sandwich on whole wheat. No tomato, please." I handed her my menu and she took it, purposely brushing my fingers with her own.

She bent her knee, popping her hip out to the side, and tilted her head as she tried to gain my attention. When it failed to work, she bit her thin bottom lip — a possible method of flirting in her world — and batted her eyes as she spoke. "I'll bring it right up." I suddenly felt dirty from the double entendre I knew her words were intended to hold. She walked away, and I kept my eyes on the table since I knew she was expecting me to watch her sway her hips suggestively.

Billy reached across the table and punched my shoulder. "She was totally hitting on you, man."

I picked up my coffee and took another drink. "Thanks, Captain Obvious. I hadn't noticed."

Billy narrowed his eyes at me, grabbing a surprisingly small amount of fries from his plate. "So, what are the plans for tonight? Inviting me and Alex over for guy-time?" I cocked an eyebrow and stared at him blankly for a moment. "What? What else are you gonna do?"

"I have *plenty* to do," I said adamantly. The truth was, Cassie and I still had a lot to work through if I was going to get her to agree to our summer vacation in California in the next couple of weeks.

Billy scrunched up his face in disparagement. "Come on," he whined, further reminding me why he was Charlie's favorite uncle. "We never just hang out anymore."

"Bullshit," I countered. "Just last Friday we went to the pub after work."

Billy rolled his eyes and spoke facetiously. "Ooooooh, B.F.D. You know what I mean."

His comment forced me to think back to the last time we truly hung out. He was right; it had been quite some time, and that made me feel bad. "You're right," I told him. "Tell you what. Give me the weekend. There's some shit I need to work through at home, and then we'll set something up, all right?"

Billy's eyes showed his momentary displeasure before they lit up and he smiled wide. "Deal. You better hold your end of the deal, asshole," he ordered, pointing his finger at me in warning. "I can still take you."

I laughed heartily and reached across the table to grab a few of his fries. Billy's eyes dropped to my hand, and he stared in complete disbelief at my actions. "What the *fuck* do you think you're doing?" he demanded.

"I'm eating some of your fries. I'm starving."

Billy shook his head, pulling his plate toward him like a territorial animal, ready to fight for his food. "Nuh uh. That's your own fault," he growled. "You were late; you eat when that fine waitress brings you back your food."

Her ears must have been burning, because she

headed over to our table in an instant. "How's everything going here?" she inquired softly, placing her hand on the back of my chair. It made me uncomfortable. "Can I get you more coffee?"

I looked at her briefly and smiled so as not to appear rude. I'd hate to have her spit in my food...especially since Billy was so unwilling to share. "That would be great, thanks."

She disappeared quickly and Billy watched after her, obviously ogling her ass. I reached across the table and grabbed a few fries to toss at him. "Would you fucking stop that," I whispered harshly.

"Whoa," he started, shaking his head. "It was one thing when you *stole* my food...now you're just wasting it."

Our server came back over with the coffee pot, and much to my pleasure, my meal. I grabbed my napkin off the table and unfolded it, placing it across my lap, before I thanked her. Picking up the first half of the sandwich, I licked my lips before digging in gluttonously. I was completely famished.

The rest of lunch was filled with talk of Billy's upcoming wedding. "Sarah wanted to know if Charlie would like to be the flower girl?" I smiled at the image of Charlie all dolled up and walking down the aisle, scattering rose petals delicately before Sarah's grand entrance — because let's face it, anything Sarah chose to do was always considered "grand."

"Well, I can't speak on behalf of her, but I can only deduce that she would be your most willing participant," I told him with a light laugh as I finished my lunch. Reaching onto my lap for my napkin, I wiped my mouth before crumpling it and tossing it onto my plate. "So, what are you doing tonight?" I asked as I reached into my wallet for some cash.

Billy frowned at me again. "You mean besides

not having guys' night? I guess I'll allow Sarah to rope me into more wedding planning. I think tonight is cake tasting, so I guess that's pretty fucking awesome."

"How was everything today, gentlemen?" our server asked, appearing from nowhere. Truthfully, she was starting to worry me a little.

"Everything was great. Thank you," I replied, offering her a kind, but not flirtatious, smile.

Her cheeks flushed a deep crimson as she reached into the pouch of her apron, pulling out the billfold and setting it on the table. She held the leather folder in place with the tips of her fingers and locked gazes with me for longer than necessary. "Well, please let me know if there's *anything* else I can do for you." She slid the bill toward me and then sauntered off.

Billy's eyes widened as he slowly turned his head to me, and then they dropped to the folder between us before rising up to meet my gaze once more. "No fuckin' way," he muttered, reaching for the billfold. He snatched it before I had the chance, which was pathetic since it was right there in front of me. "Holy shit, dude! She gave you her number!"

I pulled my wallet out of my back pocket and grabbed a couple of bills before grabbing the receipt from him. Her name, Lauren, was scrawled along the bottom along with her phone number and the words "call me." I stuffed the cash into the little leather pocket inside the folder before turning toward the exit.

Billy watched me with suspicion as we walked across the parking lot toward our vehicles. "So," he began, dragging out the word a little. "Everything okay, man? I mean...you seem a little, I don't know, off?"

With a quiet laugh, I scoffed. "Yeah. I'm fine. I guess I'm just a little stressed. Things around the house have been a little more strained than usual."

Billy nudged me with his elbow. "Come on, Charlie's too cute to be the cause of your funk."

"What?" I asked, looking at him in confusion. "No, it's not Charlie. It's just..." I sighed, not really knowing if I should talk to him about what was troubling me. How could I even begin to explain that everything I thought I knew — everything I thought Cassie and I had — was so beyond broken that there might be no way to save it?

"I'm sorry. I didn't mean to pry. I only ask because I'm concerned," he said, turning to me when we reached my car.

I ran my hand over my weary face, expelling a huge gust of air from my lungs. "It's Cassie," I whispered, unable to meet his stare.

"Oh." His voice was so quiet that I almost didn't hear him. I felt his hand on my shoulder. "I understand how hard things have been. We all do, you know?" I nodded, slowly looking over at him as we leaned on the driver's side of my car. "Everything will be okay, man. I know you'll figure things out, though. You have to."

I looked up at him, grateful that he seemed to be optimistic for me. The details of what was going on between Cassie and me were private, but you had to be blind not to notice it. She wasn't just absent from her home life, she frequently missed dinners and parties with friends and family, too. She wasn't just withdrawing from her life at home, but life in general.

"Thanks," I sighed sadly and met his empathetic stare. "Look, I should head home. I'll call you later, all right?"

Billy backed away from my car, allowing me to

hop in, and I exited the parking lot. The entire way home I felt guilty that I had said anything to Billy regarding my issues with Cassie. It was really nobody's business but ours, and I hoped Cassie wouldn't be too upset with me.

"What's wrong?" Cassie asked as soon as I walked into the living room.

I raised my eyes from the floor to find her still sitting on the couch, book in hand and a worried look on her face. "Nothing, I just..." I shook my head and swallowed my guilt. "No, it's nothing. Everything is fine."

"You're sure?" she asked softly, narrowing her eyes at me.

I nodded and made my way over to her. Once I stood before her, I leaned forward and lifted her bent legs and slipped beneath them. "I missed you," I told her, and she giggled softly. I bathed in the sound, and Cassie began running her slender fingers through my hair.

"I missed you, too."

I moved my body closer to hers until she was practically on my lap and I laid my head on her shoulder. As I lay there, listening to her soft breaths, I closed my eyes and breathed her in until I fell asleep.

For the first time in as long as I could remember, I felt at peace. It felt as though we actually stood a chance.

Chapter Eight
crossing the line

When I awoke Monday morning and Cassie was still by my side, I was shocked. Usually she was gone before I even woke up. Maybe she was tired of everything. Maybe she really was going to make more of an effort.

"Will you be home for dinner?" I asked quietly as I finished buttoning up my shirt.

With a slight smile, Cassie stood from the bed, the leg of her plaid bottoms falling from around her knee until they hit her mid-calf where they belonged. She stood in front of me, helping me with my tie. "I can't tell you one way or the other. You know that."

And just like that, everything we had accomplished over the weekend turned to dust, and my heart shattered as I looked into her eyes. "Cass..."

"I'm sorry, Jack. You know I can't commit to that. It's not that I don't want to be here, I swear to you. It's just not always possible." She made one final adjustment to my tie and offered me a smile before cradling my face and stretching onto her toes to kiss me softly. "I'll try. I always do."

Every part of me ached. I wanted to believe her, but it felt all too familiar. Like the wonderful weekend we had just shared together was no more than a dream.

Not wanting to argue and start the day off on the wrong foot, I pulled her into my arms and inhaled deeply. "All right," I whispered into her hair. "Please try. Charlie would really enjoy some time with you."

Cassie worked her way free, and with a nod, she ushered me out of the bedroom so I wouldn't be late for work. "Have a good day," she said happily from the front door.

I faced her with a smile and replied, "I will." I had just turned from her again before suddenly remembering something. "Don't forget about California in a couple weeks." She had just begun to protest when I interrupted. "Just...see what your schedule is like, and we'll figure it out. We'll talk tonight. I love you."

With a quiet "I love you," in return, she closed the door and I walked to the Audi and headed for work. Upon arriving at the office, I found Sienna and Jill having a cup of coffee at the front desk.

"Jack!" Sienna called elatedly. "Have a good weekend? You must have, you look rested."

I chuckled. "Now, why is it when a woman tells a man he looked tired we don't think twice about the backhanded compliment? But if we were to say the exact same thing to a woman she'd have an epic temper tantrum?" I asked as I reached for the cup of coffee Jill had just poured for me, nodding my thanks as I waited for my answer.

Laughter filled the air as Sienna successfully avoided the justification to one of the many double standards that plagued the sexes. Instead, she turned to Jill. "Please hold all my calls for the next half hour."

Jill nodded, flashing me a brief smile, before Sienna looped her arm through mine and led me to her office. Once inside, she led me to the chair adjacent her desk and perched herself on the edge before me.

"So, how was your weekend?"

This felt oddly like a therapy session—one I hadn't agreed to. I moved to stand up, but Sienna was quick to stop me. "Relax, Jack. I'm asking as your friend and colleague. Not as a therapist," she said in an effort to comfort me.

Eyeing her skeptically, I sipped my coffee. "My weekend was fine. Yours?"

"Fine. Thank you for asking," she responded with a smirk and an arched brow as she pushed herself off her desk and moved to sit behind it. "What did you do this weekend?"

"Hung around the house mostly," I replied. "Had lunch with Billy. Nothing too exciting."

"Well, I'm glad you had a lazy weekend. You deserve a little time off. You must be excited about your trip, huh?" she asked as she turned on her computer.

With a despondent shrug, I met her eyes. "I guess. I mean, yeah, it'll be great to go back and have some time with the family. Cassie's parents will be there, and we don't see them as often as we should even though they only live a few hours away."

"Oh, that'll be nice. Charlie must be very excited."

I chuckled at the memory of her enthusiasm at dinner on Friday. "That she is."

Sienna fidgeted nervously; it was almost as though she wanted to ask me something but was afraid for my reaction. I leaned forward and rested my mug on her desk. "So, what's up?"

With a dry laugh, Sienna shook her head. "It's nothing."

"Bullshit," I countered. "Something's bothering you. Now what is it?" I watched as Sienna uncharacteristically fidgeted before meeting my gaze again.

With a deep breath, Sienna seemed to steel her resolve. "It's unnerving how you seem to read people, you know." I gave her a cocky grin and nodded for her to continue. "I'm concerned, Jack. You've been distant lately."

"I've been busy. Getting Charlie to my parents, picking her up and keeping her routine...I've been doing it all. It's very time consuming," I explained. The pain I experienced just saying out loud how *alone* I felt in my life was all-consuming, and I felt as though I was drowning in that anguish.

Sienna folded her hands on the desk in front of her in a very professional manner. "I know. And I don't mean to pressure you in any way, but just know I'm here if ever you need someone to talk to. I'd hate for you to feel as though you have to deal with everything by yourself." The room was silent for a moment, and Sienna furrowed her brow in worry. "I just don't want to see you lose yourself. Not with everything that's coming up in the next few weeks. The beach vacation, Charlie's birthday." Sienna took a deep, shaky breath, and I knew what her next words would be before she said them. "Cassie's birthday. I know that day has always been hard for you in the past few years. Ever since..."

Inhaling sharply, I stood in one fluid movement and offered Sienna an appreciative smile before grabbing my mug. "Thanks for the concern, but everything is going to be fine."

"I hope so," Sienna whispered solemnly as I exited her office and headed for my own.

As I sat there before my first appointment, Sienna's concerned words kept replaying in my mind. The wound from the miscarriage was still open from when Cassie and I had argued on Friday night, and Sienna's words were acting like salt, aggravating it and making the burn unbearable.

I didn't even realize that a tear had fallen down

my cheek until my phone rang. Quickly wiping the wetness from my cheek, I snatched the receiver off the cradle. "Yes, Jill?"

"Dr. Martin, Miss Chambers is here for her appointment," Jill cooed in return.

"Thank you, please send her in." Standing from my chair, I refastened the buttons of my suit jacket and came out from behind my desk just as my next patient opened the door and entered.

"Aah, Marly. How've you been?" I asked as I crossed the room and motioned for her to have a seat on the leather sofa across from my chair.

"Better, actually. I felt our last session really helped me work through my insecurities," she said happily. "Tom and I have been communicating one hundred and ten percent better."

I smiled and leaned back in my chair with her file in my lap. "I'm glad to hear it."

The next hour was spent talking about Marly's upbringing and why she felt so insecure in her relationship. As it turned out, the poor girl's parents' marriage imploded due to her father's indiscretions. It made sense why she didn't trust her fiancé to remain faithful when away on business trips.

After our morning appointments, Sienna and I grabbed lunch down the street at a little cafe. I tried to keep the subject matter light and off of my personal life, so we talked about work and her upcoming plans with her sisters. Thankfully she hadn't seen her sisters in months, so her excitement over the upcoming festivities was enough to have her monopolize the entire hour.

My afternoon was back-to-back appointments, which was great because the time seemed to pass by much more quickly; I was anxious to pick up Charlie. She'd stayed weekends with my parents, Cassie's parents, and even her aunts and uncles before, but no matter how often her weekends away occurred, I still missed her dearly.

"Daddyyyy!" Charlie squealed as I walked into my parents' house. She leapt off the step in the entry very enthusiastically and directly into my arms.

Closing my eyes and laughing, I pulled her tightly and kissed her cheek. "Hey, bug. How was your weekend?"

"So much fun! We baked cookies...and Gramma teached me how to make play dough that can be eaten. And then, Gramma and Grampa took me out for ice cream last night! And I got to go over to Seth's place, and we played in the sandbox for the whole afternoon. Oh! And then, when Grampa was at work, Gramma took me to the mall and we got to hold the puppies at the pet shop!" she rambled on in one excited breath. I pulled her tight once more before setting her back on her feet.

"She was an absolute joy," my mother stated as she entered the room and knelt before her. "Okay, sweet girl, why don't you go find your grandfather in his office and say goodbye?"

"Okay, Gramma!" Charlie squealed before hotfooting it up the stairs.

"Thanks again for keeping her this weekend. She seems like she really enjoyed herself," I said as I picked up Charlie's bag and jacket.

Mom offered me an apprehensive smile and then glanced up the stairs to ensure we were alone. "Jack, I think she needs to see a counselor," she told me point-blank. Her voice was smooth and sure, her tone never faltering, which led me to believe she wasn't just suggesting it.

My eyebrows knit together as my anger slowly escalated. "Excuse me?"

"I don't know. I just think that Charlie might benefit from sitting down with, maybe Sienna or someone else in your practice. I think she needs to talk to someone about what she's going through. It concer—"

"She's fine," I snapped. "I think I'd know if something was going on inside Charlie's head."

She narrowed her eyes in challenge, and this only served to fuel my rage. "Be realistic, Jack. She's gone through a lot in the last couple years, and it's not like she can just push her thoughts into your head. You may be a psychiatrist, but you're not a mind reader."

"You don't think I'd know if something were going on with my own daughter...in my own home?" I demanded.

My mother shook her head quickly. "No, that's not it at all." She put her hands up in surrender and conceded. "You know what, forget I said anything. I really don't want to argue about this right now. Your father and I were just concerned, that's all."

"Daddy? Are you and Gramma fightin' again?" Charlie asked from the foot of the stairs, her voice quiet and barely heard. One look at her tugged on my heart. Her eyes were watering and red-rimmed as she chewed on her lower lip—just like her mother.

I brushed past my mom and knelt before Charlie, pulling her into my arms. "No, baby. Grandma was just telling me something, that's all."

Charlie dropped her gaze from mine, her curls falling in a delicate curtain around her face, and nodded softly. "Okay," she whispered in a trembling voice.

I scooped her up in my arms and headed for the door. Turning back to my mom, I looked at her apologetically and instantly regretted how I had spoken to her. "I'm sorry. I'll talk to you later?"

My mother only nodded, pulling her arms tightly around herself. "All right. Get her home."

I felt like shit. Not only had I snapped at my own mother for merely being concerned—concern that, honestly, wasn't misplaced—but I managed to upset my reason for existing in the process. After strapping Charlie into her seat, I kissed her forehead, my brow furrowing slightly as she sniffled.

We drove home in silence...again, and I couldn't stop my ever-expanding guilt from swallowing me whole. As soon as the car was parked, Charlie unbuckled herself and waited for me to open the child-locked back door so she could walk to the house. Watching her walk slowly to the house broke my already-shattered heart even more. When I first saw her, she was so happy and full of life, and in the span of five minutes I was able to burst that bubble.

Maybe the problem wasn't Cassie at all. Maybe it was me.

My self-revelation hit me like a ton of bricks, and my pace soon mirrored Charlie's. I watched from the entryway as Charlie headed straight to the couch after kicking her sneakers off and putting them away. She lay with her back to the room, completely unmoving until I called her for dinner.

After pushing her food around for ten minutes and not taking a single bite, I sighed and set my fork down. "Bug, are you upset by my disagreement with Grandma?" I asked softly so as not to make her sullen attitude even worse. It didn't get worse, but it most definitely wasn't any better. Charlie shrugged and set her fork down, dropping her hands to her lap. "She just thought that maybe you needed to talk to someone." I placed my finger under her chin and coaxed her wet eyes up, swallowing my pride for a moment. "Do you, baby?"

She only shrugged again, and her refusal to actually talk worried me. I scooted off my chair and knelt on my knees beside her chair, turning it until she faced me. "Bug, you can talk to me," I assured her.

The right corner of her mouth turned up, but it was the furthest thing from a smile. She sighed heavily and looked out the dining room window before saying anything. "Does Mommy love me?"

I gently turned her face to me. "What?" I asked incredulously. Had I really just heard her right? The reason I questioned it was because she spoke so softly.

The tears that had been threatening to fall from her bright eyes finally did. "Baby, of course your mama loves you. Why would you even ask that?"

"I dunno," she said with another shrug. "I told Gramma that I miss Mommy." She paused for a moment, her brow furrowing with a combination of sadness and confusion. "They said that Mommy was really sad for a long time, and that she was sick. Is she, Daddy? Is Mommy sick?"

I bit back the rage I currently harbored toward my parents for sticking their fucking noses where they weren't welcome. Who the hell did they think they were?

Once I was sure my seething fury wouldn't be audible and scare my poor, sweet baby, I brushed Charlie's tears away from her cheeks and tucked her curls behind her ears before cupping her cherubic cheeks in my hands. "That was a very, very long time ago," I assured her softly. "Believe me when I tell you that Mommy loves you more than anyone could ever understand. Both of us do."

"So, she's not sick?" Charlie asked, still focusing on something she shouldn't have had to hear about for many years—if ever.

"No, baby. Mommy's not sick anymore." I watched as relief rolled over her, quickly washing the sadness from her eyes.

I kissed her forehead and smiled. "There's my girl. I need you to understand, Charlie, that you can talk to me whenever you need to, okay?"

"Okay, Daddy."

With that behind us, we returned to our dinner. However, I was anything if hungry. As I sat there, stabbing the vegetables on my plate, all I could think about was my parents' betrayal. How could they justify telling Charlie about Cassie's past? That was for Cassie and me to do...*not* them.

Charlie and I went about the rest of our evening routine before she reminded me after bath time that I promised to play the piano for her last week. As always, she looked up at me with her big blue eyes, pushing out that plump lower lip, and I was putty in her little hands. She pulled on her nightie and we went to sit on the bench together.

I played her a lullaby I had composed just for her when she was just over a year old, and by the time it was finished, she was fast asleep with her head resting on my arm. Replacing the fallboard quietly, I carefully shifted and picked her up so as not to wake her. As I carried her toward the stairs, I saw Cassie standing in the foyer.

A warm smile graced her face as she looked at our sleeping daughter draped in my arms. "Hey," she whispered, stepping forward and kissing Charlie softly on the forehead.

"I'm just going to run her up to bed. I'll be right back down, okay?" Cassie nodded, kissing me on the cheek as she passed by me and headed for the living room.

After tucking Charlie into her bed, I flipped on

her night-light and stuffed her little kitten-teddy under her arm before exiting her room silently. Once I had returned to the living room, I flopped down next to Cassie and rested my head on the back of the sofa.

"What's wrong, baby?" Cassie asked soothingly as her fingers ran through my hair.

"Charlie thinks you don't love her." Once the words left my mouth, I looked over at Cassie and the pain in her eyes destroyed me. "I told her you did, of course. But that was when she told me that my *parents* told her that you were sick."

A violent tremor slithered its way through Cassie's frame and she squeaked, "I was."

"That's not the fucking point!" I cried, standing up and pacing the room. "It wasn't their place!"

"Jack, calm down before you wake her up. She doesn't need to hear you so upset."

"Calm down? How is it you're not as furious as I am?" I demanded, looking down into her pleading eyes. She simply sat there, staring up at me as though I had no right to be upset. I had every right.

With a shrug, she sighed. "Because they're right. I was sick. Sure, maybe you didn't want Charlie to hear about it, but maybe she said something and your parents grew concerned."

"They want her to talk to someone," I continued, really hoping that Cassie would at least take my side on that.

She didn't, though. "Maybe she should."

"She can talk to us!"

Cassie jumped to her feet and cradled my jaw in her tiny hands and began rubbing hypnotic circles on my temples with her thumbs. "Calm. Down," she commanded softly. "It's just their opinion on what is best for Charlie. Charlie is growing up to be a fine and respectable young lady; I'm just sorry I've missed so much of it."

I had just gotten a hold of my emotions when the phone rang. Pulling free of Cassie's wonderful head massage, I leaned over the coffee table and scooped it up. "Hello?"

"Hey, sweetheart," my mom said sweetly into the phone, and in an instant I saw red again.

Cassie, sensing my ire, rushed to pull me to the couch where she promptly sidled up to me and began running her fingers through my hair. Motions that usually calmed and soothed me did no such thing as I began to lay into my mother.

"Where the hell do you get off telling Charlie about Cassie?" I demanded.

"Jack!" Cassie hissed next to me, quickly pulling her arms back. I met her appalled expression with one that said I didn't care how that sounded. I needed my mother to understand that what she did was not okay.

On the other end of the phone, I heard Mom sigh sadly. "Jack, it was never our intention to say anything about Cassie's condition—"

"Past," I said through gritted teeth, jumping to my feet again. "*Past* condition."

"Yes, I realize that. But some of the things Charlie was saying... Jack, she deserves to know what Cassie went through back then. It might help her understand why..." her words trailed off as she tried to justify her interference. "We're just worried, Jack."

"Mother, I assure you there is nothing to worry about." I shook my head in aggravation. "Just, stay the hell out of it. I'll tell her when she's ready."

"Ja—" I hung up the phone before she had a chance to say anything else and tossed it across the room. It hit the mantle before exploding into a million tiny pieces that scattered along the floor.

Narrowing her eyes at me, Cassie stood up and crossed her arms. "Well, I hope that made you feel better."

"Not really," I seethed, kneeling on the floor to clean up the plastic shards. I definitely didn't feel *better*. Pissed off. Ashamed. Remorseful. Sure...but "better?" Not even close.

Cassie's feet came into view as I picked up the last few pieces, and I sat back on my heels to look up at her. She looked cross with me, and she should have. I had never spoken to my mother like that before. It wasn't how I was raised.

"You're slipping, Jack. Fast. You need to fix this."

Frustrated with myself, I clenched my jaw and reached into my pocket for my cell phone. There was no way I could leave things like that with my mom. I dialed their number and my father picked up on the first ring.

"I assume you've called to apologize?" he guessed. His tone was monotonous as he spoke, and he was obviously — and rightfully — displeased with my behavior. "You've really stepped in it this time, Jack."

I had to bite the inside of my cheek before I lost it with him, too. After all, it wasn't *just* my mother who had betrayed my parental rights and told Charlie about Cassie. He was just as guilty, and a large part of me wanted to remind him of that fact. Instead, I took a deep, cleansing breath and closed my eyes as I responded. "I know," I told him calmly. "Can I speak to Mom, please? I'd like to apologize."

"Helen?" he called, covering the mouthpiece as they conversed for a minute.

I heard the shuffle of the phone passing hands, followed by her faint breathing, but she didn't speak. It didn't surprise me. With a deep breath, I spoke.

"I'm sorry, Mom. I shouldn't have yelled at you and blamed you." I had to pause for a moment when my voice cracked. "I understand why you said what you did...I just wish you'd have talked to me about it first."

"You're right," she agreed quietly. The tremble in her voice gave away just how deeply I had hurt her. I felt awful—for the second time that day I had hurt one of the most important women in my life. "We shouldn't have told her without talking to you first. I'm deeply sorry for overstepping our bounds. We were just worried."

I nodded as though she could see me. "I know, and I appreciate that you guys worry, but I assure you there's nothing to be worried about."

There was a heavy silence between us, and as I waited for her to say something, I looked up at Cassie and smiled weakly. Her hard expression only softened minutely. Clearly, she was still not entirely pleased with my outburst.

"Jack?" Mom said quietly. "I know you tell me there's nothing to worry about...but you know that you can talk to us about anything, right?"

I nodded silently for a minute before I realized she couldn't see me. "Of course I know that. Look, I should go. I'll see you tomorrow, all right? Goodnight. I love you."

"I love you too, sweetheart. I'll see you in the morning."

After ending the call, I placed my cell on the coffee table and turned back to Cassie. "I'm sorry for being an asshole."

The hard lines on her forehead softened completely and she uncrossed her arms. "I suppose I can forgive you. But promise me one thing?"

"Anything, love."

Cassie moved across the floor fluidly and took my hands in hers before looking up into my eyes. "After seeing the way my past has disrupted the peace between you and your mother," she paused, her eyebrows knitting together with worry as she bit her bottom lip and continued. "Swear to me that no matter what happens, you won't ever let me get in the way of your happiness. Especially when it comes to our family."

Chapter Nine
breaking free

"Swear to me that no matter what happens, you won't ever let me get in the way of your happiness. Especially when it comes to our family."

How could I promise that? Cassie was my life...my future...my *happiness*. How could I promise to not let her come in the way of herself? It was an insane thought—a thought that seemed to be coming full circle. Right back to Cassie. It made me dizzy, like I'd been riding around and around on a carousel that was moving entirely too fast. Even though it seemed a little crazy, I promised—but I had to in order to offer her some peace of mind that her past would no longer cause a rift between my parents and me, or be a problem for Charlie.

For the first couple of days after my disagreement with my mom, facing my parents was awkward, to say the least. My mother would barely meet my gaze, her embraces fell flat, and she hardly spoke two words to me unless it concerned Charlie. She put up a good front for Charlie so as not to upset her, but the strain was still there.

By Thursday, I was grateful that Jennifer and Alex had stopped by my parents' house, because I was able to ask them to take Charlie to the park for a bit so I could talk to Mom and Dad. Once we were all seated around the table, I apologized face-to-face, knowing that a phone call was clearly inadequate considering the severity of the situation.

"It's just...I don't know. I kind of wanted to shelter Charlie from Cassie's illness a little longer. We just didn't want her to know until she was old enough to really understand," I continued, finally bringing my eyes up to meet their stares.

My mom reached across the table and held her hand over mine. "I know, and I'm sorry. But she woke up from her nap crying for Cassie." She sniffled as a lone tear trailed down her cheek. "When I finally reached her, Jack, she lost it. She was kicking and screaming over and over that she wanted her mom. I've never seen her do that before."

I balked at my mother's recollection of the events that had prompted their talk with Charlie. "Why didn't you tell me this?"

Her eyes fell briefly and the air in the room was heavy with her remorse. "You never gave me the chance," she replied softly.

While I knew her words to be true, it still upset me. "You could have called," I said breathlessly as my chest began to tighten with anxiety at the mere thought of Charlie's episode.

"She told me not to, and I figured it best not to upset her further. I intended to tell you Monday when you picked her up. But after you reacted the way you did—"

"Because you opened with telling me my daughter needed therapy," I interrupted in a harsh tone. Feeling my anger level elevate, I took a deep breath, reminding myself that wasn't why I was here. "I'm sorry. That's not the point. Please, go on."

After a brief pause to gather her composure, she continued in a shaky voice. "Thankfully your father was home. He came rushing in, and we were finally able to calm her long enough to talk to us."

"W...what did she say?" I croaked, completely horrified by what I was hearing.

"Well," my dad interjected when he saw my mother's inability to go on. "She said she didn't think that Cassie loved her, and that's why she's not home with her anymore." I nodded in understanding as Charlie had told me the same thing when I got her home on Monday. Dad continued. "We told her that was absurd and that Cassie absolutely loved her." As I absorbed my father's words, I sat there for...well, I wasn't sure how long, actually. All I knew was that my poor, sweet baby missed her mother so much that she broke down.

Rubbing my hand down the length of my face in an attempt to erase the horrified expression I knew I wore, I nodded. "Okay. Well, the California trip will change everything. I think it will bring everyone back together and put Charlie's fears at ease." I could hear the denial that laced my words, but I chose to ignore it. While I desperately wanted California to be the cure-all we needed as a family, I knew it wouldn't be that simple.

It didn't escape my notice that my parents exchanged a glance, having their own silent conversation with their eyes. However, before I could say anything more, the front door opened and Charlie came barreling into the house.

"I won!" she cheered, her voice echoing through the hall as her aunt and uncle followed her inside.

"That's because you and your aunt are cheaters," Alex said matter-of-factly.

"Oh, Uncle Alex," Charlie cooed sweetly. "Don't be such a sore loser!" Soon the house was filled with the sounds of her giggles, and as I rounded the corner, I found Charlie on the floor at the mercy of her uncle's tickling.

It was refreshing to see her happy again, as though nothing plagued her. After Alex ceased his attack, Charlie jumped to her feet, gasping for air between her residual giggles, and hopped into my arms.

"Daddy, I raced Uncle Alex all the way from the park and I beat him!" she exclaimed excitedly.

Touching my nose to hers and winking, I chuckled. "That's because he's not as fast as us," I whispered. "Even back in high school, Uncle Alex couldn't outrun me." Charlie giggled again and Alex feigned hurt, sticking out his bottom lip and everything.

Alex arched his right brow, the right corner of his mouth curling up in a smirk as well. "You know I'm going to want a rematch, Charlie," he told her.

"You're on!" she screeched as she wriggled out of my grasp and flew across the empty space until he hoisted her up and hugged her tight.

"Auntie Jennifer and I have to go, but when we go to the beach? You better believe you and I are gonna throw down," he said with a wink.

Charlie giggled. "Bring it." Hearing those exact words fall from a four-year-old's mouth made everyone in the room burst out into a hysterical bout of laughter. "What's so funny?" she asked seriously.

I shook my head softly, my laugh dying down. "Nothing, bug. Come on. Let your Uncle and Auntie go home. I'm sure you'll see them tomorrow."

Charlie slid out of Alex's arms to give Jennifer a tight hug, and we stood in the entry as they said their goodbyes and left. I looked down at Charlie as she leaned against my thigh, a bright smile still on her face, and she looked up at me in return.

"I suppose we should head home, hey? Let your grandparents have a quiet evening to themselves?" I inquired. Charlie quickly agreed before kissing my parents and rushing out to the Audi while I said goodbye.

I turned to them both, and my mother offered me the first genuine smile in days as she pulled me into her arms. "I am sorry," I told her.

"Me too," she replied softly as she pulled away and kissed my cheek. "Go on, get her home. We'll see you in the morning."

I said goodbye to my father and then headed out to the car and checked Charlie's car seat straps before sliding behind the wheel and heading for home. Our evening was no different than any other: home, dinner, bath, and bed. Shortly after I tucked Charlie in, Cassie made it home, and we talked more about Charlie and the trip to California in the coming weeks.

"I still don't know, Jack. I get that you think this will be good for Charlie, but I fail to see how my being around won't actually make things worse," she argued as we lay on our bed staring up at the roof.

It didn't surprise me that she was still trying to find a way out of the trip. I turned to her and propped myself up on my elbow. "Baby, my parents said she freaked the hell out because she wanted and *needed* you. How on Earth do you think being around you won't be positive for her?"

Cassie pulled her bottom lip between her teeth and turned her head to face me. "Just trust me when I tell you that including me in your family vacation won't end well. For anyone."

"Cassie, we have to go. Please," I begged, sidling up next to her and working my right arm under her body so I could wrap them both around her before snuggling my head into the crook of her neck. "Come on. Think about it. The sun? Sand? Water? Our families sitting around the table three times a day."

Cassie laughed and began to run her fingers through my hair. "I thought you were trying to come up with reasons to convince me to go, not run far, far away," she teased as we tilted our heads to lock eyes. "The sun burns. Washing sand out of places that God never intended for it to wind up isn't pleasant. The water is cold...plus: sharks. And, I don't know if you realize it, but our families are...well, I'd hate to use the term crazy, but..."

I chuckled and placed a kiss to her bare shoulder before stroking the sliver of her lower abdomen that was showing. Back and forth, my hand moved across her skin, up over the swell of her hip and back down as my finger lightly traced the barely visible c-section scar above her pelvis. Her skin quivered at the ticklish sensation, and I laughed against the flesh of her shoulder before looking up at her through my lashes.

"Baby..." I said softly, dragging out the word and trying to pull her into my eyes in hopes of dazzling her the way I used to be able to.

"Jack," Cassie warned, cocking her eyebrow at me and twisting the right corner of her mouth up.

I stilled my hand on her hip and pushed my body up to kiss her softly on the lips. "You're right."

"I am?" she inquired, lifting her eyebrows in shock at my admission.

With a sly smirk, I shrugged. "Sure," I told her. "You do tend to resemble a freshly cooked lobster after five minutes in the sun." She laughed and slapped my chest playfully as I continued. "Digging sand out of my shorts has proven to be a bitch in the past. And cold water doesn't tend to be too forgiving in certain departments." Cassie's fingers found their way back into my hair. My eyes began to lull shut, and I yawned. "Oh," I said through the yawn. "And our family? Totally nuts." I looked up at her again.

"But we need this."

"And I want to be there. I just don't get how you think it's going to help," she repeated.

The fear I had felt the last couple years came rushing forth again, coupled with something else...something I refused to even acknowledge. If I did, everything I'd built would come crashing down and smother me. "I'm afraid," I confessed.

"Afraid of what?" Cassie inquired, her forehead creasing with worry.

I exhaled slowly. "I'm afraid that if you don't come, I'm going to lose you," I told her truthfully.

With a soft kiss, I felt my fear and apprehension start to disappear. "I told you; I'm not going anywhere as long as you need me."

My eyes fell shut, and I sighed softly against her skin as sleep threatened to take hold of me. "I'll always need you, Cassie."

"Now I'm afraid," she said breathlessly into the top of my head, and I almost didn't hear her as I fell fast asleep, wrapped in Cassie's arms, her hands in my hair and her soft voice soothing me.

Chapter Ten
three leaps back

It had been two long weeks, and every night it was the same. Cassie wasn't giving me an answer one way or the other, but I was certain she'd cave. It was Saturday, and Cassie was gone before I woke up. We were scheduled to leave shortly after Charlie's nap. Our parents were going to stop by the house because Charlie had expressed an interest in riding with them in the van they had rented so they could all travel together, and Jen and Alex would ride in the Audi with us.

On my way out of Charlie's room, I grabbed her suitcase and headed to my room to grab my own. With both cases in hand, I headed down the stairs and found Cassie standing at the foot of the stairs. The look on her face showed nothing but sadness and regret.

"I can't go," she informed me, her voice so soft I almost didn't hear it.

Clenching my jaw, I walked past her, ignoring her statement completely. "Are you packed? We're leaving as soon as our parents get here for Charlie." I set the suitcases down on the floor next to the door and turned, not once looking her in the eye.

"You're not hearing me, Jack. I can't go with you guys." I heard her follow me to the kitchen, but I still refused to look at her.

I froze in my tracks and closed my eyes as I took

a deep breath. "Cassie, don't do this." Turning slowly to face her, I exhaled my breath and opened my eyes. "Cassie we need this trip. Do it for Charlie," I pleaded.

She shook her head violently and wiped at her eyes. "I can't. Don't you get it? I *want* to do this for her...for you...for *us*. But this isn't something I can just do." A sob broke free as she continued. "I need you to understand I love you both...*so much*. But this trip won't change anything. When you get back, things won't magically go back to the way they were. I won't change...I *can't* change." Her head fell back, and she looked up at the roof as she continued on with a dry laugh. "God, how I wish I could just take it all back! But I can't. I can't undo the things I've done—the mistakes I've made—and even if I could, you would never forgive me...forgive yourself."

I rushed forward and grabbed her by the upper arms lightly. "Cassie, what the hell are you talking about?" I demanded, my voice shaking with fear that the last few weeks had all been for nothing. That she had merely been toying with my fragile emotions.

"I need you to accept that this is over. That it's been over for a long time. I need you to let me go," she said, her big blue eyes pleading with me to do as she asked. "You deserve so much more than what I can offer you. You need to move on and find someone who makes you happy. Who makes Charlie happy. Think of her...for me."

Releasing my tight grip on her arms, I cradled her face and forced her to hold my gaze. "I am thinking of her. Of all of us, Cassie. Damn it, how do you not see that? She needs you to go on this trip as much as I do." Cassie tried to shake her head in my grasp, but I held her as still as I could without causing her any harm.

"Let me go, please," she sobbed, her delicate hands coming up and encircling my wrists. "I just need—"

In an act of sheer desperation, I pressed my lips to hers. My lips worked against hers, trying to force them to mold to mine as she sobbed. Eventually, she uncrossed her arms from her body and brought them up until she fisted the front of my shirt, pulling my body into hers.

I released her face and dropped my hands until they were on the small of her back, holding her firm against my body, unwilling to ever let her go. She was unnaturally still against me, so I released her and took a step back.

As I looked over her, I noticed her arms fall and hang loose at her sides in defeat, and her brows were knit together in remorse. "I...I..." I stammered for a moment, pushing my hands through my hair and tugging once I reached the back of my head. "I can't believe you're leaving me."

"You had to see this coming," she said, trying to justify her total disregard for our family.

My anger bubbled, and my blood boiled beneath my flesh as I lost complete control. I swept my arm across the island in the kitchen, tossing the half-empty wine bottle, a single glass, and a bowl to the floor. They shattered upon impact, the wine splashing the light wall and staining it a rich shade of burgundy.

"No!" I shouted, causing Cassie to jump with a slight whimper. "I didn't see this coming! I thought we were making progress in our relationship, and now you tell me you want to fucking leave?"

"No," she whispered with a single head-shake. "I'm telling you I need you to let me go."

I stared at her for a moment as I tried—and

failed — to see the difference in what I asked and what she wanted. Finally, after a long moment of silence, I screamed in aggravation.

"Jack, keep it down. Please. You're going to wake Char—"

I thrust a finger toward her, my rage-fueled glare burning into her sad eyes. "Don't," I ordered. "Don't you even say her name," I snarled venomously. She acquiesced with a short nod and looked at the floor nervously. "Why didn't you just say all this a few weeks ago?"

"I tried!" she cried, raising her red eyes to mine again. "I told you I was lost. That we couldn't get back what we had. And what did you say?" She paused momentarily as I searched my memory for the answer, but she spoke before I could even open my mouth. "You told me that you needed me and that I wasn't going anywhere." She spread her arms wide and laughed dryly. "Well, here I am. As fucking requested!"

I stared at her, completely dumbfounded for a moment as she blamed me for her staying all this time. "So what? We're done then? Is that what you want?"

"No," she sobbed, wiping the tears from her eyes roughly. "It's not what I want. But it's what you need…to be happy. I have to go."

"And your decision to leave? That makes you happy?" Asking her that question, to me, felt like the equivalent of having my heart ripped from my body, and then watching as the life was squeezed out of it in front of me.

Cassie shrugged sadly, her frustration fading quickly as the sadness in her eyes returned. "My happiness is completely irrelevant at this point. I've caused you so much pain that I don't deserve to be happy."

"That's bullshit, and you know it," I told her angrily. She didn't contest my opinion, instead she stood before me with resolve clearly etched into every part of her expression. Her mind was made up. She was done with this...with me...with *us*.

I shook my head with a dark laugh. "You know what? Fine. You want out? Go. Get the hell out of my house!" I screamed, pointing down the hall behind me toward the door.

"Jack!"

I jumped in fright as a familiar voice called out my name sharply. When I turned around, I was face-to-face with my parents, Cassie's parents, and a terrified-looking Charlie hugging Gayle's thigh, her little face half buried into the fabric of my mother-in-law's skirt. My gaze drifted between each of their faces, but all of their expressions were the same: confusion and, most predominantly, fear.

I looked back at Cassie as she bit her bottom lip and began shaking her head at me, a gesture that indicated she didn't want me to continue our disagreement in front of our family. Charlie's sob forced my eyes back to her as she looked up at me; she was completely terrified by what she had just witnessed, and I felt horrible since I had always made it a point to never argue with Cassie in front of her.

"I...I need to get out of here for a minute," I explained quickly as I moved toward the bodies blocking my access to the front door.

"Jack?" my mother said softly, laying a hand tenderly on my forearm.

"No, Mom. I can't keep having this same fight with her." I lifted my eyes to Gayle and Frank, whose confusion seemed to be escalating by the minute. "Maybe you two can talk some sense into your daughter, because I've had it."

Gayle inhaled sharply, tears quickly welling in her eyes as her hand snapped to her mouth, and her husband's brow furrowed with concern. It hadn't occurred to me until just that moment just how much he seemed to have aged lately. I couldn't remember for the life of me when the worry lines in his forehead deepened or the grey in his hair multiplied. Even Gayle seemed a little worn out as she sobbed into Frank's shoulder.

"Jack," my mother tried again, but I pulled out of her grasp.

"No. I have to get some air. If she wants to leave, let her. I'm done." I waved my hand dismissively behind me at Cassie. I'd had enough, and so had she.

"Who's leaving?" my mother asked quietly, pressing her hand over Charlie's exposed ear gently.

"Cassie, who else? She wants to leave us. Leave her family." Again, I felt the physical pain of the words in my chest.

My mother promptly picked Charlie up and stared at me, her mouth agape. The entire room fell eerily silent, and minutes felt like years before anyone spoke. My father stepped forward and laid a firm hand on my shoulder, pressing lightly until I looked into his brown eyes.

"Son, Cassie's been gone for two years," he told me in a shaky voice.

My eyes narrowed and I scoffed. "What the hell are you talking about?" I asked him skeptically. When I turned back and looked at Cassie, I watched in horror as she clutched her stomach tightly and folded in on herself. As she fell to her knees on the kitchen floor, she was gasping for air and looking up at me, fearfully shaking her head back and forth. "She's right there!"

Cassie's head shook slowly now, and this time I knew why. I inhaled sharply, not wanting to believe what I already knew was true. "No," I whispered. "Cassie, tell them."

"I'm sorry," she squeaked. "I can't."

Chapter Eleven
reliving the past

The trees along the highway whirred by as I stared out the car window wondering what the hell was going on. There was really no describing just how confused I was by everything that had been said yesterday afternoon when my parents showed up at the house. It was all a complete blur as I tried to recall anything real from the past couple of years. Had it all been in my head? Just how fucked up was I?

Gone. They said she was gone.

I still couldn't wrap my foggy brain around the thought. How could she have been gone? And for two years? I saw her *every day*, and they were telling me she left us two years ago? It just didn't make sense. My brain hurt even trying to remember the events that had brought me to this point.

"Sweetheart?" my mother said softly from in front of me, saving me from my own insanity.

I pulled my arms tighter across my chest as I shifted my face to hers. "Hmm?" As my eyes finally settled on her, I saw just how distraught she was by everything that had happened. Blinking rapidly in an effort to clear the haze from the outer edges of my sight, I shifted my gaze to my father as he navigated his way through the city streets.

"How are you feeling?" she asked, turning and reaching back between the two front seats to place a delicate hand on my knee.

I swallowed what little saliva was in my increasingly dry mouth thickly and licked my lips. "Tired," I rasped in a gravelly voice. I found it hard to focus my gaze on her. No matter how many times I blinked, it didn't seem to help.

"That's the meds, son," my dad spoke up, glancing briefly over his shoulder to offer me a reassuring smile. Sadly, it fell flat in light of *why* I was heavily medicated.

Gone.

"I know," I sighed in defeat, allowing my head to loll onto the headrest of the Mercedes' backseat. After telling me that Cassie had been gone for two years, I became upset. Actually, that was an understatement; I went completely bat-shit crazy.

Before Charlie could witness what was rapidly unfolding, my mom and Gayle retreated up the stairs with her while my father and Frank worked to subdue me. Dad wound up calling in a prescription for a mild sedative because I refused to listen to reason and was well beyond rational. There was nothing anyone could say to me that would make what was happening any better.

After taking my first dose, I headed upstairs to find Gayle and my mom sitting on either side of a sleeping Charlie in her bed. The red around her eyes was the key indicator that my poor, innocent baby had cried herself to sleep after having witnessed the complete loss of my sanity downstairs. How had I let any of this happen? How had I not put two and two together?

I climbed up onto the bed next to Charlie and pulled her into my arms so I could hold her as I allowed the meds to do their job. It wasn't long before I fell into a dreamless, coma-like slumber.

When I awoke in the morning, Charlie could be

heard downstairs talking softly and scurrying around. I stayed in her bed for a few minutes, staring up at the ceiling, as I tried to get a grip on reality before facing the consequences of my actions the day before. There was a part of me that thought it was all just a bad dream, that I would go downstairs to find Cassie and Charlie playing like the last two years of fighting weren't real either. That everything was perfect. The small smile that spread across my face was short lived as I sat up and the fog in my head reminded me of the medication I had taken the night before.

It was all frighteningly real.

Gone.

Still a little groggy from the sedatives, I didn't actually remember much from yesterday. So, when I trudged down the stairs to find my mother tidying up the mess I was apparently responsible for, I felt horrible. I offered to help, but was quickly shooed away by her and Gayle. Instead, I went and sat on the living room sofa and stared blankly at the wall ahead until I was called for breakfast.

I couldn't eat, though. I sat with my hands clasped in my lap and stared at the quickly cooling food that sat on my plate while everyone around me ate. Once we all finished eating the breakfast that Gayle had made, she and Frank offered to take Charlie for the day while my parents and I went on the little road trip we were on.

I had questions about what happened, and there was only one way to get the answers.

"How long until we're there?" I asked softly as I turned to look out the window again. We were entering the city, and my body instantly stiffened as my apprehension took hold. I already knew it wouldn't be much longer, and I felt the fear of reality sinking in with every second that passed. The car suddenly felt like it was shrinking around me.

"We should be there in about fifteen minutes," my dad replied softly.

I sucked in a deep breath and held it until my chest ached. As we weaved through the city streets, I heard my mother sobbing softly. I shifted my eyes forward just in time to see my father reach his right hand across the center console and hold hers to offer her comfort. I looked down at my own hands and felt empty inside. There was no one to comfort me in my own time of need.

The next fifteen minutes felt like an eternity, but we finally pulled up in front of the hospital. It loomed over me as I looked up through the tinted window of my father's luxury sedan. I reached for the handle and had just popped the door when my mother reached between the back of her seat and the car frame to grip my wrist.

"You're sure about this? You don't want us to come in with you?" she inquired, her eyes reflecting her anguish.

I shook my head and offered her a weak smile. "No, this is something I should do alone. You guys go and park the car. I'll see you in a few."

"Okay, we'll meet you inside, then," my father said.

After taking a deep breath, I found my nerves and stepped out of the car and into the sun and warmth that Denver offered this time of year. I walked with reservation up the long, intimidating walkway toward the entrance. My heart started beating wildly in my chest as I passed doctors and nurses who were walking past me, looking at me, judging me... Okay, so they probably weren't judging me, but given what just happened, it felt like I was under a microscope and everyone was taking turns looking through the glass to see if they could figure out what was going on beneath the surface.

The doors opened automatically, causing me to balk in surprise. It shouldn't have affected me like that, but I was so wound up. I passed through the oversized doors and headed for the admissions desk where a woman sat clicking away on her computer keyboard.

She must have seen me approach through her periphery, because she turned to me with a wide smile. "Good afternoon, what can I help you with today?"

I placed my hands on the counter and gripped it tightly as I spoke. "I'm Jack Martin. I, um, well, my dad called earlier?"

"Oh, yes! Mr. Martin, of course!" she said animatedly as she began leafing through the small pile of folders on her desk until she found the slip of paper she was looking for. "You're going to want to go to the fifth floor. The elevators are just straight ahead, and when you reach fifth, turn right and head down to the South wing. Just check in at the nurse's station and they will guide you from there." She placed a slip of paper up onto the counter before me and held out a pen. "I'm just going to need you to sign here, and then you're free to go on up."

"Thanks," I told her monotonously as I signed the form she handed me and returned it. After giving her a curt nod, I made my way for the elevator and pushed the button. There were people moving all around me, bustling through the halls as I waited eons for the doors to open up. It felt as though they were all moving at a mile a minute, but I was frozen in time, forced to watch them all live their lives and go about their days when I had nothing left to live for.

When I finally arrived at the fifth floor, I turned right and headed for the nurse's station. The hall looked long, and I felt a little disoriented as I set forth on the next leg of this little journey. The dizziness wasn't the worst of it, however; as I made my way down the corridor, the walls appeared too close together, and my heart thundered painfully against my ribs. I finally arrived at my destination, and when I did, all the nurses there seemed to stop what they were doing and stare.

I suddenly felt very anxious and my palms were sweating, which was unusual for me. "Um, I'm Jack Martin," I stated. Upon learning my identity, I was met with nothing but sympathetic stares, which made me even more uncomfortable.

"Hello, Mr. Martin. I'm Nurse Collins. Please come with me," a friendly looking, middle-aged woman said sweetly.

I walked with her a little further down the hall until she stopped in front of a door marked "523," mumbling something about me going on in because she had to go and find Dr. Richards. Offering her an appreciative smile and a nod, I waited until she walked away before I closed my eyes and took a deep breath. I held the breath for an extra beat before letting it out and opening the door. When I stepped into the brightly lit room, the first thing I saw was the perfectly made bed with crisp white linens beneath the barred window.

The walls were pretty bare and were painted a pale shade of green. I assumed it was meant to be cheerful, however, I couldn't help but find it depressing. I continued to take in my surroundings, and when I looked to the left, I saw a familiar face sitting in the rocking chair that was placed in the far corner of the room. She was dressed all in white, and her blonde hair cascaded around her pale face like a soft curtain. Her hands were fidgeting as they rested on her knees, and her eyes were drawn to the other window in the room as she looked out into the day.

Even though I knew where I was and why I was here, I stared at her with hope. Hope that maybe what I was told to be true wasn't at all. That I would go home and everything would be back to normal.

Once the soft click of the door latch catching behind me was heard, she turned to me and the corners of her mouth twisted up into a smile. "You came."

I flopped down on the bed opposite her and dropped my eyes to the floor. "I didn't really have a choice, now, did I?" There was a heavy silence between us before I could continue. "I need you to tell me everything. No tiptoeing or sugar coating any of it. I need to hear it from you. Why?"

"Baby," she whispered, her voice so soft and beautiful. "You know what happened."

I laughed, almost maniacally as I lifted my head. "I thought I knew a lot of things...but apparently everything I thought I knew wasn't real. How...? I just don't understand...*why*?" I repeated, my voice straining.

"It's a long story."

Cocking an eyebrow, I straightened my posture and looked her dead in the eye. "I'm pretty sure I've got the time."

Cassie stood gracefully and moved to sit by my side. She placed her hand over mine and, with a sigh, she began to tell me everything, and my memory started to come back...

""I'm going to go and get the sleeping pills that Sienna prescribed. I'll be back in fifteen minutes, okay? I'll see if my mom can keep Charlie tonight, too," you whispered before standing and walking toward the bedroom door, stopping to say, "I love you." I knew the words you spoke

to be true, but I was just so...so broken from what had just happened.

"I couldn't move. I wanted to run to you and to apologize for putting you through such grief. It killed me that you were so upset by the miscarriage. Even though I was physically and emotionally drained, I remember wiping my eyes and lifting my head to let you know that no matter how badly I had failed you as a wife and Charlie's mother, that I felt the same way. "I love you, too," I said with a sniffle. I did...do love you, Jack. But after everything that happened, I didn't deserve your love in return. I still don't.

"I don't know how long I stayed in bed for after I heard the door downstairs lock and the Audi speed off down the street, but I remember with crystal clarity that my thoughts never once strayed from how I wished I could take back every negative thought I had about being pregnant again. I was scared — terrified beyond belief — because I remembered what I was like after having Charlie, and I refused to live like that again. The fear consumed me, and you just kept pushing and pushing — "

I interrupted her for a moment. "I didn't intend to push. I just thought that with some gentle prodding, you'd come around...maybe remember how great your first pregnancy was," I explained softly, realizing she wasn't entirely to blame for everything that had happened.

It was because of me that she fell over the edge and into the crashing waves that drowned her.

Cassie offered me a sad smile and ran her fingers through my hair. I sighed as the sensation caused every hair on my body to stand on end. "I know your intentions weren't to hurt me. You were excited...who wouldn't be? I just couldn't wrap my mind around everything that was going on...it was too much. And then, when I miscarried...?" Cassie dropped her face from mine, and I heard a small sob escape her. When she returned her gaze to mine, all I saw was anguish and shame. "I was relieved. For that one fleeting moment, it was like this huge weight had been lifted from me. And I felt guilty because, while I ultimately got what I thought I wanted, you were suffering."

As she confessed her true feelings to me, my breathing faltered slightly and my chin quivered. "I need you to continue," I said, my voice wavering with uncertainty that I could even handle what I was about to be told.

Cassie nodded and carried on with her story.

"I finally pulled myself out of bed to use the washroom, and when I looked into the mirror I didn't even recognize the monster staring back. My eyes were lifeless, my face gaunt from not eating all week. I was caught in a riptide, and as I stood there, staring into eyes that were no longer mine, I couldn't breathe. The walls felt as though they were closing in on me, and I fell to the ground hyperventilating. That's when you came home and rescued me.

"You ran up the stairs when you heard me crying and picked me up off the floor. You took me to bed where you sat me in your lap and moved us back and forth while I sobbed into your shoulder. While you made me feel safe and loved, I couldn't help but think that maybe your concern for me was misplaced.

"Being around you was the hardest thing I ever had to do in the following days. You were so distraught over losing the baby, and the only thing that killed me was that you were upset. That you would eventually blame me because I never wanted the baby. Even resent me somewhere down the line. I wouldn't have been able to live with you hating me.

"I assured you I was fine, though, and you believed me so easily...or maybe you had just stopped caring. Charlie

continued to go to your parents' house while you went to work, leaving me alone with my thoughts. The only thing I could think was how things had changed so drastically from the miscarriage. I rarely spoke to you or Charlie. She was only three, and I completely shut her out...who the hell does that? You would bring her home, and she would run to me all excited about her day with your mother...and I walked away, Jack. I turned from her and walked the fuck away."

Cassie reached up and wiped the fresh tears from her cheek, sniffling as she remembered everything. "Then, after you put her to bed, because I refused to read to her, we got into a fight. Granted, it wasn't the first...but the things we said to each other? They altered me in ways that I can't even begin to apologize for.

""For fuck's sake, Cassidy!" you screamed as you stood mere inches from my face. "I get that you're upset, but you don't need to take this out on her! She has no idea what's going on, and she needs you! I need you to at least pretend to care."

""Fuck you!" I shouted, and your head snapped back as though I had slapped you...and in truth, my lashing out at you verbally was far worse. "I know she needs me, I'm sorry if I can't be as fucking perfect as you! I never asked for any of this. You did." Even though I said I was sorry, I wasn't...but I should have been.

"*The way you looked at me as I screamed at you was agonizing. I could see your disappointment in how I was behaving – your anger at how I was treating our daughter; and while it pained me to hurt you and Charlie, a part of me just didn't care anymore. That part of me was fast becoming dominant. I can't even describe it...I knew I was acting like a crazy person. The depression was so thick it choked me, but I was so terrified to be medicated for it. I just, I don't know...I figured it would pass.*

""I don't even know what to say to that, Cassidy." Your eyes narrowed, and for the first time in all our years together, I felt your hatred toward me. It burned like acid eating its way through my heart — my soul — taking it all away along with your love. "I can't even look at you right now. I'm going downstairs for a bit. Do whatever the fuck you want."

"Before you left the room, though, you set the bottle of my sleeping pills on my night stand and walked away from me. You always gave me just enough to help me shut my emotions off so I could sleep, but that time...

"In my heart, I knew you weren't hinting at anything, but in my current state of mind — and after the epic screaming match we had just engaged in — what else was I expected to believe? Pulling my legs up and crisscrossing them in front of me, I sat on the edge of the bed staring at the pills, waiting for a sign that I should go and get you. That I should confess to you the fucked up things that were clouding my better judgment, but that voice...

"I just wanted it to stop! Can't you understand that? I had a brief moment of clarity, and I ran to the bathroom with the bottle of pills clutched tightly in my hands. I stood over the sink, popped the top and held it at an angle, ready to dump them down the drain and tell you how I was feeling, and ask for you to help me...to save me from myself.

"But something kept picking at me. It picked and picked and picked...until finally the voice told me you wouldn't understand...that no one would and you'd put me in...well, here. Tears flooded from my eyes, clouding my vision as I held my free hand out under the mouth of the bottle. Our fight continued to loop in my mind like a broken record, making me feel unworthy of you — of our dear sweet Charlie — and in an instant, it was like I was watching everything happen from a third-person perspec-

tive. Like, I had left my own body and watched as I dumped the pills into my shaking hand. So many tears continued to spill forth onto my cheeks, only to make room for more that impaired my vision further.

"I didn't need to see, though. I knew what I was doing. Kind of. I guess the closest way I can describe it was like having an out-of-body experience. I watched myself — even tried screaming for you — but the part of me that was watching couldn't be heard. So I opened my mouth, slipped the handful of pills in, and filled a glass with water, chugging it back. All the while you were downstairs playing your piano. The ominous and angry tones from your music floated through the house, and I could hear the pain — the anger — behind the composition. Every note entered my body and vibrated, making me feel as though I had chosen my true path."

My panic level started to rise rapidly as Cassie told me in vivid detail what she had done. I could feel the color drain from my face, and I felt like I was going to be sick. I started shaking my head, denial rearing its ugly head.

It wasn't real. It couldn't be real.

Regardless of how hard I tried to wake up or snap back to reality, Cassie swallowed thickly and took a shaky breath. "That was the last time you played...it wasn't the night I told you I didn't want more children." She paused again, offering me a weak smile. "You seem to have forgotten a lot more than just that, though..."

"As I became drowsy minutes later, I was unaware of anything. The pain seemed to dissipate, and I felt at peace. That didn't last for long, though...

"You know when they say your entire life flashes before your eyes in the face of death? Well, as I stared into the

mirror, my reflection becoming increasingly blurry, I saw you. The melody that was echoing through our house suddenly shifted into the song you composed for me, and our entire life together played back in my head like a movie on fast-forward. And then I saw Charlie. Sweet, beautiful Charlie. I remembered the joy she had brought into our lives from the minute we found out we were expecting her. Her sweet face, tiny toes and fingers. How she would grip onto our fingers so tightly, and how she allowed us to see directly into her innocent little soul.

"Then I felt something I never thought I would. I felt grief for the loss of our unborn baby. Imagined what he would have looked like had he made it. Would his eyes have been blue? Hazel? His hair brown or blond? When he smiled, would he have your same mischievous grin?

"It was in that moment, I found the love I was supposed to have for him – and I felt that love ripped away just as quickly..."

Cassie dropped to her knees before me and gripped my cold, clammy hands tightly. "I screamed out your name...do you remember that? I was finally able to cry out for you as I pushed myself away from the counter. On trembling legs, I rushed to the toilet to force myself to be sick, but it was too late. Too much time had passed with the pills in my system, and my legs gave out on me. I fell to the floor, shattering the glass I still clutched in my hands, and unconsciousness took hold..."

My eyes never strayed from Cassie as she sat before me, her eyes glistening with a fresh onslaught of tears. "There's no way I will ever be able to express how sorry I am for what I've done to this family," she sobbed, bringing my hand up to her mouth and peppering my skin with her soft kisses.

My heart strained painfully, and tears fell furiously from my eyes as I, too, began to sob with every touch of her lips across the back of my hand. "I still don't understand."

"You do. You just can't admit it to yourself. You will, though. The first step is just...letting go." Her voice was quiet, hiccupping slightly from the violent sobs that forced their way from her lungs. "It's your guilt that won't allow you to move forward and accept my fate."

"I won't ever be able to let you go. Not ever."

Cassie sighed, wiping the tears from her eyes. "You have to. Think of Charlie."

Hearing her tell me something she clearly couldn't even do enraged me. "You mean like you did?" I regretted saying it as soon as the words left my mouth.

Cassie's face twisted in pain. "And that, my love, is something I am forced to live with for the rest of eternity. Don't think it's easy for me to watch her grow and not be able to hold her in my arms. To not be able to tell her I love her and have her hear me—because it's not. I want to take her to play dates and run my fingers through her little blonde curls to comfort her after a bad dream. But I can't."

I couldn't stop the venom from spewing forth from my mouth, even though I knew my words hurt her deeply. "Because you were selfish."

She shook her head, but she seemed to take my accusation with a grain of salt. "No, because I was sick," she corrected me, and she was right. She *was* sick, and I didn't see the signs. I kept pushing her farther and farther until she finally just...broke.

I broke her. Destroyed who she was. This all happened because of me.

Not wanting to fight anymore, I pulled her into my arms and held her tightly. She had to be real; I could hear her, smell her...*feel* her. There was still a cloud of doubt that hung above me, though, and as we sat there, wrapped up in our own blanket of misery, the door opened suddenly and in popped an unfamiliar face. I stared at him blankly through my teary eyes and squeezed Cassie's hand tightly.

"Mr. Martin? I'm Dr. Richards. Are you ready to begin your session?" the kind-looking man asked softly, a tentative smile playing lightly at the corners of his mouth. When his question finally registered in my brain, I slowly turned to face my beautiful Cassie once more...

...only to find my arms empty, her absence leaving me cold.

Chapter Twelve
dreams become real

I didn't move from my spot on the bed as I stared at the empty space where Cassie was seated only moments before. The truth of everything she had just confessed bore down on me like a ton of bricks. I was having trouble breathing, and the outer corners of my vision darkened as my stomach rolled.

"Jack?"

Closing my eyes, I inhaled slowly and hoped that I wouldn't pass out. *I'm so lost.*

"Jack?" the man's voice called out again. "Are you all right?"

I opened my eyes and found he had entered my room, looking more than concerned. Hoping to assure him that I was fine, I nodded—even though I was fairly certain that wasn't the case. "Yeah," I managed to say in a rough voice. "I'm fine."

"Your parents are waiting for us in my office. Are you ready?"

When I stood from the bed, he moved to the side so I could exit the room—*my room*—first. As soon as I was out in the hall, he walked beside me. I welcomed the comfort that this action brought, even if the professional in me knew he was only doing it so that I felt as though I wasn't alone.

We didn't say anything to one another as we wandered down the hall before stopping outside a door with a nameplate that read "Doctor Kenneth Richards" on it. From the other side of the solid oak, I could hear my parents speaking. While I couldn't hear exactly what they were saying, I knew it had to be about me.

The doctor opened the door and waited for me to go in first. There, standing in the middle of the room were my parents. My father looked exhausted, but he was at least able to contain the distress that I was certain he was feeling. My mother, on the other hand, could not—not that one could blame her; this was entirely fucked up. As soon as her eyes landed on me, they welled with tears, and her forehead furrowed with worry. She rushed across the room and wrapped her arms around my neck.

"Mom, everything's going to be okay," I whispered as I embraced her in return. Even though I wanted the words I spoke to be one hundred percent true, I wasn't completely convinced, either.

Having loosened my grip on my mother, it wasn't until Dr. Richards cleared his throat that my mother released me. When we looked up at him, he indicated to the sofa in the center of the room. Taking me by the hand, my mom led me to the sofa where she and my father sat on either side of me, and Dr. Richards took his place in the leather seat across from us.

The position I suddenly found myself in unnerved me because I wasn't used to being "the patient." It seemed to be affecting me on much more than just a psychological level, too, because as I sat with my parents beside me, my arms were tucked in tight to my sides with my shoulders slumped forward. In the back of my mind, I knew that this was the posture of someone who felt defeated...someone who felt like they had nothing left and was trying to guard what little control they still had. I had seen it more times than I could count in my own office. Patients would come in, completely down on themselves and needing my assistance to help them figure out where to go from there. And yet...here I was; completely unable to help even myself. I was in no way capable of counseling others.

A quiet, dry laugh escaped as I realized this, and I could feel my parents' eyes drift to me. "Sorry." I shook my head as I issued my apology.

The three of them waited in silence for me to explain my little outburst, but I refused to share. They already knew I was crazy; I didn't want to cement their feelings on the subject. Instead, I just dropped my gaze to my fidgeting hands and waited.

"Okay, so, Jack, your parents have told me a little as to why you're here... Would you like to elaborate further?" Dr. Richards finally asked, breaking the maddening silence.

"Not particularly," I replied, my tone returning to its previous dark tenor as reality came crashing back down around me.

Dr. Richards simply nodded, knowing he wouldn't be able to force anything out of me at the moment. "Okay. That's quite all right. We don't need to discuss it today. I'd be more than happy to wait until your first session...or whenever you're ready to talk about it." He was trying to make me feel at ease. It didn't work.

I clammed up again, allowing my parents and Dr. Richards to discuss the plans for my "recovery." *Fuck, how had it come to this?* I could feel the nausea churning in the depths of my stomach, and had to swallow thickly to try and hold it at bay. My saliva thinned and was unnaturally warm, tasting of bile as it flooded my mouth, and I could no longer hold it back. I threw myself up off the couch and hunched over the trash can that was by the door.

Because I hadn't eaten anything since...I wasn't even sure, actually...I was mostly dry heaving into the bag. Every muscle in my back and stomach started to ache as my body convulsed, and I could barely hear the muted voices of my parents and Dr. Richards behind me. The tremors in my body finally subsided, and I pushed myself up on shaky limbs before turning back to the worried stares of my parents and an extremely nervous-looking doctor.

"I'd like to go back to my room now?" I stated, posing it more like a question since I wasn't sure if that was even an option.

"Of course," Dr. Richards finally said. "I'd like to see you tomorrow for the first of your private sessions. And if it's all right with you, I'd like to do weekly family sessions. Having them here would be most beneficial to your recovery."

It was that word that caused me such distress; I suddenly felt queasy again, but this time was able to hold the sickness at bay. "Of course," I managed to choke out. "What time tomorrow?"

"Ten AM."

I nodded and reached for the brass doorknob, my anxiety refusing to relent; instead, it seemed to be heightening exponentially by the minute. The reality of Cassie's...of Cassie's...*absence* was suffocating me. It felt like all the air had been sucked from the room, and I had to get the hell out of there.

"I need...I need to go," I stammered breathlessly.

As I rushed from the room, I heard my father ask something about a medication routine. I probably should have cared, but I just couldn't focus on anything except wanting to see Cassie. The need for her — even if she wasn't real — was all-consuming.

The door to my room slammed against the wall behind it as I threw it open and rushed inside. I was wrong to find it institutional earlier. It was where I last saw Cassie; therefore it was where I wanted to be.

My eyes searched frantically for her, but she was nowhere to be seen. Hot tears spilled forth onto my cheeks as I flopped down on my bed.

"Jack?" I looked up to find my terrified parents standing in my doorway. "Son, are you all right?"

"No. I...how...? *Why?*" My brain was a mess of jumbled thoughts...and memories...and *questions*... I couldn't make sense of any of it. As my panic and anxiety continued to rise, I could feel the remnants of my earlier dose of medication wearing off.

My dad understood what was happening and stepped forward, reaching into his pocket. "Dr. Richards will prescribe your regular meds tomorrow, but having discussed everything with him, he's okayed your taking two more Librium to get you through tonight." He dropped the pills in my hand, and I just stared at them.

It was ironic, really; pills had started this whole mess, and here I was—medicating myself...with a *sedative.*

Not wanting to feel anything for the moment, I opened my mouth and swallowed the pills without any water. My father laid his hand upon my shoulder and squeezed lightly. "I'm in the hospital tomorrow, I'll stop by after your session to check on you," he told me softly before heading for the door.

Without saying a word—most likely because there was nothing more to be said, or she was just far too emotional—my mother wrapped her arms around me once again. Before leaving, they turned to me. "We love you, son," my father reminded me. "We know you can do this. For Charlie."

My chin quivered, because I suddenly missed my baby. My baby, who never asked for any of this. She didn't deserve to lose her mother. She didn't deserve to go through everything she was being forced to go through in her short, almost five years of life.

"For Charlie," I repeated in a voice barely above a whisper as my mom and dad closed the door with a soft click behind them.

And then, I was alone.

Chapter Thirteen
making progress

Time stands still as I run up the stairs. The sound of the glass shattering from the floor above me haunts me and makes me think the most horrible things. I have tunnel-vision. I can only think of one thing, and it's the most terrifying, mind-numbing thought a person can have. My feet feel as though they are trudging through molasses as I hit the top stair and try to bolt down the hall toward our bedroom.

The sound the door makes when it slams against the plaster as I throw it open is loud, but I don't focus on it. I'm focused on the empty bed as the tenor of the last ominous note I played on the piano echoes in my head. The blankets are rumpled; Cassie's pillow has an indent where her head probably rested only moments before.

But the room is empty.

That's when I see the bathroom door slightly ajar. There's light coming from beneath the door, and I am suddenly frozen in fear. What will I find behind that door?

I move forward and lay my hand flat on the cool panel of wood and push it open slowly...

"And then what happens?"

My hands were clenched tightly in my denim-clad lap as I spoke quietly about the dream I had quite often. Dr. Richards's voice brought me back to the present, and I raised my eyes to his. There was no judgment there. Only empathy.

After waking alone that morning, my brain still foggy from the Librium my father made sure I took before bed, Dr. Richards had come to escort me to our first private session. Walking back into his office was daunting, and my heart was thundering so loud I was sure he'd hear. Even though I was still feeling the effects of the sedative, it didn't stop my anxiety from creeping in just a little. We crossed the room, and Dr. Richards indicated for me to have a seat on his leather sofa while he took the chair across from me.

With him seated in his leather chair, his legs crossed and his yellow legal pad in his lap, we sat in silence for a few minutes before he asked me how I was feeling. His posture conveyed his confidence as he watched me with warm, caring eyes while my apprehension consumed me wholly. I wasn't nervous about his presence; I was nervous because of where I was, and more importantly, *why*.

We sat in silence for a few minutes before Dr. Richards asked me how I was sleeping. It was that question that got me talking about my dreams.

I loosened my hands and offered him a shrug. "I don't know. That's usually when I wake up."

"So, you're saying this—what you told me—was just a dream?" Dr. Richards leaned forward in his seat and really focused on me.

"Isn't it?"

"You tell me, Jack."

His tone was familiar, and it made me chuckle dryly as I sat back and ran my hands through my hair. "Nice one." As a therapist, I could recognize what he was doing. He waited, as we were supposed to, until I took the bait off the hook he had cast.

"I honestly don't know what I'm supposed to believe anymore," I admitted quietly.

"Tell me about her. Tell me about Cassie." He sat

back in his chair again and set his pen down on his notepad.

What was I supposed to tell him? Tell him about Cassie when we met? When we got married? How she was after having Charlie? How she was before—

"I can't," I croaked, cutting my thoughts off and feeling the tears burning the rims of my eyes.

Dr. Richards nodded in understanding. "That's fine. I can wait until you're ready." He looked at the watch that circled his left wrist and frowned. "I hadn't realized our hour was almost up. Is there anything else you want to discuss?"

With a sigh, I began picking at the sleeves of my grey cable-knit sweater. I could feel my anxiety level start to elevate again, and he must have picked up on it. "Your father said he had been giving you Librium? How do you feel they're working?"

"They work fine, I guess."

"Do they make you drowsy?" I nodded once. "Do you feel anxiety when you're not taking them?" I nodded again. "Do you think you need something stronger?"

I shook my head quickly. "No. Definitely not." As a doctor who had prescribed my fair share of anti-anxiety medication, I knew that they could be addictive. I could already feel the effects of this, and I knew that I would have trouble without them...when I was ready.

Dr. Richards nodded and made a note in my file. "All right, then. I will keep you on them. You'll get them on a schedule. The nurses will bring them around for you when it's time to administer meds. How are you feeling now?" he asked, his eyes dropping from mine.

I followed his gaze to where I was wringing my hands in my lap nervously. Sucking in a sharp, nervous breath, I parted my hands and rubbed them down my thighs and over my knees before offering him a forced smile. "I've, uh, been better," I told him honestly.

Dr. Richards nodded in understanding. "I'll send the nurse around to you soon, then." He stood fluidly, and I followed his lead. I crossed my arms across my torso and walked with him to the door. "Your father mentioned he might stop by today? I hope the two of you have a good visit. I'll see you tomorrow."

"Thanks," I croaked quietly before walking past him. "Tomorrow, then."

Even though the walk to my room wasn't terribly long, it felt as though it took ages. Once inside, I sat in the chair I saw Cassie in the day before and stared out into the day. The sky was overcast—nothing new there—but I could see a hint of the morning sun behind the darkening clouds as they threatened rain. The weather seemed fitting with my mood, and as I stared out into nothingness, my mind began to drift until it settled on Charlie.

"I wonder what she's doing right now," I wondered aloud.

"She's with Gayle and Frank for a few more days," my father responded, startling me as he entered the room without my hearing him. He offered me a smile when I turned to him, and I raised the right side of my mouth in an attempt to do the same.

"How was your session?"

With a shrug, I responded. "It was all right, I suppose."

His forehead wrinkled with worry, and he seemed to be debating something in his head. "And you're doing...okay?"

This time, both sides of my mouth turned up, but the sound that came out of me was far from jubilance.

My laugh was dry and rough. "I've checked myself into the psych ward...so, I'm going to go with 'not good.'"

"Of course. I didn't mean anything... It's just...we're terribly worried about you." Dad entered the room and planted himself on the edge of my bed, dropping his head into his hands.

I could see that this entire situation was taking a toll on him as much as it was me. "I know," I whispered. "I don't know when...or even how any of this happened. I don't... I'm having trouble remembering."

My father lifted his head and met my eyes. He looked exhausted — like he hadn't slept in days. His complexion was unnaturally pale, and there were deep circles under his eyes. "You can't remember?"

I shook my head in response as I prepared to speak. "If it's anything close to what I've been told... I don't know that I want to."

"Told? By whom?" He paused momentarily before realization struck. "Cassie," he breathed softly. "Son, you know she's — "

"Gone. Yeah, I got that," I rushed to finish for him. I wasn't ready to hear that she had...that she was... I shook the thought from my mind. I refused to allow *that word* be a part of my vocabulary. "So, Charlie is with Frank and Gayle? How is she? I mean, does she understand what's happening?"

At first, my father didn't seem thrilled that I was skirting the issue of Cassie's...absence, but I gave him a pleading look that hopefully conveyed how much I needed to know that my daughter wasn't going to be negatively affected by any of this. He seemed to understand as he clasped his hands in his lap.

"I spoke with her last night before she went off to bed," he answered.

"And?"

"She's confused by everything, Jack." He took a deep breath and waited a moment before he continued nervously. "I'd like your permission to explain some of what has happened to her." Considering where I was, it seemed foolish that he'd have to ask my permission. I understood why he was asking; I had made a pretty big deal about him and my mother overstepping their bounds recently. However, given everything that had happened, I probably wasn't the one who should be making any decisions when it came to Charlie's well-being.

"Of course. Do what you think is best. It can't hurt her any more than I already have," I responded. "I'd, um...would it be all right if I talked to her? I mean, she could call me...*here*? Or maybe, I could...?"

For the first time since he arrived, there was a familiar spark in my father's eyes, and his smile was wide and genuine. "I think she'd really love that." He reached into his pocket and pulled out his cell phone. My heart began to soar as I watched him punch in a series of numbers that I prayed were Frank and Gayle's.

I sucked in a breath when he held the phone to his ear and waited.

"Hi, Gayle," he greeted happily. I could hear her speaking from where I sat, but I couldn't make out what she was saying; all I heard was my father's side of the conversation. "Is Charlie around? I think there's someone here she's been wanting to talk to."

My palms began to sweat in anticipation, and when he handed me the phone, I expelled the breath I was still holding.

"Hello?" The tiny voice chirped into the phone. My tense posture softened as her gentle voice permeated every fiber of my being, and I found myself sighing with relief.

"Hey, bug," I said softly.

Charlie squealed with delight. "Daddy! Gramma! It's my daddy!"

"Well, talk to him, silly," I heard Gayle urge.

"Are you having fun with Grandma and Grandpa?" I asked, hoping to keep our first talk since...*the incident* light.

"Uh huh! We're going to a movie today. After lunchtime!" I could imagine the look on her face as she vibrated with excitement. It was likely that she was turning in circles as she spoke with me—it was something she usually did while talking on the phone, and I envisioned it perfectly.

"That's wonderful, sweetheart." I could feel my emotions catching up with me, and I fought to hold back the onslaught of emotions that came over me. However, my quivering voice betrayed me. "I miss you."

"Me, too, Daddy. When are you coming home?" she asked, her excited voice turning sullen.

I lost my fight with the hot tears that were threatening to fall. "I don't know yet, bug. There's some stuff I need to take care of first."

"Okay. I love you, Daddy."

"I love you, too, bug. I'll talk to you soon, okay?" We said our goodbyes, and when I hung up the phone, I didn't feel any better than before. In fact, I felt worse. Like our phone call was merely a tease. I dropped my face into my hands, digging my palms into my eyes to stop my tears of grief and guilt. Everywhere I turned, I was hurting someone else that I loved. I was a monster.

"I'm sorry, I thought that would help. I didn't mean to upset you further," Dad said softly.

"No. It was nice to hear her voice. I'm just pissed

at myself for allowing this to happen at all," I admitted sadly.

He sighed and stood from my bed. "Jack, you do know that none of this was your fault, right?"

With a scoff, I rolled my eyes. "You all keep saying that, but I fail to see how I couldn't have prevented any of this."

Placing a hand on my shoulder, he tried to offer me some kind of comfort. "I understand how you might feel that way, but you need to know that you didn't do anything wrong." Looking down at the pocket of his white coat, he groaned. "I'm being paged. Would you be okay with another visit a little later?"

I nodded. "Sure. I'm pretty tired, anyway."

As if on cue, the nurse knocked on my door and walked in with two small white Dixie cups—my meds. With promises to return later, my father left and I took my Librium willingly. It wasn't long before I felt the effects of the tiny capsules entering my bloodstream, calming me a little.

The rest of my afternoon was...different. Lonely—which was ridiculous, because in reality I'd been alone for the last two years. Not wanting to stay cooped up in my room alone, I wandered the halls, ignoring everyone I passed if I could. The nurses seemed all too willing to hopefully strike up a conversation with me when they noticed how withdrawn I was. However, I wasn't feeling particularly chatty, so I mumbled apologies and eventually fled back to my room.

Dinnertime came, and the food they brought me got ignored as I refused to get out of my chair. When the sky outside darkened, and my meds were administered, I crawled into bed.

My chest ached as I lay on my side staring at the

empty side of the bed that Cassie should have occupied. It felt as though my heart had been ripped from my chest, and I wasn't sure how I was supposed to move on.

She's gone. How can I live in a world where she doesn't exist?

Chapter Fourteen
back sliding

"*For fuck's sake, Cassidy!*" I shouted at Cassie as she plopped herself down on the edge of our bed.

I had just finished reading a bedtime story to Charlie – after Cassie outright refused to spend some time with her. Yes, I knew that Cassie was going through a rough time, but so was I. We were a team; when Cassie experienced something, I experienced it. This marriage was a partnership, and she was pulling away physically in the past few days just as much as she was emotionally. The worst part was that she didn't even seem to care that she was missing out with her daughter. Again.

"I get that you're upset," I told her, running my hands through my hair. "But you don't need to take this out on her! She has no idea what's going on, and she needs you! I need you to at least pretend to care."

Cassie's eyes narrowed at me, and to be honest, I was grateful because it was the first real emotion I had seen Cassie express in days. "Fuck you!" she shouted. Even though I was relieved to see that she cared enough to engage in this disagreement, my head snapped back at her words. "I know she needs me, I'm sorry if I can't be as fucking perfect as you! I never asked for any of this. You did."

I knew that another baby wasn't something she wanted. I had accepted it, even. But, the fact remained that she was pregnant. Yes, I was happy about it while Cassie was *scared beyond words, but it didn't change anything. Hearing her remind me that I was the only one who wanted this upset me.*

"I don't even know what to say to that, Cassidy," I told her, my eyes narrowing. I had reached my limit; I needed a break. "I can't even look at you right now. I'm going downstairs for a bit. Do whatever the fuck you want." I reached into my pants pocket and fisted the bottle of sleeping pills so that Cassie could get some sleep. The bags under her eyes were still dark, and I worried that she wasn't sleeping enough, even with the pills. I was fairly certain that her mood swings were the direct cause of her sleepless nights.

I slammed the bottle of sleeping pills onto the nightstand and stormed out of the bedroom. It used to be that Cassie and I never fought; that if something was bothering either of us, we'd sit and talk about it until we resolved the issue.

But now?

The stress of the pregnancy, then the miscarriage — it was proving to be too much on our relationship. It wouldn't have been so bad if it was just the two of us, but we had Charlie to worry about, and Cassie was pushing her away.

I found myself pacing in the living room, my heart pounding furiously against my ribs, and my blood boiling in my veins. I tried taking deep breaths in an effort to cool my rage before I gave into the urge to destroy...something. I ran my fingers through my hair in frustration, gripping it tightly and clenching my teeth as I tilted my head back and stared up at ceiling. Directly above where I stood was our bedroom. I couldn't hear anything, so I could only assume Cassie had taken her meds and went to bed.

I dropped my eyes from the stippling on the ceiling, and when my eyes fell to my piano that had been sitting abandoned for the last couple months, I exhaled a deep breath and released the tight grip I had on my hair. I sat on the bench, my hands on my knees as I stared at the glossy black fallboard hesitantly.

The last time I had played was the night that Cassie told me she didn't want any more children. So much had happened since then.

Almost as though I were afraid it would bite me, my hands trembled as I lifted them to the sleek, black wood. Closing my eyes and holding my breath, I raised the fallboard and placed my fingers on the keys. The sounds that came from the piano as I played were dark and angry as every pent-up emotion from past few weeks was released through my music.

As the music poured from my soul, I remembered everything that had happened these last couple weeks. Finding out Cassie was pregnant while we were at the beach — I was so happy and she just...wasn't. Then, the night of her birthday, when she miscarried. I should have picked up on it that night. Something wasn't right with her even then; she was way too calm about the whole situation.

But, that's just Cassie. She's always been calm in the face of a crisis.

Suddenly the music filling the room changed into a familiar melody as my memories shifted from the darkness of the last few weeks to the lighter times we'd shared. The song I had composed for Cassie warmed me through, and I found myself smiling. A part of me hoped that maybe she was still awake and could hear the love behind each note — that she'd know we'd get through this...together.

My optimism was quickly torn from my body only to be replaced with mind-numbing fear as Cassie cried out for me. "Jack!" There was something in Cassie's shrill scream that chilled me to my very core, and I flew off the piano bench, sending it clattering to the floor behind me as I rushed for the stairs. The sound of glass shattering forced me to move up the stairs even faster.

When I entered the bedroom, the first place I looked

was our empty bed...then my eyes shifted to the nightstand—where Cassie's sleeping pills used to be.

"No no no no no no no no no no," I said frantically, shaking my head with denial as I turned toward the bathroom door. It was open just a sliver, and as I moved forward, time seemed to slow. Once I made it to the door, I pushed it open...

The scene that lay before me left my blood cold.

I shot upright in a flash, my entire body slick with a light sheen of sweat, and my body trembling violently in light of what I had just dreamt...or *remembered*.

"Hey, you," a soft, familiar voice said. My head snapped back toward the window. There, perched on the narrow sill, was Cassie. I was instantly overcome with relief as my body softened. Kicking my thin blankets to the foot of the bed, I got out as quickly as I possibly could and rushed toward her, pulling her into my arms.

"You're back," I whispered into her soft hair as I continued to hold her close.

Cassie stretched her arms around my neck and wove her fingers into the hair at the nape of my neck. "Shhh," she whispered. "It's going to be okay."

"It was...we...and then you were..." I couldn't seem to form a coherent sentence as I held her, breathing her in.

Her fingers continued to thread through my hair. "I know, baby. I know."

"I'm so sorry," I whispered. "For everything."

Cassie worked herself free and cradled my face in her hands. I couldn't look her in the eye, though. I was ashamed of what I had done; of who I had become. "Look at me," she coaxed. As I raised my gaze to hers, she smiled and rubbed her thumbs over my cheekbones. "Baby, you're exhausted. You need to sleep."

I shook my head against her hold on me. "I don't want to," I told her. "Cassie, the things I saw... If I go to sleep, I'm afraid you won't be here when I wake up."

"That's the way it's supposed to be."

"I can't accept that." I moved my hands to her hips and gripped her firmly, confirming her existence.

Cassie's eyebrows knit together, but the smile never faded from her face. "You will. It's going to get easier." Her words were meant to comfort me, but I failed to feel that way.

Instead, all I heard was that the rest of my life would be spent without her.

I wasn't ready then... And I'm not ready now.

Chapter Fifteen
breakthrough

The next few days were a blur. My only constant was Cassie—and even she wasn't around often. While it was rare that she left my side, there were times that she was nowhere to be seen. It worried me on a number of levels because I was afraid she wouldn't return. Sometimes she even accompanied me to my sessions—not that I acknowledged her. There wasn't a doubt in my mind that I had gone completely off the deep end, but I didn't need to reaffirm this to Dr. Richards or my parents. That wasn't to say that I thought I was fooling them in any way, whatsoever—because I wasn't.

My sessions were...well, they probably would have been productive if I were to cooperate and allow the process to work. It had been five days since my arrival, and I still had trouble accepting the way things were.

Dr. Richards wanted to see me daily in an effort to get to the root of my issues. It didn't surprise me that he knew more than I had told him; he and my father worked in the same hospital and happened to be friends. Over the first few visits, I skirted the topic of Cassie, but by my fourth session—he wouldn't allow for it.

"Jack, tell me about Cassie," he pushed calmly. When my eyes snapped up to his, I felt fear. Not because I was afraid of *him*, but because I was afraid of finally vocalizing the truth.

"Sh...she's my wife," I stammered quietly. I averted my gaze and looked around the room, trying to find anything to focus on. "She's Charlie's mother."

"And where is she now?"

My eyes narrowed and my nostrils flared as I felt rage bubble beneath the surface of my skin. "She's gone," I answered through gritted teeth, clenching my fists tightly in my lap. The sting of my nails biting into the palms of my hands was the only thing keeping me lucid enough that I *didn't* rush across the room and deck him.

Dr. Richards removed his glasses and smiled at me. "I'm sorry if the question upsets you, Jack, but I need for you to talk to me. How can we work through this if you won't open up?" I nodded in understanding and waited for him to continue. "Now, your father told me a few things that concern me on a number of levels."

A dark chuckle escaped my body as I rolled my eyes. "I figured as much."

"Do you care to tell me what you think we've talked about?"

My eyes moved back to the doctor's, and I shrugged flippantly. "Cassie?"

"Can you be a little more specific?"

My lips formed a firm line and my eyebrows lifted slightly. "If I had to hazard a guess, I'm going to go with the fact that he and my mother—along with Cassie's parents—walked in on the two of us arguing."

Dr. Richards dipped his head slightly, but it wasn't a nod...it was more like a gesture that said he knew all this and just needed me to continue for my own sake. "Hmm... Now, didn't you just say that she was 'gone'?"

"I did." My lips curled back as I spoke, and I sighed in aggravation, not wanting to talk about this anymore. My chest was beginning to feel tight as an anxiety attack threatened. "Look, I don't want to talk about this right now."

Dr. Richards leaned forward and placed his notepad and pen on the table before resting his arms on his knees and clasping his hands before him. "That's fine, Jack." He watched me carefully for a moment, and there was something in his eyes that told me he wasn't quite finished with me yet. I was proven right less than five seconds later. "So, you've been here almost a week, Jack," he stated. I nodded once in response, the action slow and unsure. "Tell me, are you still seeing her?"

I was certain the guilt was written all over my face as he waited for me to answer, so I dropped my eyes from his and back to my lap where my hands lay still. Cassie's hand slipped into my view, and she offered me a gentle squeeze. With her hand on mine, I felt whole again. My world wasn't so bad with her still in it.

"No," I lied.

Cassie's hand disappeared from mine, and I shivered at its loss. "Jack," she sighed sadly. "You need to be honest. They're going to know, and they won't let you out of here until you're better. Think about Charlie. She needs you."

It wasn't until I made the mistake of allowing my eyes to drift in Cassie's direction that Dr. Richards caught on. "Jack," he scolded. "Is she here now?"

I wanted to lie. Nothing good was going to come from knowing the truth. However, I couldn't. I knew Cassie was right. I turned my head completely away from her and nodded at Dr. Richards's question.

"Is she saying anything?"

Cassie moved until she was standing right in front of me. Our eyes locked, and she silently encouraged me to open up.

"She's telling me that I have to be honest in order to get better," I said in a shaky voice. Cassie's mouth curled up into a smile as I took this one small step. I didn't want to go down this path. This path was dark and winding. Tree roots were upraised, and I knew I would catch my foot on one...and there would be no one there to catch me when I fell, because the only person I trusted was gone. Anxiety clawed at me like gnarled tree branches, and I had to look away from her.

Dr. Richards hummed in agreement. "She sounds like a very bright woman."

A smile broke across my lips, and a single tear fell from my eye. "She was." The minute the words left my mouth, my head snapped up in shock. It was the first time I had spoken about her in the past tense—the first time I had admitted to *myself* that she was...that she was...*gone*.

Cassie stared back down at me, but she wasn't angry at me like she should have been for speaking of her in that way. I expected her to slap me; to yell at me, maybe? Anything but what she did. Cassie dropped to her knees before me, clutching my hands in hers, and her smile widened.

The doctor cleared his throat. "So, why is it you feel it's so important to lie?"

With a deep breath, I turned to face my doctor. "Do you want my professional opinion?" I asked, to which Dr. Richards nodded once. "I can't let her go."

"Why not?" he pressed.

"Because I feel guilty." There, I said it. And it still didn't make me feel any better. Dr. Richards waited for me to continue. "I should have seen the signs. I shouldn't have..." I choked on my own words as bits and pieces of my most recent recurring nightmare — or rather, a repressed memory — came rushing back. "I shouldn't have yelled at her and stormed out like I did. She was upset, and I just walked away."

Dr. Richards didn't say anything else for a moment after that. He remained motionless and watched me carefully. I wasn't focused on him, though. No, I was looking at Cassie, still kneeling before me. My eyes bore into hers as I silently begged for her forgiveness.

"There," she whispered angelically. "Was that so hard?"

I dropped my head until our foreheads rested against each other, and I closed my eyes. "Hardest thing I've ever had to do," I replied softly.

Not seeing a reason to go any further today, given the "breakthrough" Dr. Richards insisted I made, he ended our session early and personally walked me to my room. Once inside, I sat in the chair by the window and didn't move.

Cassie perched herself on the sill and looked down at me with a wide smile gracing her gorgeous face. Dressed all in white, and the way the sun was beaming into the room behind her, she looked like an angel, the golden halo of sunlight above her head lighting up every one of her stunning features.

"I'm proud of you," she told me. "Everything you accomplished in your session today? It was wonderful."

"I'm glad you thought so."

Her smile vanished, and she tilted her head to one side as confusion flashed in her eyes. "You don't?"

I took a deep breath and closed my eyes. With every day that passed, there were more and more people who told me that she wasn't really real, and it was starting to take its toll. I knew she wasn't really there, yet I didn't want her to leave me again. Without her, I had nothing to live for. My entire reason for existing was gone.

Because of me.

"Jack?" a small voice called into the room from behind me. I turned around and saw my mother and father standing in the open doorway. It wasn't until I offered them a half-smile that my mother's expression relaxed and she rushed forward.

I stood from my chair and was nearly knocked over by the force of her embrace. "Hey, Mom," I whispered into the top of her head as I wrapped my arms around her in return. I acknowledged my father over my mother, and he nodded in response. "Where's Charlie?" I asked, really hoping that after almost a week away from her, that they'd have at least brought her with them to visit me.

"With Jennifer and Alex, dear. We didn't think she was ready just yet," she said, working free of our embrace.

"Oh, okay." My spirits fell impossibly lower at hearing that they didn't feel I was well enough to see my own daughter. "So, uh...how've you both been since, um...?" I honestly had no idea when the last time I had seen them was. My days were all blending together. I knew how long I had been here, but as to what happened on what day? Not a clue.

"We've been well, son," my dad said as he rested his hand on my shoulder. "And you? How are your sessions going?"

What he really meant to say was, "Are you still delusional? Still seeing the apparition of your wife?"

"You know that's not true," Cassie said from her perch on the sill, knowing what I was thinking without me having said it.

I tried ignoring her—couldn't be having another episode in front of them, after all. "It went well today. Dr. Richards seems to think I've made progress."

"You have," Cassie chimed in again. I had to clench my eyes shut and turn my head so I could no longer see her in my periphery. Of course, my parents noticed this and became concerned.

"Jack?" Dad inquired quietly. "What is it? What's wrong?"

"Nothing. I just have a headache. I didn't sleep well last night." It wasn't a lie; I was still having that same dream where I was at the piano and I heard the glass shatter above me. I looked down into my mother's all-knowing eyes and tried to smile. "I know you guys travelled all this way, but I'm really tired. Would you mind if..."

A tear fell from her left eye as she shook her head. She tried to mask the disappointment in her voice, but I still heard it. More guilt weighed down on me. "No, of course not. We understand. Get some sleep. We'll see you tomorrow for our family session."

"Right," I said monotonously. I had almost forgotten that we were scheduled for a family sit-down to discuss how everything was going, and how it got to where it was.

Suddenly dizzy, I nodded and headed for my bed where I sat on the edge, my eyes locked on a black speck in the tile in hopes that I could make the room stop spinning for just a moment. "You'll..." I cleared my throat when it cracked slightly. "You'll tell Charlie I love and miss her very much?" I heard Cassie hop down from the window sill and move to my side. She laid one of her chilled hands on my shoulder, and I tried my hardest not to acknowledge its presence.

"We will," my mother promised, leaning down to hug me one more time, just missing Cassie's hand as she reached around my neck.

As soon as they were gone, I changed into a T-shirt and a pair of flannel pants before crawling into my small twin-sized bed. I left the corner of the coverlet turned down and looked up at Cassie expectantly. She remained motionless before me, staring into my eyes with hesitation.

"Please?" I whispered with need.

With a solitary nod of surrender, Cassie climbed into the bed with me. She lay facing me, our legs bent so that our knees were touching, and she started stroking my hair while I raised the blanket up over her. We didn't say a word for a few minutes; we just stared into each other's eyes.

"You need to let me go," she finally whispered. Her words didn't come as a shock. Not anymore. I now understood the weight that was behind them. I knew she was right, but I couldn't bring myself to do it. I needed her. I was nothing without her.

I shook my head, still keeping my gaze locked on hers. "I can't, Cass," I whispered.

"Try? For me? I need you to get out of here...and I can't go with you." While her words upset me, she didn't seem fazed by them. She had accepted what had to happen here. I hadn't, though.

"We won't be apart. I need you. Without you, I..." Tears fell from my eyes, and my hands fisted the fabric of her white shirt tightly, pulling her to me, securing in my mind that she was really here with me.

Cassie allowed me to pull her body toward mine, and she wrapped her arms around my neck as I buried my face into the front of her shirt and held her tightly. "I'm so sorry!"

"Shhh," she soothed into my hair. "Everything's

going to be okay, I promise."

I couldn't seem to find the words that could properly convey exactly what I was sorry for, and eventually, I had fallen asleep in Cassie's arms.

Chapter Sixteen
wide awake

The door to the ensuite bathroom creaked as it swung open, causing me to shudder at the sound. My eyes scanned the countertop to find it spotless, moving next to the tile floor. Nothing seemed out of place at first, but as the door opened wider, Cassie's feet came into view...then her calves...her thighs... My breathing hitched in fear as I pushed myself through the door and pulled her limp body into my arms.

With her turned face-up, her head lolled back over my arm as I shook her gently in an effort to rouse her. "Cassie?" I cried. I could feel the tears beginning to burn my eyes the longer she didn't respond to me. "Cassie!" This time, I leaned my face down to hers and raised my voice, hoping beyond hope that that would work.

Her body felt heavy in my arms, and my panic level increased—even though that shouldn't have been possible without causing a heart attack. My instincts finally kicked in, and I leaned my face to hers, turning away from her to listen for her breaths. The tears that were threatening finally fell when I realized she wasn't breathing.

"Cass, honey! Don't do this to me!" I set Cassie back down on the tile floor and checked for a pulse. Nothing. I felt my heart strain as I struggled to remember what to do next. I felt as though all the air had left the room, and I was starting to see spots before my eyes. How did this happen?

Taking a quick look around, I finally saw the glass

that I had heard shatter only moments before, and lying amidst the debris was an empty pill bottle.

The pill bottle I had left with her. The one that was almost full. "Fuuuuck," I groaned quietly, the nausea rolling in the pit of my stomach. After taking a few deep breaths, I looked back down at my unmoving wife. I stared at her, not once looking away or blinking as shock set in. I had no idea what to do...where to go from here. I pulled my cell phone out of my pocket and quickly dialed 9-1-1.

"9-1-1, what's your emergency?" a female voice answered.

I swallowed thickly, still watching Cassie; praying that she'd wake up any second and we'd laugh about how I had overreacted again.

She didn't. We wouldn't.

"It's my wife."

"Okay, sir. What about your wife?"

"She's not moving," I responded, my tone unnervingly calm and collected while every part of my insides was screaming in protest against it. "I...I heard a glass break. Then I came upstairs and she was on the bathroom floor. Not... She's not moving..."

"Is there a pulse, sir?" the 911 operator asked softly. I shook my head. "Sir? Is there a pulse?"

"No," I croaked. "She's not breathing either."

There was a pause that was probably only a few seconds in reality, but it felt like a lifetime before the operator spoke again. "Have you tried CPR?"

My head shook sadly, more tears leaking onto my cheek. "CPR," I sighed. "I know CPR..." Setting the phone down on the floor, I bent over Cassie's lifeless body and tilted her head back and began the process. I puffed air into her body from my lungs and thrust down on her chest in an effort to bring her back to me.

"Come on, baby. Come back to me, please," I chanted, my words jolted by the chest compressions. Minutes had

passed, and I was getting no response. I found myself working more furiously, a combination of sad and angry tears streaming down my face, when suddenly there was a loud crack, forcing me to snap my arms back as if I was being held at gunpoint.

With wide eyes, I stared at Cassie, wondering which rib I had just broken and whether or not I had caused her irreparable damage that even the best doctors wouldn't be able to fix. I leaned over and picked up the phone, my eyes never leaving Cassie's body.

"I...I think I broke one of her ribs," I stammered into the receiver. I suddenly started panicking, nothing I said was coherent, and I could barely make out what the woman on the other end of the phone was saying.

"Sir, you have to remain calm. I have dispatched an emergency unit out to you. They should be there soon. All I ask is that you don't move the body."

I froze in an instant upon hearing her final words, the bile churning like tidal waves in my stomach as I became catatonic. I stared down at my wife's broken body, her eyes closed and her tank top riding up to settle just under her breasts. I fell back onto my backside, the phone clattering on the tile next to me. I lost the fight against my nausea and scrambled for the toilet quickly, spewing the contents of my stomach into the porcelain bowl.

Time stood still, or at least, that's how it seemed. It could have been seconds, minutes, even hours before I heard the sound of sirens. It wasn't until I saw the flashing lights of the ambulance through the bedroom windows that I blinked my now-dry eyes and remembered Cassie's attire.

"Let's..." My voice cracked, forcing me to clear my throat before I continued. "Let's fix you up before they get up here." I whispered, reaching down gently to tug her shirt down so as not to overexpose her midriff.

Once she was covered up, I stood from my spot on the floor and backed out of the bathroom slowly, stumbling over my own feet a couple of times. I then walked down to the front door and unlocked it just as the paramedics were rushing up the walk. "She's upstairs," I rasped as they rushed past me, traipsing in mud from the recent storm we'd had. As I followed them up the stairs, I explained where they should go, my entire body numb to what was going on.

They dropped to her side and began hooking her up to a heart monitor. The steady BLIP I expected to hear from the portable device was absent, and this caused a tremor to rock through my body. They felt around before they started administering CPR, and once again, I found myself holding out hope that she'd wake up and we'd be smiling and laughing again in no time. That she'd forgive me for the terrible fight we'd had.

Nothing.

With a sharp gasp for air, I sat upright in bed, sweat pouring down my forehead, and my hands death-gripping the thin blankets to my chest. Each intake of oxygen burned, and my lungs struggled every time. My eyes were focused on the soft light coming in through the narrow window on my door as I struggled to take in my surroundings and remember where I was.

"Jack? What's wrong?" Cassie asked, suddenly appearing at my side.

Closing my eyes and swallowing thickly, I answered. "I...I think I'm remembering *more*." It wasn't until I felt Cassie's cool hand on the back of my neck, teasing the short hairs there, and her other over top of my own that my breathing eventually evened out and I lowered the blankets to my lap.

"I found you..."

Cassie nodded, watching her hand intently as it moved through my hair. "Yeah, I know."

The memory lingered like smog in my brain, polluting something pure; the only difference was that the images were crystal clear, and not hidden behind a thick cloud of poison. It choked me.

"Talk to me," she gently prodded, her fingers working like magic on my scalp. The tension in my muscles released, and I leaned my head down onto her shoulder with a sigh.

"I don't want to talk. I just want to stay here with you," I confessed, kissing her bare shoulder softly.

Cassie's lips grazed the top of my head, breathing me in. "I can't stay," she whispered, the hand she had in my hair never stopping.

"Why not?" I asked, pushing my face up to look her in the eye.

Cassie bit her lower lip and sighed. "Because I'm not *good* for you, Jack. My being here with you is only hurting you and those around you. You can't possibly want that."

She was right. But how could I want her to be gone...*really* fucking gone? My life didn't make sense without her in it. No, wait... I had Charlie, and in that way, my life totally made sense. But without Cassie, I was nothing. A shell. Empty.

"I want you," I whispered breathlessly, my lungs feeling tight as my anxiety returned.

"I know. But, that's just not possible."

Even though her words cut like a knife to the heart, I knew that ultimately she was right. "Wh...what happens once you leave?"

"You move on," she responded softly, her hand ghosting over mine.

Chapter Seventeen
the truth comes out

Falling back asleep was difficult. It wasn't until Cassie started humming softly, laying sweet kisses on my forehead while her fingers trailed lightly through my hair, that I was finally able to find the peace that sleep brought. It was restless, though; the dream I had...*the memory*...recurred every time I closed my eyes. What happened that day would continue to haunt me, and I could feel my grip on reality slipping every time I woke up in a cold sweat. I knew that it was *supposed* to be a good thing—my remembering—but, it didn't feel that way. It felt like it was the beginning of the end for me...for *us*, and I tried to will it all away. To forget once more.

All I knew was I couldn't live in a world where I had allowed *that* to happen. Yet, I knew I needed to be there for Charlie. I couldn't have both; I couldn't escape without leaving Charlie. She meant the world to me. *Ugh!* It was all so confusing. Real, fantasy, fantasy, real. The two worlds I knew were slowly becoming one, and I wasn't sure which one I would ultimately choose...which one I *wanted* to choose. In one, I was a husband and father with a fantastic life. In the other, I was... I was a monster who let his wife...

No, I couldn't be that person. How could I accept that?

I had been awake for a while, just lying in bed thinking about all of this, but it wasn't until the morning sun broke through the clouds and streamed through the window that I sat up. I ran my hands over my weary face, feeling the stubble that had accumulated there over the last five days. I briefly contemplated shaving, but figured such luxuries probably weren't available to the depressed and delusional.

"What are you thinking about?" Cassie inquired, sitting up behind me and running her hands over my shoulders.

With a chuckle, I turned my head until I could see her through my periphery. "Shaving, actually."

When she laughed, my heart ached because it was a sound I missed so very much. If I were to allow my therapy to work, I would have to say goodbye to it. Forever. I wasn't sure I could do that.

"I should, um, get ready. My parents will be here soon." I turned to face her fully, my eyes pleading and afraid. "You'll be here when I come back, right?"

She uttered those six words I had heard far more than I ever wanted to. "You know I can't promise that."

"Try?" I begged softly. "I'm...I'm just not ready right *now*."

"Okay, okay," she said, offering me a smile to assure me that she would be here. "Everything's going to be all right."

I kissed her lightly and stood from my bed, grabbing a change of clothes so I could grab a quick shower before my appointment. After cleaning myself up, I pulled on my black sweater and jeans, then headed back to my room and found Cassie sitting on my bed, cross-legged and smiling. We didn't say anything to one another. Instead, I climbed back up onto the bed and rested my head on her shoulder as we sat in silence.

"Mr. Martin?" I lifted my head as the door opened, and in walked the nurse with my parents at her side. "Your parents are here."

I pushed myself off the bed and wrapped my arms around my mom. "Hey, Mom. Dad. How've you guys been?"

My dad clapped his hand down on my shoulder, and when I looked up at him from in my mother's arms, I noticed his gaze was directed toward my bed. Letting go of my mom, I turned to look at my bed. Cassie remained there, motionless, and it appeared as though he was looking right through her. "What?" I inquired nervously.

Inhaling a deep breath, he turned to me with a smile. "It's nothing." He suspected; I could feel it in my blood. It wasn't surprising, especially considering how I had been sitting when they entered, but it still frightened me. "Well," he said, breaking up the brief, uncomfortable silence and pretending like it really was nothing. "We should get going."

I walked with my parents down the corridor, my mother's arm looped through mine the entire way and talking like it was just any other day. "Frank and Gayle are dropping Charlie off tonight. She's very excited to see you again."

"Me, too," I responded softly, silently wondering when that might be. I was just about to ask when they'd be bringing her by, but the door to Dr. Richards's office opened.

"Good morning," he greeted as we crossed the threshold into his office, closely flanked by my father.

Releasing my mother's arm from my own and wrapping my arms tighter around my body, I nodded my greeting and made my way to my spot on the sofa. I allowed my gaze to stray from their usual focal point on the coffee table toward the door where my parents and doctor conversed for a moment.

"How is he?" I heard my mother whisper. I was

certain she didn't mean for me to hear, but I did.

I also didn't miss the quick glance that Dr. Richards shot in my direction. He offered me a warm smile before turning back to my parents and assuring them that things were going quite well. My eyes wandered back to the coffee table where they fixated on the small bowl of silk flowers that Dr. Richards kept there.

A few more moments had passed, and he and my father shared a moment, discussing my treatment and medications. Dr. Richards, while his friend, was also a professional and said he wasn't at liberty to share details, just that things were going along as planned.

When they finally joined me, I was lost in thoughts of Cassie. Memories of some of the happier times we had shared.

"So, Jack. How've you been since yesterday?"

I shrugged in response to Dr. Richards. "All right, I suppose. No better, no worse."

"Did you sleep well?" I raised my eyes to his, and he knew as soon as he looked into them—noticing the dark circles that lined them—what the answer was. "Are you still dreaming?"

I nodded once. "The dreams...they're changing," I confessed. My parents turned to face me as I spoke to Dr. Richards, and I grew anxious. I started wringing my hands in my lap as I continued to tell my doctor about the newest dreams. "It used to be that I would just be coming home—sometimes with Charlie, sometimes without. I think my fear manifested that scenario. I...I would hear that glass shatter and I would bolt up the stairs. But I always woke up when I reached the bathroom door."

Dr. Richards leaned forward, clearly hearing everything I had said and drawing a conclusion in his mind. "So, are you saying you've since passed that threshold?"

Swallowing thickly, I clenched my burning eyes shut. The memory of Cassie lying on the cold tile floor, broken glass around her, flashed briefly behind my closed eyelids, and I nodded as I choked back a sob. "I have. I couldn't save her. She...she...*died* before I even got there. It was all my fault."

Cassie's hand slipped into my view as she knelt before me, and I instantly felt at peace now that she was there with me. "It's okay," she assured softly. "You can do this."

I tried to look away from her; tried not to acknowledge her, but I felt the carefully constructed walls that I had built when around other people start to crumble. "I tried to save you...but I was too late," I whispered in a hoarse voice, my eyes returning to our hands as they twisted and twined together. "You stopped breathing. I tried—so hard—to bring you back."

"I know, baby. I know," she whispered, freeing one of her hands to use the pad of her thumb to wipe my tears away.

I took a deep, cleansing breath before I continued. "She was unresponsive to my efforts," I said, this time speaking to Dr. Richards, whose eyes were wide having just witnessed me talking directly to my dead wife. "I grabbed my cell phone from my pocket and dialed 9-1-1. I tried time and time again to revive her. I even broke one of her ribs because I refused to stop chest compressions."

I looked back to Cassie, who was still holding my hand with one of hers and stroking my cheek with the other. She gave me a gentle smile. "I'm so proud of you, baby."

"No," my father interjected quickly, looking between Dr. Richards and myself. "Jack, the paramedics…they were able to bring her back. She was in the hospital for a while before she… I'm so sorry."

"No, I *remember*. They got there and there was no pulse…" I shook my head, my eyes not once straying from Cassie. She gave me the strength I needed to continue. However, the look in her eyes told me that what my father was trying to tell me wasn't entirely untrue.

When I looked back over at my dad, he looked at me sadly. "No. Son, you're not remembering everything…"

Nothing.

There was no sound coming from the monitor. I felt my entire world crumbling beneath me, and my legs started to tremble. The paramedics began to administer CPR, and I fisted my hair tightly in my hands, frustrated that I was unable to do anything.

"Daddy?" The world snapped back into focus as the tiny voice called out from behind me. When I turned in the direction it came from, I saw Charlie standing in the doorway, her little pink blanket in her hands as she rubbed the sleep from her innocent eyes.

"Bug, what are you doing out of bed?" I asked in a strangled whisper as I knelt to scoop her up into my arms. I whisked my two-year-old daughter out of the bedroom and out into the hall where she couldn't witness what was happening.

"I hadda ba' dweam," she mumbled sleepily as she rested her head on my shoulder.

"Aw, baby. It's okay. Daddy's here." I hugged her close to me and started moving back and forth until she dozed off again. I continued to coo "Daddy's here," over and over again, and each time I said it, I knew that it would only ever be me…

"I've got a pulse in here!" I heard a medic call out.

When the words registered, my head snapped in the direction of the bathroom. I rushed back into the room with Charlie still cradled in my arms, to find Cassie still unconscious. The sounds coming from the machine weren't as steady as they should have been, but it was beeping, which meant her heart was beating.

The rise and fall of her chest concerned me, as she seemed to be taking short and shallow breaths. I felt a minute feeling of relief wash through me. True, we weren't out of the woods, but this was a start. It had to be.

The paramedics loaded her onto the gurney as they told me they were taking her to the hospital. Once they left, I loaded a sleeping Charlie into her car seat and followed the ambulance. I called my parents and let them know what was going on. They offered to come to the hospital and watch after Charlie while we waited. I was appreciative because I didn't know what to expect.

She had a heartbeat, though. She was breathing. That had to be a good sign, right?

"While they got her breathing and her heart beating again, the damage had already been done. She was in a coma for a few weeks before you had them take her off life support. She passed within hours of the order," my dad explained solemnly.

"I killed my wife," I said breathlessly. Through the corner of my eye, I saw Dr. Richards shake his head and open his mouth to speak, but I cut him off as I continued to stare deep into Cassie's warm eyes. "Maybe not directly, but...I gave the order."

"It was what she wanted," my mother spoke up, placing her hand on mine.

Dr. Richards interrupted this time. "You feel as though you're wife's death is your fault? Like you pushed her over the edge?"

"Didn't I? We said some pretty cruel things to

one another. I left her alone after hours of fighting. I may as well have dumped the pills right into her waiting hands."

Cassie shook her head vehemently, disagreeing with everything I was saying. "Jack, no."

My parents were both stunned into silence beside me as they listened to what I was saying. My mother looked terrified, and I hoped it was fear of the situation and not of me. There was a long, heavy pause in the room, and I waited for anyone—Dr. Richards, my parents, or even Cassie—to say something else to me. But no one did. They waited until I spoke. What I had to say, though, wasn't toward them.

I looked deep into Cassie's glistening eyes and spoke, pushing past my trembling voice. "The reason I can't let you go..." My mouth dried instantly and my voice cracked, so I cleared my throat before I felt I could continue. "The reason I can't let you go is because, if I do, you're gone. And when you're gone...it's because I let you die. I promised to protect you, and I let you down. You were my entire reason for existing. Admitting all of this makes your death real; and when you're not there... I don't feel whole. Cassie, I can't live in a world where you don't exist."

Tears fell from Cassie's eyes now. "Charlie is your reason. Live for her, Jack. None of this was your fault. Not once did I ever feel like you let me down. I let myself down. I was weak."

"Jack?" Dr. Richards forced his way into the conversation I was having with Cassie, and I turned to him. He looked at me with deep concern, and I was certain he could see the fear in my eyes.

From a professional's standpoint, I was certifiable. I had no doubt that he was going to recommend they lock me up and throw away the key. The mere thought of this jolted me back to reality, and I thought of poor, sweet Charlie.

"Yes," Cassie whispered. "Think of her. Be there for her. She needs you."

I released Cassie's hand and turned away from her so I could face my doctor completely. "I want to be better," I assured him. "For Charlie. I need to be better for her. I'm no good for her this way."

Dr. Richards smiled. "Then let's start from here."

Feeling completely overwhelmed from everything I'd learned in the last twenty-four hours, I sighed, running my hands over my face. "I don't know if I can talk about this anymore," I admitted quietly.

"Jack," my mother prodded softly, laying her hand over top of mine once more. "We know this is hard for you—"

"Mrs. Martin, if he doesn't want to talk right now, that's all right." I shot Dr. Richards an appreciative smile as he jumped to my defense. My appreciation was short lived, though. "When did you guys start to notice that things seemed, well, for lack of a better word, *off*?"

What an interesting question. Suddenly curious myself, I turned just in time to witness my parents' exchange a glance. How long had this been going on? Had I been delusional since the day I found her? When *did* I breakdown?

My eyes drifted down to where my father encased my mother's other hand within his own, and I listened as he spoke. "Not long, actually. Everything seemed...well, *normal* seems like a pretty inadequate term to be using considering everything that has happened to our family..."

I had to agree with him there. What was *normal*, anyway?

"When all of this first happened, Jack was completely beside himself with grief. It was as though he had lost the other half of his soul—"

"I had," I interrupted in a hoarse voice, my eyes catching Cassie's once more. My mother squeezed my hand gently in an attempt to comfort me, but all I could do was offer the room a gloomy smile and squeeze her back in assurance.

"We know," she breathed softly.

There was an overwhelming silence in the room as, I assumed, my father didn't know how to proceed after my interruption. Finally, he cleared his throat and resumed what he was saying. "It took some time for him to come to terms with Cassie's actions that day; but he did. He's been a fantastic father to Charlie."

"So, when did you and your wife suspect that he had relapsed?"

My face scrunched at Dr. Richards's choice of words. "Whoa, whoa, *whoa*," I said in rapid succession, shaking my head and clenching my eyes shut. "Relapsed would mean that I'd have originally had to have…oh, I don't know, *lapsed*."

When no one said a word, dread settled in my veins like cement, weighing me down.

Chapter Eighteen
the pain of healing

I heard my parents both swallow thickly, and Cassie dropped her gaze. "Oh, God," I exhaled.

"It, um..." My mother scrambled for words, turning from my father to face me completely. She bent her left leg and propped it up on the couch between us as she took both of my hands in hers. "It started about a week after the, um, the funeral. Your father and I had plans to come over to visit you and Charlie and —"

The memory hit me so hard that, had it been physical, it would have knocked me on my ass.

Charlie was upstairs in her room, napping, while I stood at the sink washing up the dishes we had dirtied at lunchtime. Every sound I made when I placed the clean dishes in the drying rack echoed through the empty house, reminding me that halls that were once filled with her laughter wouldn't be...for a very long time.

I was unaware of how many days had passed since... since... Ugh, I couldn't even think it without my entire body trembling with anxiety. I dropped the plate that was in my hand and it sunk to the bottom of the soapy water as I clung to the side of the sink basin to keep from falling to the floor. I stared at the bubbles that floated on the surface of the water for longer than any sane person should have, but the way the bubbles continued to pop and disappear as though they'd never existed was...depressing, and I could feel my chest tighten. Cassie was gone. She was just —

"How was your day?" The sound of her voice startled me; I hadn't been expecting her...at all, actually. I closed my eyes tightly because I knew this couldn't be real. Slowly, I turned around, and when I opened my eyes, Cassie was seated at the island, her arms folded atop the marble countertop. Her smile was bright and familiar.

In an instant, every feeling of grief left my body. I dropped the hand towel I was using to dry my hands and ran around the island, sweeping Cassie off the stool she was perched upon and swung her around the room.

"You're home!" I exclaimed between feather-light kisses. "You have no idea how much I've missed you. Charlie's been asking about you. I...I didn't know what to tell her," I confessed, releasing my hold on her just a little; I never wanted to let her go again.

Cassie sighed, prying herself from my arms and backing away. Her eyebrows knit together, and she spoke quietly. "The truth, Jack. You should tell her the truth."

"How...?" I shook the new memory from my mind. "How long was the first episode?" I asked, my voice cracking slightly.

Mom shrugged slightly, squeezing my hands in hers. "We can't be one hundred percent certain, but I'd say about a week. You called us that afternoon and said we should come over another time. After everything that had happened, we understood that you probably weren't ready for company, so we agreed. We never thought..." She allowed her words to trail off as I absorbed what she was telling me.

With my eyebrows still pressed together, I bobbed my head slowly. "And, when you found out the first time...? What happened? Was I *here* before?"

My dad interjected. "No. What happened before was much less severe than this time. Last time, you knew what was real. But this time... Well, you seem to have created a world where Cassie still exists. Where she didn't—"

I closed my eyes tightly and shifted my head away from him. "I'm going to ask you not to finish that sentence. I... I can't hear it again." The pain of his impending words struck me, and I had to stop him before I broke down even more. I had already come to terms with what happened; but one could only take so much in a day.

"Of course," he said softly. "The day we found out, we had just arrived to pick up Charlie for the weekend. You were in the kitchen, and we could hear you talking." I opened my eyes and glanced back at him as he began to tell me the story. "At first we thought you were talking to Charlie, but as we got closer, we knew that wasn't the case..."

"So, what do you want to do this weekend?" I asked Cassie as she sat on the countertop before me. The way her eyebrows arched with confusion made me chuckle. "Charlie is going to my parents' place, so it'll just be you and me."

The last few days having Cassie back with me this way was...a relief. Like nothing ever happened to take her away from me. It was just her and me, and I wouldn't have had it any other way. I wouldn't share her with anyone even if I could have.

"Oh," she said with a smile, relaxing her forehead. "Well, I'd suggest going out, but..."

"Right," I rushed to agree. "Good call. Movie night, then?"

"Sounds perfect."

"Jack?" My mother's voice appeared out of nowhere, causing me to turn frantically to where she and my father had just entered the kitchen. "Sweetheart, who are you talking to?"

I looked from Cassie to my parents, and Cassie's face

reflected the sorrow that I felt inside. Like on some level we knew this—us—would never last. "I...um..." I dropped my head into my hands and confessed everything to them.

"When you told us that Cassie had come back to you, we were more than concerned. It was discovered that you weren't sleeping, and you were suffering anxiety attacks that brought on your delusions of Cassie returning." I continued to stare blankly at my father as he reminded me of just how broken I was two years ago.

"This wasn't the first time I've been medicated," I announced, knowing without a doubt that I was right. Flashes of me taking pills several times a day came and went through my memory. "It's the Librium that keeps her away from me." I was suddenly angry. At them for taking her away from me. At *myself* for both allowing them to, and not being strong enough to let her go on my own.

"We hadn't realized you had come off of them recently," my mother confessed in a voice that was barely above a whisper. "We suspect it was the impending anniversary to...well, everything that set you off."

I had just arrived at my parents' place after a particularly exhausting workday. Sometimes I found it quite emotionally draining to do what I did. I was quite looking forward to getting Charlie home and spending some time with her before I put her to bed so I could just relax.

On the drive to the house, I had this nagging feeling like I was forgetting something I had to do, but I couldn't put my finger on it. By the time I pulled into the driveway, I had all but given up trying to remember whatever it was I forgot. My focus was on seeing my baby girl—who wasn't really a baby, anymore.

As always, she greeted me with so much enthusiasm when she opened the door and leapt into my arms. She was the light that kept me going. It had been almost two years since our lives spiraled out of control, but Charlie kept my feet planted firmly on the ground.

Our night was fairly routine. We would eat dinner, Charlie would have a bath, we'd read a bedtime story, and then I would put her to bed. However, when I was alone, I was at my worst. Yes, almost two years had passed, but not a moment went by that I didn't think about Cassie. In fact, two weeks from today would mark the one month countdown to the second anniversary of the day we lost the baby. That was the day that started it all...

Knowing Charlie was sound asleep, I stood from the couch, flicked off the television, and headed for bed. As I made my way toward the stairs, I swear I heard my name being whispered, and every hair on my body stood on end. While most normal people would have been a little freaked out by this, there was something about this *particular whisper that calmed me. I stood as still as a statue and waited for it again. When I didn't hear the soft voice, I shook my head, chalking it up to exhaustion, and moved up the stairs slowly to pull my weary body into bed.*

After I quickly changed into my pajamas, I went to the bathroom to brush my teeth and take my medication. I placed my toothbrush into the holder and opened the medicine cabinet to grab my prescription bottle.

*"Shit," I mumbled when I opened it to find it empty. I had completely forgotten that I had taken my last dose the night before last, and was meaning to pick up a refill...on my way home from work...*tonight*. "I knew I was forgetting something."*

With muttered promises to myself to pick up my prescription tomorrow, I exited the bathroom to go to bed. As I pulled the blankets back and crawled beneath them, I froze and listened... really *listened. Coming from Charlie's room was a quiet melody of whispered song lyrics.*

"Cassie?" Just as soon as her name left my lips, the soothing sound of her voice stopped. That night, I had trouble falling asleep because I kept waiting to see if I would hear her again — which I didn't; and when I finally did doze off, it was a completely restless sleep.

The next morning, my mind was going a mile a minute. I couldn't stop thinking about how I thought I heard Cassie the night before. Though I knew it to be impossible, there was this tiny part of me that wanted it to be true. Then I got to thinking what life would have been like if Cassie was still around...

My mind was so preoccupied with those thoughts that my day went by fast. Work came and went; dinner and playtime with Charlie seemed to fly by faster than I would have liked; and the whole time I was thinking about Cassie. Charlie was the mirror image of her mother in so many ways, too. Her big, blue eyes; the way she pulled her plump lower lip between her teeth; even the way she overanalyzed everything she did was pure Cassie.

That night, I stood in Charlie's doorway watching her sleep soundly. Her soft blonde curls framed her cherubic face as she snuggled her little stuffed kitten close to her heart and smiled. Every breath she took was precious — this I knew. As I stood there, watching over my sleeping angel, I remembered my life from the very moment I met Cassie in high school. Our courtship. Going to college together and the hurdles our relationship overcame in those trying years. Getting engaged. How stunning Cassie was on the arm of her father as she made her way down the aisle to me...toward her future. I smiled when I reminisced about the day she told me she was pregnant, even silently chuckled at the memory of her thinking I would be upset by that fact. Then, the day Charlie was born...

Such beautiful memories of our happy life together.

"Hey," a soft voice said from behind me. I closed my eyes and tried to will it away, knowing it wasn't real. That her being here could only mean trouble for the life I had worked so hard to rebuild.

It took only a few seconds before I gave up trying, though. I wanted her to be here... I wanted her to be real.

I closed Charlie's door before turning to Cassie. The moonlight that shone through the window in the hallway cast a silver glow across her perfect features and she offered me an apologetic smile. "You're late." There was no hiding the slight anger in my voice. None of it happened, I willed, wanting it to be the truth.

She tilted her head to the side and placed a hand on my cheek. "I'm sorry. I'm here now, though."

I brushed past her and headed to our bedroom. Her soft footfalls were heard behind me as she followed. "For tonight," I said, closing the door once she had crossed the threshold. How long can this last?

Reality finally slipped away...

And like every other night for the last two years, we argued until we were both too tired to say anything else.

All the air left my body as the vision assaulted me. "Holy shit," I gasped, falling back onto the leather couch and running my fingers through my unruly hair. I was suddenly extremely overwhelmed by... *everything*. Staring up at the ceiling, I tried to catch my breath as I willed the room to stop spinning.

My mother looked back at my father and then redirected her attention on me. "What is it, dear?"

"Jack?" Dr. Richards's concerned voice caught my attention.

I swallowed thickly as the realization continued to sink in. I remembered that night with vivid clarity, but until now hadn't *really* thought about it. "What...?" I shook my head and sat back up, turning to face my parents again. "When did you guys figure it out?"

"At first, we didn't," Mom confessed with a sad smile. "There were a few things you said here and there. The beach house fixing everything, for one. We weren't aware that there was anything that *needed* fixing." She took a deep breath, her face clearly reflecting her struggle to voice her next statement. "However, it wasn't until Charlie spent the weekend that we grew even more suspicious."

"We asked Sienna to speak with you; see if maybe she could pinpoint any strange behavior." My eyes shot to my father as he started speaking.

"You spoke to Sienna?" It suddenly made sense; the day Sienna pulled me into her office after my weekend with Cassie. The way she had been evaluating me. *This* was why.

My father nodded. "Billy called us, also. Told us you seemed off at lunch. It wasn't really just one thing, Jack. Everyone saw it."

"Everyone but me," I whispered, my eyes finally finding Cassie again.

She sighed softly and cupped my cheek in her delicate hand. "But you know now."

"Yeah, but I wish I didn't."

Chapter Nineteen
letting go

Minutes turned to hours. Hours to days. Days to weeks.

While I now knew the truth, I still couldn't let go. I *wanted* to get better—needed to, even. But letting go of Cassie was proving to be more difficult than I had anticipated. I still couldn't accept that *this* was my life.

Once I recognized that my medication was keeping my delusions of her under control, I would tongue the capsules at the part of my day when I knew I needed her most. At night. She chastised me, sure, but who was she going to tell?

"Jack, you need to take those. They'll help you sleep," she told me firmly.

I scoffed at her as I pocketed the two pills I had tongued under my nurse's supervision. "*You* help me sleep."

With a sigh that was part exasperation and part despair, she walked toward me, cupping my face in her hands. "You know I can't stay. You need to let me go...so you can get back to Charlie. She needs you."

My eyebrows dipped toward one another, and my voice caught. "But... *I* need *you*."

"Baby," she said sweetly. "I'll always be with you in some way."

My anxiety had peaked, and I knew I should

have taken my pills—that's what they were there for, after all. But taking them meant that Cassie would leave, and I couldn't handle that. Not yet. I shook my head against her firm grasp. "No. I'm not ready. I...I need more time."

We had come to an understanding that night and Cassie pulled me down into bed with her, humming to me until I fell asleep in her cool embrace. The dreams still recurred, but this time, I knew them for what they really were—the truth. Unfortunately, my sleep was still far from peaceful, and I was admittedly exhausted more and more every day, but I was still unwilling to give up that time with my Cassie.

When I awoke the next day, my body was fatigued and moved slower than usual. I didn't want to take my meds, but I could feel the toll that going the night without them was having, so when the nurse came around, I took them, being sure to swallow and let them work.

"I'm proud of you," she whispered, wrapping her arms around my neck. "I love you." The way she spoke told me she thought this was me giving in.

"I'll see you tonight," I said, leaning forward and pressing a kiss to her forehead before she had to go.

"But—" I placed a finger to her soft lips, silencing her before she had a chance to object to what I was insinuating.

"Tonight," I whispered, only to have her nod solemnly against my finger.

When the Librium entered my bloodstream, Cassie was gone, and I was alone. I already felt the emptiness that her absence always brought, and I didn't like it one bit. There was only an hour until my next session, and I was sure my parents would be stopping by in the afternoon—they usually did, after all. As much as I appreciated their effort to check in on me, there was only one person I wanted to see besides Cassie: Charlie.

She was my only living link to my wife, and I hadn't seen her since the day I had admitted myself to the hospital. Her birthday was the next day, and I felt awful that I was going to miss it. I should have been there with her, helping her blow out her candles, taking pictures of her as she tore open the wrapping paper on the many gifts I hadn't yet bought for her...

I missed her terribly, and not a moment went by where I wasn't thinking about her; wondering what she was up to, if she missed me, if she thought about me as much as I did her. Had she changed much in the weeks I had been here? Was her hair longer? Her voice a little more grown up? So many questions and just not enough answers.

"Jack?" a familiar voice called out. I lifted my head and saw Sienna poke her head into the room, her smile bright and friendly. Not tentative in the least—which was a welcome change to most of my visitors.

"Hey," I greeted warmly, pulling her into my arms and squeezing her tightly. "How've you been?"

After ending our hug, Sienna flopped herself onto my bed and patted the empty spot next to her. "Swamped...which is why I haven't been able to come see you until now. I'm sorry. Friends don't let friends—"

"Sit in the nuthouse alone?" I finished jokingly.

Sienna laughed nervously, pushing a strand of her brown hair behind her ear. "No," she responded, her laugh trailing off slightly. "I suppose we don't do that, either. Seriously, though, how have things been going?"

As I sat in my room, with Sienna on my bed, the right side of her body barely brushing mine, I watched her every move. She wasn't apprehensive or hesitant around me, but she was working hard to try and get a read on me. When her eyes caught mine, what I once thought to be attraction was nothing more than caring and concern. *Friendship*.

"We miss you around the office."

I nodded. "Yeah, I miss you guys, too." Another beat of silence filled the room before I finally had the nerve to voice what I had to. "Did you know?"

"About Cassie?" she asked before shaking her head. "Not right away. I mean, I knew you seemed to be struggling..." I scoffed at the word she chose to describe what I had been going through. "But I had no idea that you were seeing her again."

Sienna turned to me, taking one of my hands in hers. "Jack, I feel it only right to let you know..." She took a deep breath, clearly afraid of what she had to say next. "You were seeing patients when you...well, what I mean is — "

I didn't have to be psychic to know what she was going to say before she said it. While I had been delusional and seeing my dead wife, I had also been practicing psychiatry. Clients had come to me and trusted me with their problems, and yet, none of it even compared to the secret I had been keeping. Sienna was here to tell me that I was under evaluation. "Yeah," I chuckled darkly, raking my fingers through my hair. "I was wondering when this would come up."

Sienna dropped her eyes to her now-fidgeting fingers. "I've gone through your files. Everything appears legit. There shouldn't be any problems. I just thought you should know that it's being looked into."

"And the practice?" I asked, concerned that the practice she had worked so hard to build from the ground up would be compromised.

"I'm sure it's fine. We'll figure it out. We always

do." She raised her brown eyes to mine after a beat. "I'm more concerned with you. Are you okay? I mean...are you still...?"

I chuckled as I watched her try to find the right words. "Delusional?" I finished for her.

Sienna's eyebrows wrinkled together with uncertainty, and she seemed kind of ashamed of even beginning to voice the question. "Well, I wasn't going to be that blunt, but, yeah."

Considering I hadn't even been able to fool my parents, I knew I wouldn't be able to lie to Sienna without her knowing. She wasn't just my colleague and mentor. I considered her to be a friend, and she'd borne witness to the worst parts of my marriage to Cassie. With a shuddering sigh, I clasped my hands tightly in my lap and looked down at them—silently willing Cassie to show up and give me the strength to get through this moment as she so often did.

"I still see her," I confessed, my voice a hoarse whisper.

"Are you not taking your meds? They seemed to help...the last time?" When she spoke the last three words, they came out slow and tentative, almost as though she wasn't sure I wanted to hear about the first time Cassie ever came to me.

Raising my eyes back to Sienna, I noted the heavy concern that registered in her expression. "Sometimes. I can't lose her again, Sienna. It will destroy me." Tears fell from my eyes as I admitted this to her. "I take them in the morning—after my dreams make the anxiety worse."

"Jack," she breathed softly, placing a hand over mine to calm the furious fidgeting that was going on. "The dreams are a result of your anxiety. Take the meds at night."

My head shook quickly. "No, I need her the most

at night."

"Look, I get that this is hard for you. I do. But, you look like you haven't slept much in weeks. That's not good for you. It's only going to make things worse. Think about what this is doing to—"

Knowing what she was going to say before she even said it, I cut her off abruptly. "I'm going to stop you right there. I *love* my daughter—you know that. I want to be better for her...but things are so much more complicated than that."

"I know. But they don't *have* to be," Sienna whispered softly, giving my hand a gentle squeeze. "Come back to us. And soon, okay?" Sienna's eyes shifted to her watch, and she groaned quietly. "I have a few appointments today, but—if you'd like—I can stop by again soon?"

The smile that spread across my face was small, but still genuine. "I would appreciate that."

With a bright smile, Sienna draped her arms around my shoulders again and squeezed me tightly, whispering promises to do anything she could to help—even if that meant coming to visit me several times a day.

Once she was gone, I headed to my daily session. It was no different than any other session, really. Dr. Richards could tell I was still stressed, and the deep purple circles under my eyes were a prime indicator that I wasn't getting as much sleep as I should have been. There was no reason for me to lie to him about anything; I wouldn't fool him, anyway. I confessed to tonguing my night meds, and this earned me a very disapproving look from him.

When he instructed me to start taking them, I told him I would...when I was ready. My refusal to give Cassie up was starting to concern him more and more each day, and I wouldn't be entirely surprised if he started administering an anti-anxiety medication through a syringe, or putting me on lockdown. Extreme measures, sure, but deep down I knew I was being difficult. Had I been in his position, it's what I would have done.

After my session, I had lunch in my room. Instead of eating, I pushed the food around, eating only a few bites here and there. My appetite was non-existent, and I just wanted Cassie back with me. *Five hours, thirty-three minutes,* I thought to myself as I looked up at the clock.

Yes, I had it worked out to the minute — give or take a few seconds — just how long my Librium kept me Cassie-free, and I found myself much more aware of the time when she wasn't with me. The hours dragged on and on and on...

Unable to take the loneliness of my room, I decided to walk the halls to clear my head. In the common room, a few of the other patients were watching a movie on the wall-mounted TV. I wasn't aware of what movie was playing, but I didn't want to be alone, so I took a seat in the empty arm chair and stared through the TV, not really paying attention to the bright picture. It wasn't long before my eyelids felt heavy, and my head bobbed several times as sleep threatened to take hold. Eventually, I gave in.

"Movie's over," a smooth voice whispered in my ear.

My head snapped up quickly, my neck aching from the awkward position in which I fell asleep in the easy chair. Blinking a few times, my vision finally cleared and the light, post-nap fog started to fade as I focused on the big blue eyes before me. My body relaxed in an instant, every part of me numb to the pain of her absence all day, and I smiled widely as I moved to stand up.

"You slept," she said happily, and I nodded in response.

One look over Cassie's shoulders told me the nurses were suspicious. They all watched me carefully for a moment until I indicated to Cassie with my eyes that we should head back to my room for more privacy. Taking my hand in hers, Cassie understood, and before long we were walking down the hall. The nurses kept their eyes trained on me, but as I got closer to them, the looks they gave me weren't ones of concern or fear, but of...anticipation? It was very curious behavior.

Of course, as soon as I pushed the door to my room open, I understood why their eyes never left me.

As I stepped over the threshold, the first thing I saw was a big pair of baby blue eyes, topped with a curly mess of golden curls. Tears sprung to my eyes, and I crouched down as Charlie squealed and ran forward. The force of her little body colliding with mine propelled me back until I landed on my backside with my baby girl in my arms. I pushed my nose into her thick curls and inhaled the scent of her shampoo, committing it to memory.

"Daddy! I missed you so much!" Charlie exclaimed into my ear as she squeezed me tighter around my neck. Her little body vibrated as the adrenaline from our reunion coursed through her entire body.

"God, Charlie. I missed you more than you could ever know. I'm so sorry." My apology wasn't just meant for Charlie. As my eyes drifted upward, I saw my parents standing in the center of my room. My mother's hands covered her mouth and tears spilled forward onto her cheeks and fingertips. Meanwhile, Dad had his arm around her shoulders, holding her close to his body to support her as her knees trembled from the overwhelming emotions she was feeling.

Not that I was complaining about my surprise visitor, but I had to ask. "What made you...? Why now?"

My mother was still so overcome with emotion that she was in no condition to speak, so my father shrugged one shoulder and smiled crookedly at me. "Sienna thought you might need this time with Charlie. She called us after seeing you, and after hearing what she had to say, it made sense."

I pulled Charlie closer to me, and every part of me that ached to see her again felt relief as the gaping wounds started to heal. I didn't want to let go of my baby — not ever — but she started wriggling to free herself, even giggling because she thought it was part of a game. Releasing her was the hardest thing I ever had to do, because I knew we couldn't be together yet. She would have to leave me here until I was better.

"I drew you a picture, Daddy!" she told me excitedly. She ran over to my bed — where her pink baby blanket was now folded on top of my pillow — and grabbed an eight-by-eleven piece of white poster board. I stood up and moved to my bed, sitting on the edge, and pulled Charlie onto my lap so she could present me with her gift. My emotions caught in my throat as I looked at the image she had drawn with crayons.

"This is me right there," she said animatedly, pointing with her finger to the picture of herself. "You can tell 'cause I has yellow hair. I'm wearing a blue dress because blue is your favorite color." She turned her head up to look at me. "Do you still like blue, Daddy?" Her voice wavered with the uncertainty, afraid that maybe I had changed since being here.

"Yes, bug. I still like blue," I assured her as I

tucked a loose curl behind her ear before turning my attention back to her drawing. With a smile, I pointed at the person standing next to her. "And who's this handsome man?"

Charlie giggled. "That's you, silly! Can't you see?" Charlie pointed at the other people in the picture and told me who they were. "Over here is Gramma and Grampa Martin. And then Gramma and Grampa Taylor are in the picture, too! Did you know that I got to go visit them for a weekend? It was so much fun!"

As she told me this, I realized that I had missed so much of her life in the weeks that I had spent here, and I wanted to know absolutely everything she had done in my absence. It made me more determined than ever to get better. For her.

I continued to look over this beautiful picture that Charlie had drawn for me, and one person in particular caught my attention. My brows knit together, and I brought the picture up closer so I could get a better look. "Charlie? Who's this up here...by the sun?" Charlie pulled her bottom lip between her teeth and looked hesitant. "Bug?"

"It's Mama," she whispered. "She's a angel. See, there's her wings. She's wearing blue, too, Daddy."

A tear fell onto my cheek, and I moved to quickly brush it away. "I can see that," I rasped, turning my head up to look at Cassie who was still standing in the doorway, staring in wonder at Charlie. She took a deep breath before moving gracefully to our side and placing a hand on my shoulder. I wanted to acknowledge the gesture, but knew I shouldn't.

Charlie stirred slightly, craning her neck to look at me. Her eyes were big and curious, and they drifted off to where Cassie was standing. Could she sense her? "What does she look like, Daddy?"

I drew in a sharp intake of air and snapped my head to my parents. My mom's head began to shake back and forth in denial that I had slipped—or more accurately, made no progress at all—and my father gave her shoulders a light squeeze.

My focus returned to Charlie. "Just like you, baby."

"And, she's here right now?" I looked back to Cassie as she knelt down until she was face-to-face with Charlie. Charlie seemed to be in-tune with her mother's movements, because her eyes followed Cassie's descent. It was eerie, but gave me hope that I wasn't *entirely* crazy. That Cassie was with us in some way…

"She is," I confirmed, my voice gravelly with apprehension.

Charlie sucked in a shaky breath and held it for a moment before laying her head against my chest. Her tiny fingers grasped at the loose fabric of my sweater, and when I looked down, I saw her tugging at her bottom lip nervously. With her eyes still trained on where Cassie knelt, she whispered words that melted my heart. "I love you, Mommy."

I gripped Charlie around the waist and turned her body to mine. She wrapped her arms around my neck and hugged me back as more tears fell from my eyes. Holding her in my arms felt different somehow. I knew I always loved Charlie and would die for her; but these last two years had me withdrawing from her—more so in the last few weeks when Cassie came back to me. I had reconnected with my daughter in that moment, and felt my will to live return.

I turned to Cassie and offered her a sad smile. "I can let you go now," I told her softly. She nodded her head once in understanding and stood slowly.

Once on her feet, I closed my eyes as she leaned

forward to press her lips to my forehead. They felt like a whisper of a breath against my skin. "I love you both," she whispered, and when I opened my eyes again, she was gone.

Instead of the emptiness her absence usually brought, I felt a strange sense of calm wash over me. The guilt I had harbored over her death seemed slightly less, and I felt like a new man.

I was ready to move forward into the light.

Chapter Twenty
within reach

"The dreams have stopped."

Dr. Richards cocked his head to the right. "Oh?"

It had been about three weeks since Charlie first visited me at the hospital, and after telling Cassie I could finally let her go, the dreams seemed to be occurring less and less. Instead of having them every time I closed my eyes, they slowly dwindled to a few times a week until they stopped all together.

Cassie's visits, however, stopped immediately. I took my medication as scheduled and was really making a conscious effort to move on. Yes, I still loved her with everything I had, but she was gone. Charlie was here, and she needed me more than I needed Cassie.

There were times I still struggled without her and often thought, *"Maybe I could skip this one dose... Just this once..."* That's when I would catch Cassie's disapproving stare in my memories and Charlie's face, her eyes alight with the hope that I would be returning to her soon. Harnessing the intense pain that started to burn in my veins, I took my meds. It wasn't long until they took effect, and I felt my body relax.

Everybody around me had their theories on why I was suddenly doing so well. Some thought it was the Librium that kept me anchored in this reality; others thought maybe I was stronger than before. Me, however? I liked to think it was Charlie's frequent visits; that seeing her almost every day reminded me of the work I was here to do. My parents even brought her back the next day so I could see her on her birthday.

"Happy birthday, bug," I whispered into her ear as I held her to my chest.

Charlie giggled and pushed herself free of my firm embrace. "Thanks, Daddy! Did you sleep good?"

With a smile, I nodded. "Better than good," I replied softly. True, I had my usual dreams about the day Cassie had overdosed, but I had slept better for the most part. Why? When Charlie left the day before, she handed me her pink blanket and told me she wanted me to keep it with me for as long as I was here. She told me it would help remind me of her; and while I didn't need to be reminded of her, I knew it would help me remember my silent vow to get better for her.

Charlie and I sat on my bed for a while, and she pulled out a couple of books that she had packed in her backpack for me to read to her. The ones she begged me to read were some of our old favorites that we always read together before she went to sleep. It felt good to be with her like this again – like nothing ever happened.

As we read, she leaned her head against my arm, both of us sitting with our backs against the wall. "I like the way you read to me, Daddy," she whispered breathlessly through a yawn.

I closed the book that we had just finished together and wrapped my arm around her. "You have no idea just how much I missed reading to you, Charlie."

"Hmmm," she hummed contemplatively. "This much?" She held her hands out in front of her about a foot apart, and with a chuckle, I shook my head. Her tiny brow

furrowed and her lips pursed. "This much?" she asked, pulling her hands farther apart. I shook my head again, and she stretched her arms as far as they would go. "This much?"

"'Fraid not."

Charlie dropped her arms into her lap and grunted in exasperation. "Well, that's as far as my arms go, Daddy."

"To infinity," I told her, placing a kiss onto the top of her frustrated little head.

Charlie looked up at me, her eyes wide and sparkling with excitement. "And beyond?"

My laughter filled the room, and I had to admit that it felt **good** *to laugh like this again. It seemed like it had been forever since I felt genuine happiness, and I welcomed the feeling entirely.*

"You been watching Toy Story *again?" I inquired, poking her lightly in the ribs.*

Charlie squirmed away from me in a fit of giggles. "Maybe!" she squealed. "Gramma and Grampa bought me the new one when I went to visit them. It's a good one!"

I ceased my attack on Charlie's ticklish sides and pulled her onto my lap. "Well, maybe you'll let me watch it with you when I come home?"

Charlie's giggles stopped, and her already wide smile grew even more. "Will that be soon?"

"God, I hope so, bug."

She pulled her bottom lip between her teeth, and I felt a small sting in my heart at the familiar gesture where Cassie's absence still lingered. Charlie's eyebrows lifted nervously, so I offered her a smile and used the pad of my thumb to work her bottom lip free before she hurt herself.

"What's wrong, bug?"

"Is Mama here?" Her little voice trembled as she spoke, and the pain I felt doubled.

I swallowed thickly, trying not to let the rising sorrow show in my eyes. "No, baby. Mama's gone."

"Oh." Her eyes dropped to her lap where she fiddled with the hem of her shirt. "Are you gonna miss her?"

"Um," I began, not quite sure just how far to take this conversation for Charlie's sake as well as my own. "There's a large part of me that's going to miss your mama very, very much." Charlie watched me carefully, waiting patiently for me to continue. I smiled at her, and this seemed to put her at ease slightly. "But, when I look into your eyes, I'm reminded that we'll never be without her. You remind me so much of your mother, Charlie. And while I'll continue to miss her, I know that she'll always be with us in some way."

Charlie pulled herself up and wrapped her arms around my neck tightly. Not another word was spoken for several minutes until my parents returned to the room.

Letting Cassie go—while probably one of the hardest things I'd ever had to do—was only the first step. Over the weeks, Dr. Richards had helped me work through a lot, and I was grateful for everything.

Dr. Richards cleared his throat, yanking me from my thoughts. "How long have you been free of them?" he inquired.

I thought back the last few nights and realized that it had been almost a week. I had dreamt of Cassie, but not of that night. The dreams I had, when I could remember what they were, were happy and full of the better times we'd shared.

"Almost a week," I answered, my voice registering the relief I felt at the revelation. "I feel...*good*, you know?"

Dr. Richards's mouth turned up into a smile. "That's fantastic."

My smile mirrored his, and I leaned forward in my seat. I rested my arms on my knees, my body language transforming as I spoke. No longer did I give off the impression of being weak and defeated; now I was happy and exuded the confidence I had lost. "Yeah, I think seeing Charlie again helped remind me that everything would be okay." I paused for a moment, and my doctor waited for me to continue. "I was so consumed by my own guilt over what happened to Cassie that I forgot I had a reason to live. For so long, Cassie was all I lived for. Then we had Charlie, and my focus was split.

"When Cassie died...I don't know... It was like the guilt was all-consuming. Eventually, it took on a life of its own and created this alternate reality where she was still with me. I did everything I could to hold onto her, and it alienated me from the rest of the world to a degree." As I confessed everything, I felt the weight of my past continue to lift from my shoulders, and for the first time in over two years, I felt hope.

"Charlie is the reason I'm here. She's my reason to live. If not for her...I don't know where I'd be."

Dr. Richards leaned forward and set his notepad and pen on the table between us. "You've come a long way, Jack. When we first started these sessions, I was afraid this would take longer. The guilt you felt was understandable, but what happened wasn't your fault. I'm happy to hear you realize that now."

Even though a small part of me still wondered if Cassie would have followed through had I not left her sleeping pills with her while she was in such an emotional state, I knew that I wasn't to blame for her actions. I couldn't keep beating myself up over this. I needed to get better—for Charlie.

"I just have one more question for you," Dr. Richards said, taking his glasses off to inspect the lenses. I nodded and waited for him to continue. There was something in the way he looked at me when his eyes lifted to meet mine again, and I smiled, hoping that the next words he spoke were the ones I longed to hear. "How would you feel about going home tomorrow?"

"Are you serious?" I choked out, tears of joy prickling my eyes. "Of course I'd love to go home. As long as you think I'm ready."

Replacing his glasses back on his nose, Dr. Richards relaxed back into his chair. "Well, I'd still like to see you once a week. I think it would be best." I nodded in agreement, knowing that there was still a little way for me to go before I could consider myself cured. "But, I truly feel you're ready to go home."

Ready to go home.

His words repeated over and over in my mind, and to be honest, I didn't hear much else that he had to say. He must have known it, too, because, with a laugh, he ended our session twenty minutes early.

As soon as I was alone in my room, I grabbed my empty bag from beneath my bed and opened it up. I packed up all of my belongings, being sure to leave my pajamas and an extra set of clothes out for tonight and tomorrow before zipping it up and placing it on the chair. My excitement was indescribable. My hands shook with anticipation, and the seconds weren't ticking by fast enough on the clock. It was barely noon, and I had to stick around here until *tomorrow*? How was I going to get through the day?

The nurse came by with my afternoon meds, and she stood in the room, watching me with a smile. Once again, there was that brief, *"What if?"* moment. I was so happy with my progress, and I wanted to share it with Cassie. My better judgment took hold soon enough, reminding me that I'd be a fool to throw away everything I had accomplished now, less than twenty-four hours before my release. I returned the nurse's smile before opening up and taking the Librium.

Moments later, I was alone again, and still unsure what to do. Pacing the room didn't seem to pass the time. I was too wired to sleep—even with the meds. I was anxious—but this anxiety was completely unlike anything I had experienced before now.

Deciding I should let someone know about my release, I went out to the community phone and dialed my parents' home number, knowing my mother would be home with Charlie.

"Jack!" my mother greeted enthusiastically. I could hear in her voice just how much happier she was. I knew that what was happening to me was beyond stressful for her and the rest of my family. Thankfully, that was all behind us now.

"That's my daddy?" I could hear Charlie squeal in the background. *"Please, may I speak to him?"*

"Mom, before you put her on, I just want to let you know I'm being released." My mother gasped softly, but before she could say anything, I continued. "I don't want you to tell Charlie just yet. I want to surprise her."

"Gramma! Pleeeease lemme talk to my daddy!"

I chuckled as I listened to her continuing to whine. My mother agreed to my request, a light sniffle echoing through the telephone. "Okay, you better put her on before she has a fit. I love you. I'll see you tomorrow."

The phone exchanged hands, and I had to contain my elation in order to ensure I didn't ruin my little surprise. "Daddy!"

"Hey, bug. How are you today?"

"I'm only okay, Daddy." Her voice suddenly sounded sad, and she sighed softly. "Gramma said we aren't coming to see you today."

The fact that she sounded so heartbroken by this had me ready to tell her about my homecoming tomorrow; but I held strong. "Aw, baby. We just saw each other the other day. I'm sure it won't be much longer until you get to see me."

"I know. I just really wanted to show you the new picture I drew for you."

I laughed softly and leaned forward on the counter the phone sat upon and ran my free hand through my hair. "I'll see it, and you, very, *very* soon. I love you."

"I love you, too," she replied, her voice perking up just a little at the prospect of seeing me again.

We said our goodbyes, and I spoke to my mother again. I let her know that her and my father should stay home with Charlie and that I would find another way back. They offered to send Jennifer and Alex, or even Billy and Sarah, but I told her I'd like it if everyone was there when I got home.

After hanging up the phone, I finally felt the drowsiness that the Librium often brought on, so I went back to my room and lay down on my bed in hopes that I would be able to catch a few winks and the hours would seem to just fly by. The sleep that found me was deep and peaceful, and I dreamed of the reunion that was just on the horizon.

Chapter Twenty-One
homecoming

Waking up that morning was so different than any other. Instead of lying in bed a while longer than usual, I got up right away and rushed to the washroom where I showered and shaved before dressing in jeans and an off-white sweater. After getting myself ready, I headed back to my room and grabbed my bag from the chair I had set it on yesterday, going through it to be sure I hadn't forgotten anything. Before I zipped it shut, I grabbed Charlie's blanket off my bed, folded it up tight, and placed it inside. With my bag ready to go, I took one final look around the room and smiled.

The room no longer seemed sad and depressing to me. Ever since the day I began to accept the way things were—the first day I saw Charlie again—everything in my life seemed less tragic, and I saw the world through new eyes.

"Are your parents picking you up?" Dr. Richards's voice startled me from my happy thoughts, and I turned to him with a smile.

"Um, no. Sienna's going to pick me up. I wanted to surprise Charlie," I explained. I moved for Dr. Richards and extended my hand to him. "I want to thank you again for everything you've done."

"It was you who did all the work; I simply nudged you in the right direction. Now, I don't want you thinking that this is the last we'll see each other," he told me, gripping my hand in his. "I was serious yesterday when I said I think it would be beneficial for you to continue seeing me once a week. Bring Charlie. I'm sure she has questions, and I'd be happy to talk to her about what she's going through, as well."

"Thank you," I repeated. "We will."

"Hey!" a bright voice chimed from behind Dr. Richards. Sienna entered the room with a wide smile and looked between us. "You ready to go?"

"Definitely." I glanced back at Dr. Richards. "I'll make an appointment for next week." We said our goodbyes to one another before he handed me a prescription for my anti-anxiety medication, as well as a small packet that contained a few Librium to tide me over until I got it filled, and went off to his first appointment of the day.

Sienna pulled me into her arms and held me tightly for a minute. "Aah!" she cried out happily, tightening her arms around me for emphasis. "You're going *home*! Can you believe it?"

"It does seem a little too good to be true. But I'm afraid if I let myself think, for even a second, that this isn't really happening, I might wake up in this bed, strapped down and being force-fed enough tranquilizers to take down a large herd of elephants," I confessed with a laugh as I released her from my embrace.

"So? Are you ready to go? I called your parents when I arrived and let them know we were going to be leaving shortly."

I nodded before turning to grab my bag, and Sienna led me from the hospital. I waved to all the nurses as I walked past them, saying my farewells on the way out, and once outside I inhaled deeply, absorbing the fresh air that the cool fall day had to offer. Yes, in the weeks I had been here, I had been outside.

However, today was different. The air, as it entered my lungs, was filled with the prospect of a second chance at life.

Even though I had driven the highway from Denver to Frederick more times than I could count, this time was also completely different. Everything seemed just a little bit brighter as Sienna drove and I stared out the windows. The changing colors of the leaves were a little brighter, the sky just a little bluer, and the sun just a little more golden. It was a true testament to the advances I had made in the last few weeks.

As we pulled onto my parents' street, my hands began to sweat, and I nervously tried drying them on the thigh of my jeans as I saw their house come into view. Sienna pulled her car into the driveway, and I found myself taking a few controlled deep breaths in order to calm my thundering heart. For a brief second, I felt as though I wasn't ready for this. That there was a very real possibility that I could relapse — again. What if that was to happen? What would happen to Charlie? To my parents? To me?

Sienna's warm hand on my own brought me back to the present. I looked over at her, the panic clearly written on my face. "It's going to be fine," she assured me.

"What if — ?"

Sienna shook her head and cut me off. "No. No 'what if's.' This is a happy day. Behind those doors is a five-year-old little girl who loves and misses her daddy more than anything in this world. She has no idea you're here, and when she sees you..." Sienna took a deep, shaky breath and held back the tears that had filled her eyes. "God. Her entire world is just going to stop. And when you look into her big, soulful eyes, you're going to remember that you conquered something no one should ever have to. And that you did it for her."

Sienna was right. I nodded my head and reached for my door and exited the car. As we walked up the sidewalk to the front door, I could hear Charlie inside having the time of her life. I gripped the black door handle and moved to squeeze the latch to push it open, freezing briefly to take another deep breath.

"You can do this," Sienna whispered from behind me, placing her small hand on my shoulder in a show of support.

I opened the door slowly and peeked inside the foyer. I must have timed everything just right, because Charlie came barreling around the corner, crying out for her Uncle Billy to stop chasing her. When she spotted me, she skidded to an abrupt stop, her breath catching upon locking eyes with me.

I smiled, arching my eyebrows, and dropped my bag onto the floor. "Hey, bug."

Charlie didn't move. She didn't smile. She didn't breathe. She stood as still as a statue in the foyer for what seemed like forever. Suddenly, what was happening registered with her and she let out an ear-piercing shriek.

"Daddyyyy!" She ran forward, and I knelt down to hoist her up into my arms so I could hold her. "You're here!"

Upon hearing the commotion, everyone had entered the room. Billy stood behind Sarah, his hands on her shoulders, and they both smiled at me happily. Sarah mouthed a "welcome home," not wanting to interrupt my reunion with Charlie, and I offered her a nod of thanks in return. Jen and Alex stood next to them, tears falling from Jennifer's eyes as she tried to wipe them away before anyone could see. And my parents stood just off to the side, watching happily as

Charlie and I shared this special moment.

Charlie lifted her head from my shoulder and craned her neck around to look at our friends and family that had joined us. "Did you guys know he was comin' home today?" The way she voiced the question told me she already suspected they did; she was just fishing for confirmation.

"Surprise, Charlie," my father said with a wink and a smirk in her direction.

I set Charlie down so I could remove my shoes and come inside. Sienna followed my lead upon my mother's insistence that she should stay, stating that she just had a call to make to rearrange a date that she had made for tonight.

"You don't have to do that," I assured her.

Sienna shook her head. "Darren will understand. I'd rather be here for you right now. It's what friends do."

We all gathered in the family room, Charlie perched on my lap and looking at me with excited eyes. The way she looked at me was almost as though she couldn't believe this was happening. And truthfully, that feeling I had earlier about being afraid of waking up at any minute came to the forefront of my mind, making me nervous. Closing my eyes, I pulled Charlie in for a tight hug and breathed her in until she started giggling. When I opened my eyes again, everything was exactly as it was a moment ago.

This was real.

"We're so proud of you, Jack," my mother said, breaking the silence in the room.

I offered her a wide smile. "I couldn't have done it without all of you supporting me. You've all been so great through all of this. Especially considering what I put you through." Now was as good a time as any for the final step in my recovery. I inhaled a calming breath, looked around at my family and sighed. "I'm very sorry for everything. I know it couldn't have been easy."

"Hey," Billy said, shaking his head. "We're family. As if we weren't going to support you."

Sarah nodded beside him. "Exactly," she said softly. "We love you, and we're so glad you're finally home."

My family's acceptance to everything that had happened was incredible. The way they forgave so easily... I couldn't have asked for better people to be surrounded by.

It felt so great to be surrounded by loved ones in a non-hospital setting again. I watched and listened to each and every one speak, occasionally placing feather-light kisses on Charlie's head, only to have her giggle and squirm against me. I never wanted to forget this moment...this feeling.

"All right. Dinner's almost ready," my mother announced. "Charlie, would you like to help me set the table?"

With a quick peck on my cheek, Charlie jumped down from my lap. She made it all of two steps before she stopped and put her hands on her hips. "Hey!" She cried out suddenly. Her grandmother turned to look at her quizzically. "I shoulda known something was goin' on! You even made Daddy's favorite!"

Laughing, my mom walked to her and ushered her forward. "Yes, sweetheart."

Charlie let her hands fall, and she sighed with over exaggerated frustration. "How am I gonna be able to trust you all ever again?" Their playful banter faded as they rounded the corner to the dining room, and we all laughed.

As soon as dinner was on the table, my mother came back into the room and told us all we could start eating. Upon entering the barely-used dining room, I found Charlie sitting in a chair with her legs across another—in an effort to save it to me, I assumed. Billy smirked knowingly and went to pull it out for himself, only to have Charlie scowl at him and shake her finger.

"Nuh uh, Uncle Billy! This is my daddy's seat," she informed him firmly, bending forward to place her hands next to her legs on the seat.

"But Charlie, I always sit next to you," he pouted playfully, sinking to his knees at her side and batting his eyes at her.

She merely shrugged and turned her head away from him in a dismissive manner. "That's too bad. I want Daddy to sit here this time. Sorry."

Returning to his feet, Billy laughed and rubbed his hand on the top of her hair, messing it up slightly. "S'ok, kiddo. I understand. I was only messin' with ya," he told her with a wink. "Next time, though?"

Charlie smiled and shrugged again. "We'll see."

After taking our seats, my father stood at his spot at the head of the table and smiled proudly in my direction. "Helen and I just wanted to thank you all for joining us here today," he began, nodding his head at my mother who sat directly across from him. "It means a lot to us both that you could be here to celebrate Jack's homecoming. Jack, your mother and I are extremely happy to have you back." Everyone else nodded and spoke in agreement with what my father was saying.

Looking at each and every one of them as they sat around the long table, I nodded once. "And thank you all for your continued love and support. I don't know where I'd be right now if it weren't for all of you." Once again, I found myself undeserving of them all as they assured me that it was what family did for one another, no matter what. I could only shake my head and smile as I placed my cloth napkin across my lap and started to dig in.

Dinner was phenomenal. My mother had made a roasted chicken with mashed potatoes and a steamed vegetable medley, and for dessert, one of her famous apple pies. It had been weeks since I had eaten even close to this good. After dessert, Charlie yawned and rested her head against my arm. When I looked over, her eyes appeared to be heavy, and her breathing seemed deeper.

"Son, why don't you take the Mercedes home? Get Charlie to bed," My father offered softly. "She's had a long day, and the two of you deserve a little time to yourselves."

It was exactly what I should do...what I wanted to do; but there was that part of me that was fearful of the past coming back to repeat itself. My eyes met Sienna's, and she gave me a curt nod as if to tell me that everything was going to be fine. I stood slowly, lifting Charlie into my arms, and took her to the front door where I slipped on my shoes. Everyone came to see us off as I stood in the foyer holding my sleeping five-year-old on my right hip, her head falling on my shoulder.

"Call if you need anything," Sienna told me. "It doesn't matter what time it is."

Jennifer stepped forward and stood on her tiptoes to reach around my shoulders to hug me. "I'm so happy you're back, baby brother."

"Thanks, half-pint," I said, kissing the top of her head quickly. "I'll call you guys tomorrow."

I put Charlie in the car seat my parents had put in the Mercedes while they took care of her these last few weeks, and we headed for home. As I pulled into the driveway next to my abandoned Audi, Charlie awoke slightly.

"Daddy?" she whispered softly as I opened her door.

"Mmm?" I hummed in acknowledgement as I unstrapped her and picked her up again.

A loud yawn escaped her again as she wrapped her arms and legs around me. "Nothin'. I just wanted to make sure I wasn't dreamin'."

"No, baby. This isn't a dream. I'm here. We're home," I assured her.

Once inside, I took Charlie upstairs and laid her in her bed. I hadn't planned to change her into her pajamas since she had fallen back asleep as soon as I had picked her back up, so I placed her under her comforter, grabbed her stuffed kitten, and tucked her in tight. There was a part of me that wanted to sit on the end of her bed and just watch her all night long. I missed her so much that I didn't want to miss a single minute of her life ever again. Instead, I leaned forward and placed a soft kiss on her forehead before retreating back downstairs.

As I walked the main floor, the memories of my delusions with Cassie came back, and I found myself missing her again. I rushed to my bag and grabbed the small packet of pills that Dr. Richards had given me and took two. I then went back to the living room and stood in the middle of the room, wondering what I could do to pass the time until the Librium kicked in. It was a no-brainer.

I sat at the bench behind the piano and raised the fallboard. The keys were so shiny and inviting as I placed my fingers on them and started to play. The soft melody carried through the room, and I got so wrapped up in the music that I almost didn't notice my visitor.

"Charlie? What are you doing out of bed?" I inquired, watching her rub her eyes with one hand while the other hugged her stuffed animal to her chest tightly.

"I woke up and heard the piano. I wanted to see you again," she responded, walking over and climbing up onto the bench next to me. "Play for me?"

"Always." I placed my fingers in a different position and started to play her lullaby for her. Recognizing the music instantly, she smiled and giggled, looping her arm through mine to hold herself closer to me.

"Should we head back up to bed?" I asked once the song was over.

Charlie shook her head and looked up at me. "Not yet. Can we look at pictures?"

"Yeah." I replaced the fallboard as Charlie ran to the shelf we kept the albums. Her fingers traveled along the spines until she found the one she was looking for and pulled it out. She hopped up on the couch and waited for me.

I joined her and pulled the album between us, and we went through the pictures together. As we flipped through the pages, Charlie asked questions about them. I told her about the day her mother and I got married as we leafed through picture after picture. Soon, we came to the pictures we had taken through every week of Cassie's pregnancy. Charlie was amazed at how different her mother looked from week to week as she grew inside her belly.

Going through these pictures was something I hadn't done in quite some time. I had always seen them as a painful reminder to the happier times we would never get back. It had always seemed far too horrible to look at them when all they served to do was remind me of all that we had lost.

It was that moment, sitting with Charlie and telling her stories about her mother, that I realized I had been going about this all wrong. In remembering those tragic final moments in our life together, I forgot the ones that built the life I had now.

These photos were memories of our life together. We had enjoyed the time we shared. Our relationship was beautiful, and we had captured as many of those precious moments as we could.

We loved each other. We loved the life we had created. And most importantly, we loved making the memories that I could now share with our daughter.

Epilogue
always with you

It pained me to watch her take that walk alone. I should have been there, right by her side, as she marched down the narrow pathway to her future. He stood there, waiting for her. The smile that adorned his face reached his eyes as they sparkled and shone with the happiness I knew they shared.

Seth Marshall was taking my baby girl's hand in marriage, and I couldn't have been happier or more proud. Over the years, Seth had proven his love for Charlie, and I knew without a doubt that he would cherish and take care of her forever; that I would never have to worry about her.

As she entered the room, her smile mirroring Seth's as she walked toward him, my heart both swelled with pride and ached with despair. With her long blonde hair pulled off to one side, the tight curls cascading down until they reached her waist, her blue eyes shone with excitement that only seemed to multiply with each and every step she took. The diamond white gown she wore shimmered in the pale lights of the room we had acquired on such short notice.

She looks so much like her mother.

Looking around the small room, I was pleased to see only those closest to us here to celebrate their union. Jennifer and Alex stood side by side, watching with love and joy as Charlie passed them by. Billy and Sarah stood across the slim aisle, Billy holding up his hand in hopes Charlie would give him a high-five — being her uncle's girl, she gladly obliged. The slap of their hands rang through the room, and everyone broke out into a peal laughter. Seth's mom and dad smiled at her as she continued on her way, and my parents watched on proudly, tears of joy falling from my mother's eyes.

At the tender age of twenty-three, Charlie held her Bachelor of Journalism degree. She had worked so hard to achieve the goals she had set for herself in spite of all that was going on around her. And now, she was about to pledge her love to the man before her.

Having been together since their freshman year of high school, best friends since childhood, I knew that Charlie was destined to marry Seth. Come to think of it, I was certain they were meant to be together since they were children. After graduation, Charlie and Seth parted for school, promising to remain faithful to one another while they attended university and obtained their degrees. Now that they were both done with school, they had moved back to Frederick and were ready to start their future. Together.

Seth and Charlie had only just become engaged a little over a month ago, and since neither one of them really wanted a big wedding — much to Jennifer's chagrin — they decided they wanted to have the wedding right away. For me.

"What?" Charlie cried out over the phone.

I sighed sadly, palming my face in my hand. "I'm sorry, bug."

"No," she stated firmly. "No. This isn't happening. I won't let it."

She had been away at college for a year, and upon her

leaving, I could feel myself spiraling downward. It didn't matter if I took my medication; everywhere I looked I saw her.

Cassie.

She never came to me like she did before. But the blonde across the street from the diner I had lunch with Sienna at looked just like her; the girl down the street, walking her dog at eight in the morning as I left the house, smiled at me, and I swore time and time again that it was Cassie.

I didn't keep it to myself this time; I told Sienna right away. Of course, she assumed I had gone off my meds or had started sleeping less due to an increase in anxiety from Charlie leaving. Empty nest syndrome, she called it. I told her that I was diligent with my medication, not wanting another relapse in my immediate future. But being stressed because Charlie had gone away seemed plausible. It was recommended that I up the dosage of my Librium for a bit—not something I relished doing as anti-anxiety meds could be habit-forming, but if it kept me from falling further, I'd do it.

It didn't work, though. Cassie started making appearances more and more frequently. Everywhere I turned, there she was. In the parking lot at work. The supermarket. She even waited on Alex, Billy, and me when we met for lunch. They picked up on my distress instantly, and I told them what was happening. They assured me that the waitress looked nothing like Cassie; but every time I looked at her, I saw my dead wife.

I made a doctor's appointment that week to be checked out, and after undergoing a multitude of blood work and physicals, I was ordered to have an MRI.

That's when they found the tumor.

"Charlie, it's going to be fine," I told her as I heard her sniffle and hold back a sob.

"So... What do we do?" Her voice was soft, cracking

as she spoke.

"I start radiation next week." *I still had trouble believing it all myself.* *"They're hoping to shrink the tumor before surgery."*

"Surgery?" she shrieked.

I sighed into the phone, running my fingers through my hair. *"Charlie, everything's going to be fine. It's a procedure that's been done many times before."*

Charlie couldn't hold back her crying anymore, and she had trouble speaking through the sobs. *"But not to you. You're my daddy."* *Her voice dropped to a hoarse whisper.* *"You're my whole world... If anything were to happen to you — "*

"Stop. Nothing's going to happen." *I wished I could believe the surprising conviction in my own words.*

"I'll fly out tomorrow," Charlie stated with a loud sniffle. Her voice sounded a little more stable, but, even over the phone, I could tell she was just putting on a brave face.

"Bug, you have school."

"And it can wait. I need to see you... Be with you for this. I'll meet with my profs tonight and let them know."

I tried arguing with her, but her mind was made up. She was terribly stubborn — just like her mother. After conceding, Charlie told me she had to go and see her professors before they left for the day.

True to her word, Charlie arrived at Denver International the next night. I picked her up from the airport, but instead of a happy reunion, ours was filled with tears of fear for the future. The ride back to our Frederick home was long, and Charlie continued to ask questions about what the plan for the week was. I told her I was to meet with my oncologist and a neurosurgeon to go over the procedure. I told her she was welcome to stay with her grandparents, as they'd be happy to see her, but she told me—quite adamantly—that she was coming to every appointment I had while she was there.

The oncologist seemed fairly optimistic that they could get the mass with invasive surgery, but it sounded risky. He said without the surgery, I'd be lucky to have more than a month left. After sitting down with my family, we decided that surgery was the best option.

Even though she didn't want to leave me, Charlie had been away from school for a few weeks. With promises to call when I had a date scheduled for surgery, she gave in and booked a flight back to Hanover... Yes, Charlie was a Dartmouth girl, through-and-through. It was as though it was bred into her.

Radiation kicked my ass; I wouldn't sit around and say it sounded worse than it was. It was a horrible thing to go through, but in the end, they were able to shrink the growth enough that the surgery was manageable.

After having the tumor removed, I had to undergo regular scans and tests to make sure everything was fine. And it was.

For a while.

About three months ago, I started seeing Cassie again. The tumor had returned with a vengeance and brought with it my hallucinations. I was told it had something to do with the position of the tumor pressing on the temporal lobe that caused me to see her. When I decided not to undergo the radiation and another surgery, Charlie argued with me. She was downright angry with me for my refusal to put our family through this again. I'd never seen her react that way—not even in her trying teenage years.

"So what? You're just giving up, now?" she cried,

angry tears rolling down her cheeks. Instead of wiping them away, she kept her arms crossed tightly across her chest as she glared at me.

"Bug, surgery isn't going to solve the problem. It'll take it away for a bit and then we'll be right back here."

Charlie's eyes widened, and this time she did wipe the tears from her cheeks. "You don't know that."

"Yes," I told her softly. "I do."

Charlie's head shook with denial. "You can't leave me," she rasped.

I rushed across the room and pulled Charlie into my arms. I held her to me tightly as she cried into my shoulder. Her hands clutched at the back of my shirt in an effort to hold onto me for as long as possible.

"I'm sorry." While I meant them, the words just didn't seem like enough in that moment.

A sad tear rolled down my cheek at the three-month-old memory, and Charlie stopped where I remained seated, too weak from the disease to walk her down the aisle. Kneeling before me, she placed a kiss on my cheek. "I love you, Daddy. Thank you. For everything." A few stray tears fell onto her cheek, and I lifted my hand to wipe them away.

"No tears, bug. Go on. Get yourself married," I told her softly, leaning forward and kissing her forehead.

With a short nod, Charlie stood, straightening the skirt on her dress, and turned to her fiancé and the minister. Taking a deep breath, she moved forward until she stood at Seth's side. He took her hand in his and smiled.

"You look sensational," he said, the smile never breaking from his face.

The minister began the service, and I, along with the rest of our guests, listened with rapt attention. My mother's hand slipped over mine, and she gripped it as we listened to Charlie and Seth exchange their vows.

By the end of the ceremony, I felt completely drained. The overwhelming emotions of the day had taken their toll, but I wasn't ready to let the day end just yet. I had one more duty to fulfill today, and I was going to do it.

"Son?" my father asked, the concern heavy in his voice. I turned to face him, and his eyes widened with worry. "Are you all right? Do you need to go back to your room?"

I shook my head. "No. I need to be here with her."

"You need to rest," he insisted firmly.

It only took one look to get him to back off. I got that he was just concerned, but this was something I had to do. I had to make sure I was there for her while I could be.

I sat back while Jennifer and Sarah enlisted the help of their husbands to move the chairs off to the side. This small community room at the hospital served to be the perfect place for a small, intimate wedding. Sure, it wasn't ideal, but since I needed to be here under constant care, it worked out great. Jennifer really made the small space beautiful. It didn't even look like a room you'd find in a hospital.

The lights had been turned down low, and there was soft music coming from the speaker system that Billy had hooked up. Charlie and Seth danced around the room, smiles still spread wide across their faces. Nothing could ruin this day for them.

Well, almost nothing.

When their song ended, Seth leaned forward and kissed Charlie softly. Just one more reassurance that she was loved and that he would take good care of her in my absence.

Charlie turned to look at me with a smile before Seth released her hands and she moved across the room to me. She sat next to me and took my hand in hers, laying her head on my shoulder and sighing softly.

"Thanks for today, Daddy."

My eyebrows knit together. "This isn't how I wanted this day to go for you," I whispered, placing a soft kiss into the hair atop her head.

Charlie's head shook against my shoulder. "Maybe not. But it was perfect. I got to spend it with the people I love most in the world." She raised her glistening eyes to meet mine, and when she smiled, I felt a new onslaught of tears prickle my eyes. "And most importantly, *you* got to be here."

I looked over to where Billy stood and gave him a nod. With a sly smirk, he turned to the stereo system and fiddled with the CDs for a moment before a soft, familiar melody wafted through the room.

A sharp gasp of surprise escaped Charlie as she brought her trembling hands to her mouth. I stood up slowly, turning to face her and extending a hand. "Dance with me?"

Charlie dropped her hands from her mouth, offering me her right hand so I could pull her to the middle of the dance floor. I had recorded Charlie's lullaby before being admitted to the hospital with the intention of giving it to her before I had to leave her. As the music filled the room, I placed my right hand on her hip while gently holding hers with my left, and I guided us around the room.

I'd had just enough energy to make it through that song before I had to sit down again. Everyone kept telling me that I should retire for the night, but I just couldn't. I felt the need to experience this entire day with Charlie.

"Hey," Seth said happily as he pulled up a chair next to me. "How are you doing?"

I chuckled at my new son-in-law. "Are you going to tell me I should turn in now, too?"

"Hell, no," he laughed. "Look at her. I wouldn't want to miss this day if I were you, either."

Charlie was in the middle of the dance floor with my sister and Sarah, dancing to some ridiculous song. Their laughter could be heard over the pounding dance beats, and I had to admit that it was the first time in months that I had seen Charlie truly happy. It had been a rough journey, but I felt hopeful that she was already on the road to her own recovery.

I was proud of myself for holding out until the celebration was over. Everyone had said their goodnights to the newlyweds before coming to me. It had become a daily ritual that they not only tell me goodnight, but also remind me of how much they loved me. It might be their last chance, after all.

Seth and I shook hands once more before he gave Charlie and me a moment to ourselves. We walked down the hall to my room, Charlie's arm looped through mine as we walked, and talked about the day as we often did.

"I love you, Daddy," she said when we stopped outside my door. "I just...I don't know how to say—"

"I love you, too, bug," I interrupted, knowing she was having trouble voicing her goodbyes as she often did. I hugged her once more, inhaling deeply before pulling away and holding her face in my hands. "Can I ask you something?" She nodded against my gentle hold on her. "Are you happy?"

"I am."

It felt as though a weight had been lifted from my shoulders, and I sighed with relief. "I need you to know that I love you more than anything."

"I know." Her chin quivered, and her voice trembled as her hands came up to cover mine. With one blink, several tears fell down her cheeks and she closed her eyes, leaning her face into my right hand. "I don't want this to be the end."

I pulled her back into my arms and held her as tightly as I could. "Aw, sweetie. It's not. This is just the beginning for you. This isn't goodbye, Charlie. No matter what tomorrow brings, I'll always be with you."

Even though she was still crying, her body seemed to relax slightly upon hearing that she would always hold me in her heart. After a few moments, Seth returned, and Charlie was reluctant to let me go. I told her it was time, and she simply nodded sadly, her eyes never leaving mine.

I remained outside my door as I watched Seth wrap his arms around my baby girl, supporting her, as they walked down the corridor toward the exit. Once they were out of sight, I turned and opened my door, only to find the most welcome surprise.

Bathed in the silver glow of the full moon, Cassie stood by the window, looking out at the night sky. She quickly turned to me, her familiar smile gracing her face. I couldn't help but feel the comfort and peace her mere presence brought me, but I still had to ask, "What are you doing here?"

Cassie crossed the room to me, reaching her hands out to take mine. "I'm here to take you home."

A.D. Ryan

Remember When

Other Books by AD Ryan

The Blood Moon Trilogy

Blood Moon
Wolf Moon
Blue Moon *(July 2015)*

Coming Soon

Just a Number *(October 2015)*

About the Author

A.D. Ryan resides in Edmonton, Alberta with her extremely supportive husband and children (two sons and a stepdaughter). Reading and writing have always been a big part of her life, and she hopes that her books will entertain countless others the way that other authors have done for her. Even as a small child, she enjoyed creating new and interesting characters and molding their worlds around them.

To learn more about the author and stay up-to-date on future publications, please look for her on Facebook and her blog.

https://www.facebook.com/pages/AD-Ryan-Author

http://adryanauthorblog.wordpress.com

Made in the USA
Charleston, SC
11 April 2015